Sequins, Saddles and SPURS

DESIREE HOLT
REGINA CARLYSLE
CIANA STONE

ELLORA'S CAVE
ROMANTICA PUBLISHING

TROUBLE IN COWBOY BOOTS
Desiree Holt

Stranded in Mesa Blanco, Texas, with no money and no prospects, Emily Lathrop hires on as the cook at the Lazy Aces Ranch. Two problems—she can't cook, and owner Wyatt Cavanaugh is so hot she nearly burns herself just standing near him. Trying to keep her hormones under control is a problem when Wyatt seduces her into his bed and teaches her the real meaning of erotic love.

Now proper Emily finds herself shockingly addicted to the BDSM games he likes to play, her body craving the bondage and domination that pushes her thermostat past the point of combustion even though she suspects it's all going to come crashing down any moment with a big, painful thud.

TROUBLE IN A STETSON
Regina Carlysle

Lola Lamont leaves Vegas with two pals, never imagining they'd break down in small-town Texas. So what's a former showgirl to do when she runs smack dab into the hottest sheriff south of the Mason Dixon line? Why, jump his bones, of course!

Sam Campbell takes one look at the Vegas Bombshell and knows damn good and well she belongs in his bed. She probably has the words *gold digger* tattooed to her ass but he's ready to take what the sexy blonde has to offer. Vowing to protect his heart, Sam rocks her world. Too bad she's rocking his right back. Sam is more than ready to handle some sass, spunk and sex, but is he willing to gamble on love?

TROUBLE IN CHAPS
Ciana Stone

Roxie may have broken down in Middle-of-Nowhere, Texas, but she darn sure doesn't plan on staying any longer than it takes to get the land yacht she arrived in up and running.

But you know what they say about the best-laid plans. Cliff was a complication she hadn't counted on. The man looks like walking sex and he's determined that before Roxie hightails it out of town, she'll share his bed. So he offers her a job at his bar, Chaps, to keep her close—and adds a sexy bet on top of it.

If she wins, he finances her escape from Nowheresville. If *he* wins, she stays for six months, keeping bar by day and keeping him warm at night. It's a wager she can't resist—and one she can't lose.

An Ellora's Cave Romantica Publication

www.ellorascave.com

Sequins, Saddles and Spurs

ISBN 9781419964190
ALL RIGHTS RESERVED.
Trouble in Cowboy Boots Copyright © 2010 Desiree Holt
Trouble in a Stetson Copyright © 2010 Regina Carlysle
Trouble in Chaps Copyright © 2010 Ciana Stone
Edited by Helen Woodall and Meghan M. Conrad.
Cover art by Syneca.

Trade paperback publication 2011

With the exception of quotes used in reviews, this book may not be reproduced or used in whole or in part by any means existing without written permission from the publisher, Ellora's Cave Publishing, Inc.® 1056 Home Avenue, Akron OH 44310-3502.

Warning: The unauthorized reproduction or distribution of this copyrighted work is illegal. Criminal copyright infringement, including infringement without monetary gain, is investigated by the FBI and is punishable by up to 5 years in federal prison and a fine of $250,000.
(http://www.fbi.gov/ipr/)

This book is a work of fiction and any resemblance to persons, living or dead, or places, events or locales is purely coincidental. The characters are productions of the author's imagination and used fictitiously.

SEQUINS, SADDLES AND SPURS
ಬ

TROUBLE IN COWBOY BOOTS
Desiree Holt
~9~

TROUBLE IN A STETSON
Regina Carlysle
~105~

TROUBLE IN CHAPS
Ciana Stone
~187~

TROUBE IN COWBOY BOOTS

Desiree Holt

ဆ

Dedication

To my very own personal hero, who dared me to be myself. And to Regina Carlysle and Ciana Stone, my cohorts in fun. You rock, ladies.

Trademarks Acknowledgement

The author acknowledges the trademarked status and trademark owners of the following wordmarks mentioned in this work of fiction:

Blackberry: Research in Motion Limited Corporation

C-4: The Great American Tool Company Inc.

Cadillac: General Motors Corporation

Coke: The Coca-Cola Company Corporation

Lone Star Beer: Lone Star Brewing Company

Lucchese: Lucchese Boot Company

Stetson: John B. Stetson Company Corporation

Chapter One

એ

Emily Proctor slammed the hood of the car and looked at her two friends.

"I don't have a clue what's wrong with this clunker, but I jiggled everything I could. See if it starts now."

They'd set out from Las Vegas, the three of them, refugees from downsizing, with nothing but this whale-sized bucket of bolts, a few possessions, prepaid cell phones for emergencies and the grand total of three hundred dollars between them. West, there was only California and LaLa Land so they'd headed east, away from the desert heat. They'd expected the car to break down somewhere, just not on a highway with nothing around them except pastures and cattle. They hadn't even passed another vehicle in almost an hour. And it was hotter than nine kinds of hell.

Emily'd pulled her thick mane of sable hair back into a pony tail. Now she lifted it off her neck where it rested limply and used it to fan her skin. If this was a nightmare, she wanted to wake up right this minute.

Lola Lamont wriggled in behind the wheel. One blonde curl from the mass of curls piled haphazardly on her head and held in place with a clip fell forward onto her forehead and she brushed it impatiently away. Stretching out her long, showgirl legs and straightening the t-shirt that barely concealed breasts that were the envy of every other girl in the shows, she worked herself into place on the seat. Letting out a long, slow breath, she carefully turned the key. The motor coughed, gurgled, groaned and finally turned over with a sound that set all their teeth on edge.

"At least it started again." Lola sighed. The 1966 pink Cadillac convertible was her contribution to their road trip. "This old gal has been very good to me."

"It may be time to put her to sleep," Roxie snorted.

"Roxie!" Lola did her best to look affronted.

"I'm with Rox," Emily put in. "You think this hunk of junk will at least get us to the next town?"

Leaning against the car, Roxie fanned herself with her hand. "It better, or we're gonna burn up like fried chicken."

"All right." Emily dusted her hands off on the seat of her jeans shorts. "Rox, get in the car. Lola, you drive. Roll all the windows down to catch some kind of breeze and pray as you never have before that we hit civilization before this thing rolls over for the last time."

The grand adventure they'd tried to make this was turning into a grand pain in the ass. If they didn't light somewhere soon they'd be in bigger trouble than they'd had in Vegas.

No one said a word as they rolled down the highway, each mile unwinding beneath them with unbearable slowness. Emily knew they were sending up silent prayers to the gods and the fates and anyone else who would listen.

Please, please, let us land somewhere safe.

Just as the engine was beginning to make threatening noises again, signs of life emerged. Smack in the middle of the highway sat a town. If you could call it that, Emily thought. A far cry from the glitz and glitter of Las Vegas.

But it had a main street, cross streets running into it and, lord have mercy, a cafe, where the car heaved its last and died.

"At least we'll be able to get something cold to drink," Roxie sighed.

"You better hope it's cheap," Lola warned. "Maybe we could all share one."

Trouble in Cowboy Boots

"Maybe we could just go inside and see what's what." Emily blew a stray hair away from her face. How in god's name had she ever thought this would be fun?

"'What's what' better be a way to get that hunk of junk fixed," Roxie said, climbing out of the car.

"As if." Lola tugged on her very tight white shorts and brushed at her hot pink tank top. "The only way that's gonna happen is if we rob a bank or win the lottery."

"Right now we don't even have money for a lottery ticket," Emily reminded her and sighed. "Okay. Let's go see what's inside. Hopefully they have air conditioning or we might sweat to death."

The inside of Blue Belle's looked so cheerful Emily almost threw up. Booths among one wall were upholstered in what she could only call an electric blue and the scattering of tables and chairs had cheap vases of artificial blue flowers on them. Every available space on the wall was filled with more pictures of bluebonnets than she'd ever seen. Not that she'd seen that many.

At three o'clock in the afternoon the place was mostly empty. The first thing Emily noticed was the blast of cool air that greeted them. The second was the three men sitting at a corner table. They all looked up as the women trooped in. If Emily had been in a better mood she'd have checked them out. Right now all she wanted was cold liquid, not a hot man.

The three of them plunked down in chairs at a table near the door. Roxie picked up the menus stuck between the salt and pepper shakers and fanned herself. A woman in jeans and a blouse the loudest blue Emily had ever seen came out from behind the lunch counter.

"Y'all look like you've just been dragged through hell," she commented. "What can I get for you?"

Roxie stopped fanning herself and looked at the plastic-covered menu. "We'll have the large Coke."

"All of you?" the waitress asked.

13

"One coke," Emily told her. "Three straws."

The woman stared at them for a long minute then shrugged. "Okay. One Coke. Three straws."

"Couldn't we each just get a small one?" Lola whined.

Emily bit back the retort that bubbled up. "Even a small one is more than two dollars," she hissed. "They probably think they'll get rich on strangers coming through."

The woman returned with a huge glass filled with the bubbly soda, plunked it down on the table and slammed three paper-wrapped straws beside it.

"She probably figures she won't be getting as tip," Lola giggled.

"She's right," Emily said and picked up one of the straws.

They were each taking small sips, savoring the icy cold liquid, when the waitress returned with two more large glasses of coke and set them on the table.

Emily looked up at her. "Um, we didn't order those."

"I know." The woman's voice could have curdled milk. "Your friends over there did."

"*My* friends?" Emily frowned. "I don't have any friends here."

"You do now."

The voice was deep and so smooth it sent shivers of delight dancing along her spine. She was vaguely aware of a chair scraping on the floor next to her and a body folding down into it. When she forced herself to look at the occupant she nearly lost it. A typical cowboy hat sat atop a head with thick, sun-streaked brown hair long enough to touch the collar of his chambray shirt. Hazel eyes with flecks of amber and green were watching her with an amused look. Sensuous lips turned up in a slight grin that softened the harsh angles and planes of his very masculine face. Faded jeans covered long legs that he crossed with one ankle resting on the other knee, giving her a good look at dusty, but obviously expensive, cowboy boots. Hand tooled. Emily had seen enough of them on high rollers in Vegas.

Emily was vaguely aware that the other two men had also joined them but she couldn't make herself pull her eyes away from the man next to her. The flood of moisture in her panties was her first warning sign that she might be in trouble.

"I, um, I'm afraid there's some mistake. The waitress said we were friends but I don't know you." She flicked a glance at the others. "Any of you."

She waited for Roxie or Lola to offer a protest but they were sitting there as gape-mouthed as she was. She could almost feel the thick shroud of testosterone circling them.

"Well," the man next to her drawled, "if this was a bar I'd buy you a drink. The Coke's the best I could do. Besides, y'all look thirsty enough to do more than share one."

Emily finally found a shred of her brain. She folded her hands primly in front of her and hitched her chair slightly sideways.

"We don't accept drinks from strangers."

"Speak for yourself," Lola snapped, grabbing one of the large glasses.

The man's smile widened. "Well, if we introduce ourselves we won't be strangers." He held out a hand. "Wyatt Cavanaugh."

Emily just stared at him. Finally she reached out her hand and put it in his. Immediately arrows of heat shot through her, waking up hormones she didn't even know existed. Probably she'd kept them hidden under her tailored suits.

Wyatt closed his fingers around her small hand and rubbed his thumb across her knuckles. "Now you're supposed to tell me your name," he prompted.

She swallowed. "Emily Proctor."

"Pleased to meet you, Emily Proctor," he drawled. He nodded at the man sitting with an arm draped over the back of

Roxie's chair. "Cliff Beckett, owner of Chaps, the best honky-tonk in Howell County."

Cliff laughed, a gravelly sound. "It better be. It's the *only* honky-tonk in the county."

"And don't forget those other —"

"Other bad habits of mine?" Cliff interrupted. "Let's let the ladies find out for themselves."

Wyatt looked at him strangely and turned to introduce the third man at the table.

Before he could, the man crowding close to Lola tipped his hat and pointed to the star on his shirt. "Sam Campbell, county sheriff."

"Sam was worried about three beauties traveling alone in that disaster you parked outside," Cliff said, "and wanted to make sure you were okay."

"Just doing my duty," Sam put in laconically.

"If you get drunk at Chaps," Wyatt grinned, "Sam will be the one to arrest you."

"I don't get drunk," Emily told him, then bit her lip.

My god, I sound like my fourth grade teacher.

"Well, that's nice to know. Mesa Blanco's not exactly a tourist spot, so mind if I ask what you ladies are doing here?"

The three women exchanged looks.

"Traveling," Roxie said and sipped at her Coke. "Seeing the West."

"The last time I saw a boat like that was in a junkyard," Cliff commented.

Wyatt chuckled and glanced out the big front window. "I'd have to say that limousine out there isn't in tiptop shape for touring. In fact, if I were asked, I'd have to say it rolled over and died right here outside the Blue Belle. Now you have to figure out how to give it a funeral."

"It's not dead," Lola protested.

Trouble in Cowboy Boots

"That's right," Emily added. "Just...resting." She wished Wyatt would move his chair back a little. The heat sizzling between them was scorching her more than the sun outside. She wondered if he felt it, too. When she looked at him there was a glint of humor in his eyes but otherwise his face gave nothing away.

Sam Campbell shook his head. "I have a feeling come this time tomorrow I'll have to arrest that vehicle for loitering. Now. We're honest men here and we just want to help. So why don't you tell us why you *really* ended up here."

The women heaved a collective sigh of resignation.

It's not as if we can really get up, walk out of here and drive down the road.

"All right," Roxie said. "I'll start."

With each of them contributing bits and pieces they got the whole miserable story out, all the while greedily drinking their soda, and Lola carefully avoiding any mention of the way that asshole, Nick Mantucci, had dumped her. Wyatt signaled for the waitress to bring refills for the women and more coffee for the men and they kept on drinking and talking.

At last Emily leaned back in her chair and glared at each of the men in turn, trying to ignore the sexual energy still crackling between her and Wyatt Cavanaugh.

"So. Does it make you macho men feel so much better to know we're stuck here with practically no money, a car that won't run and no place to go for help?"

"Well, now." Wyatt drained the last dregs from his coffee cup. "It could have happened in a worse place."

"Yeah?" Lola cocked an eyebrow at him. "How do you figure that?"

"We may not be as big as Las Vegas but we might be able to scare up a job or two."

"Like what?"

17

"Oh, like a cook at my ranch. My hands are getting real hungry since the last one quit."

The silence was like an elephant in the room.

A cook? Yeah, right.

"Wyatt's got a nice spread just outside of town," Cliff told them. "Ten thousand acres, right, Wyatt? Runs a nice herd of beeves. Does pretty well for himself."

"I don't need a P.R. person, Cliff." Wyatt leaned back in his chair. "But I do need a cook. For about twenty people." His glance ranged around the table. "Anyone interested?"

Before she could stop herself the words were out of Emily's mouth. "I am."

Lola and Roxie looked at her as if she'd lost what was left of her mind. A cook? They knew the closest she got to cooking was turning on the coffee maker in her condo. Before she'd lost it. She was the takeout queen of Vegas.

They're right. I've gone crazy. I can't cook and all I want to do with this man I just met is get naked and...

"So." Wyatt broke into her thoughts. He was studying her, tiny lights dancing in his ever-changing hazel eyes. "You want to cook. Ever done it before?"

"Yes," she lied. "Of course." She gripped her hands together under the table and prayed her friends would keep their mouths shut.

"So running grub for twenty or so folks three times a day isn't a problem."

She shook her head back and forth as if it was on a swivel post. "Not at all."

"Well, it comes with your own quarters just off the kitchen and a decent salary." He named a figure that was less than Emily made in Vegas, but of course she wasn't making anything at the moment so whatever the salary she was grateful. She'd just have to figure out how to cook and save up until she could get out of here.

Trouble in Cowboy Boots

Emily swallowed. "That sounds fine. When would you want me to start?"

"No time like the present. Your gear in that hunk of junk out there?"

She nodded.

"Let's get to it, then." He pushed back his chair and stood up.

Emily got a crick in her neck looking up at him. "What about my friends?"

"They'll be safe." It was the first time Sam, the taciturn one of the three, had spoken in some time. "I'll see to it. I can at least get them rooms at Mrs. Chester's for a couple of nighto. At a rate they can afford," he added quickly as Emily started to protest.

"See?" Wyatt took her elbow, his fingers singing her where they touched her skin. "All set. Let's get going."

Lola cleared her throat. "Emily, are you sure about this?"

No, but I can't say it out loud.

"Yes, if you're positive you'll be okay."

"We'll be fine," Roxie told her. "I'll make sure. *You* just stay safe. If you change your mind, we're right here. We'll figure out what to do."

"She won't be changing her mind." Wyatt guided her to the door. "This will work out just fine."

Emily cast one glance back at her friends before letting Wyatt lead her outside to a shiny black pickup and the unknown.

What have I done?

Chapter Two

Emily blew a stray hair from her forehead and turned off the hot water faucet. Standing at the sink she could watch twilight descending and see a sliver of moon emerging. Day Three at the Lazy Aces Ranch. A far cry from the Hotel Royale in Las Vegas. The sun was blistering hot, dirt from the yard and the corral flew everywhere, especially when there was a breeze, and instead of the scents common to a luxury hotel all she smelled here was cattle, horseflesh, and more animal shit than she thought possible to accumulate in one place.

Not to mention the fact that her clothes were hardly appropriate. Silk and linen slacks just didn't cut it at a working ranch. She wore her jeans shorts the first day but after listening to many wolf whistles from the men — albeit good-natured — she'd changed to the oldest pair of slacks she had with her and a loose t-shirt.

And the nickname! That was almost more irritating than anything else. Some jerk who'd seen too many reruns of *The Wizard of Oz* had started calling her Auntie Em and the others had picked it up. She'd waited for Wyatt to say something but he seemed as amused by it as everyone else.

The men had worked hard all day, moving cattle to the summer pasture, and as usual, they were hungry. She'd done her best to feed them but she was waiting for Wyatt to lose patience with her and dump her back in Mesa Blanco.

The little apartment off the kitchen Wyatt had said was hers was nowhere near the class of her condo — make that *former* condo — but it was far more presentable than she'd expected. Bedroom, bath, sitting room. Even a television with satellite hookup. Too bad she didn't know enough about her job to earn her keep.

Oh, she'd been all bluster when she first arrived, prowling the kitchen and nodding as Wyatt told her what the men liked to eat. Luckily she'd found a couple of cookbooks someone had stuck away in the pantry closet and spent the first night studying them as if her life depended on it. Which, in a way, it did.

She'd managed to get by with scrambled eggs and bacon for breakfast the next morning. Even *she* knew how to make those. After that it had been steadily downhill. Burnt biscuits. Burnt chicken. Burnt hamburgers. Burnt. Burnt. Burnt.

Emily sighed. Being assistant director for conventions at a Las Vegas hotel in no way prepared one for being a ranch cook. Maybe she should have been spending more time in the hotel kitchen. Wyatt had been giving her a wide berth but any minute now she expected him to come marching in to the kitchen and tell her to pack her things.

And then what? Lola and Roxie had called to say they'd found jobs—Lola at the Blue Belle Café and Roxie tending bar at Chaps. There probably wasn't another available job in town. But maybe she could bunk in with Roxie at Mrs. Chester's while she checked out her options. Or better yet with Lola. Belle, owner of Blue Belle's, had given her a tiny apartment behind the café. Yeah, that would probably be better.

Yeah, right. Options.

Besides, that would take her away from Wyatt, whose very presence, she'd discovered, made her panties wet with desire and her nipples so stiff she had to keep a dishtowel hanging over her shoulder to hide them. Another problem she hadn't expected—to be in lust with her boss. But the first morning after he'd brought her to the ranch, when he came into the kitchen with that loose-hipped walk of his, worn jeans clinging to long legs and a work shirt stretched across broad shoulders she'd almost licked her lips.

There was heat between them. Even Wyatt couldn't deny it. She saw it in the way he looked at her when no one else was watching. Felt it in the invisible electricity that crackled between them when they were within five feet of each other.

Not that she thought he'd be interested in taking things any further. For one thing, she worked for him. For another, she was probably as far away from the women he liked as she could get. Although in the three days she'd been here she hadn't heard him mention any, or the hands tease him about one. And no evidence that she could find of women hanging out at the ranch. Of course, she hadn't gone into his bedroom to explore. Still, she could fantasize about what sex with him would be like.

Which for some ungodly reason she'd done in her dreams. Probably the closest she'd get to it.

Am I crazy? He's no more my type than I am his.

Sighing, she went back to scrubbing the burnt pot, wondering if she'd have to pay for all the cooking utensils she was ruining. Lost in thought, she didn't hear anyone enter the kitchen and jumped when a hand touched her shoulder, dropping the pot into the soapy water with a splash. She looked up to see Wyatt reflected in the window.

"Sorry." His deep voice was a caress drifting over her. "I didn't mean to startle you."

"No problem." She picked up the pot and began rubbing at it again.

Wyatt reached around, took then pot from her hands and put it in the sink. "Leave that for a minute. We need to talk."

Emily's heart sank. This was it. In a few minutes she'd be out on her ear and then what?

"Come on." He handed her a dish towel. "Dry your hands and sit down. How about a cup of coffee?"

"Sure. Why not?" Maybe the caffeine would give her courage.

Trouble in Cowboy Boots

By the time she dried her hands Wyatt had filled two mugs and carried them to the table. He gestured for her to sit down. Wrapping her hands around the mug, she lifted it to sip the hot liquid, hoping her hands wouldn't shake too badly.

Wyatt took a swallow of his own coffee, watching her over the rim of the mug with his come-fuck-me eyes. They had darkened and the flecks of green and gold sparkled like jewels. Emily shivered under his penetrating gaze. Finally she sat up straighter and squared her shoulders.

"I think we have a problem here."

Emily's stomach lurched. Oh, yeah, they had a problem. At least *she* had one. She'd known this was a mistake the minute she'd opened her mouth back at the Blue Belle but she'd had the insane idea she could figure out how to make it work.

"Listen." She set her coffee mug down. "I want to tell you how sorry I am about…well, everything."

Was that a smile teasing at his sensuous mouth?

"Sorry that my men are lusting after you or sorry that we haven't had an edible meal since you got here?" His eyes danced with mischief. "Tell me something. Have you *ever* cooked a meal before? In your life."

She shook her head, miserable.

"Never?"

She shook her head again.

Just fire me and get it over with.

He took a swallow of his coffee, studying her over the rim of the mug. "Then why the hell did you take this job? I thought you were going to knock your friends out of their chairs you were so anxious to raise your hand."

Emily shrugged. "I didn't have any other options. I need the work. We're all broke. We told you that."

"But cooking for a bunch of roughnecks?" He shook his head. "I don't think this is exactly what you had in mind."

"As long as they stop calling me Auntie Em I won't mind it so much. There doesn't seem to be a place in Mesa Blanco—maybe in all of the county—with a crying need for a convention director."

He continued to watch her, the silence stretching out like an old rubber band.

"I know you're going to fire me," she told him, "so let's just get it over with and I'll pack my things. Get out of your hair."

"And where did you plan to go?"

Was that a grin teasing at his mouth again? Asshole!

"That's my business." If he was going to throw her out she didn't need to give him any details. She might be broke but she still had her pride.

"And mine," he told her.

She raised an eyebrow. "Oh, yeah? How so?"

"I hired you so it's my responsibility to see you don't end up on the streets."

Heat burned her cheeks. "Listen, Wyatt…"

"You're an intelligent woman. I think if you approached this like any project you've ever worked on, you could produce at least passable meals." He chuckled. "But I can't starve the men in the meantime, so I'm going to get you some help."

Her eyes widened. "Help?"

"Yeah. My foreman's wife used to do the cooking here but decided she'd had enough. I conned her into coming up here a couple of hours a day in the morning to give you cooking lessons."

"Cooking lessons? You're kidding, right?"

"Not even a little. So what's your choice? Cooking lessons or should I look around the area for you and see where else you might land?"

Trouble in Cowboy Boots

The last thing Emily wanted to do was find herself someplace else. God only knew what kind of a job he'd find for her. Besides, the high point of her day was ogling his really tight butt when he ambled along in those soft jeans of his. Followed closely, however, by the very few moment he got close enough to her that she could smell the male heat of him, feel it emanating from his body. Then of course there were the dreams she'd had the past two nights.

Sheesh! What was happening to her? Had being dumped by Nick left her so sex-deprived that she was having erotic fantasies about a man she'd known less than a week? And one she worked for, to make matters worse.

"You don't have to do that," she began.

"Oh, yeah, I do." He grinned again. "My hands will string me up from the water tank if they don't get a decent meal pretty soon. And the next cook I hire sure won't be as easy on the eyes as you are. So you still have a job. You can relax."

Her heart thumped. "Thank you, Wyatt. I promise I'll pay very careful attention during my...cooking lessons." She watched him. Something else was going on here and she hadn't a clue what it was. "If you aren't going to fire me, why *are* we sitting here?"

He set his mug down and leaned across the table, touching her free hand. The skin sizzled beneath his fingers. "I'm trying to figure out how to do this and not have you shoot me with my own gun."

Emily stared at him. "Do what? Holy hell, Wyatt, what's going on here?"

Wyatt's face was dead serious, but heat blazed in his eyes. "From the minute I saw you in the Blue Belle in those shorts and top I've been so hard it's almost painful to walk. Don't you wonder why I stay gone from the house so much? I don't trust myself to keep my hands off you."

Emily had just taken a sip of her coffee and she spewed it out onto the table. Flushed, she jumped up and grabbed the

25

dishtowel from the counter and began mopping up the mess. She couldn't look at Wyatt. She was afraid he'd see what she really wanted reflected in her eyes. "Sorry."

He reached over and pried the dish towel from her hands. "I'm guessing this is a shock to you."

"Shock?" She didn't know what to say. That wasn't the half of it. The thought wrapping her legs around that hard muscular body and feeling his cock inside her made her tremble with anticipation. "You could definitely say that."

"So is this a good shock or a bad shock?" His voice had a slight edge to it.

"I don't... I just..." She dropped into her chair. "Are you serious?"

"As a heart attack." He crossed his legs, resting one ankle on the opposite knee. "But we have a real big problem here." He paused. "Assuming you're even interested."

What was she supposed to say? No? She'd sound like a prig. Yes? Actually, totally yes? She'd sound like a slut. Finally she asked, "What's the problem? I didn't think people worried about sexual harassment out here in the boonies." She tried to make a joke out of it, but she was still stunned to find out he had the hots for her.

His face tightened. "I may be a horny cowboy but I respect a woman until she gives me a reason to think otherwise. The last thing I want to do is have you tolerate my advances because you think you have to. To keep your job."

Emily dropped her eyes and busied herself sipping from her mug. The coffee was cold and bitter but it gave her something to do while she tried to pull together her scattered wits. "So, if I said I was interested would that make a difference? And not because I want to keep my job."

Wyatt was watching her with heavy-lidded eyes. "I'd want you to think very carefully about it. I'm not offering anything here except my bed and my body. No hearts and flowers. Nothing long-term. That's not who I am. And if it

Trouble in Cowboy Boots

burns itself out and you feel uncomfortable here, I'll make sure you're set up in town with a place to stay and a job. Until you and your friends are able to leave."

"Did I give you the impression I was asking for anything?" she shot back. "And you don't have to worry about giving me anything. Look, maybe you're right and this isn't such a good idea after all."

Wyatt must have moved faster than the speed of light, because in a millisecond he was out of his chair, had pulled her from hers and was devouring her mouth as if he'd been starved for it forever. He nibbled at her bottom lip, licked around the edges of her mouth then plunged his tongue inside with possessive forcefulness.

Emily's knees weakened and her body seemed to lose all its strength. She clung to him, the heat of his body searing through her and his tongue lighting every nerve in her mouth. Her nipples throbbed and the pulse in her womb did a jungle dance. She was drowning in sensory overload. If this was a dream, she didn't want to wake up.

His arms tightened around her, pressing her breasts against the hard wall of his chest. One of his long legs insinuated itself between hers and he rubbed his thigh against her heated pussy through her clothes. She was melting, so liquid she didn't think she could stand without his arms holding her.

When he broke the kiss his eyes burned into hers.

"You want this as much as I do," he breathed against her mouth.

"Yes." It came out as a whisper. "Yes, I do."

He lifted her into his arms and strode through the kitchen to her rooms, through the sitting room into the bedroom. Hysterically she thought how glad she was she'd made the bed that day. Having sex in a messy room took the edge off things.

Wyatt stood her on the floor beside her bed and with fingers that shook slightly unbuttoned her blouse and slid it from her shoulders. His eyes fastened on the swell of her breasts and he traced the slope with the tip of one finger.

"Exquisite," he murmured. "Just fucking gorgeous." He bent his head and trailed kisses across her skin.

Emily tilted her head back and he moved his mouth to her neck, brushing against her heated skin, taking tiny nips then soothing with his tongue. He pressed his lips against the hollow of her throat where her pulse pounded and sucked the delicate flesh into his mouth.

She barely registered when he took off the scrap of silk and lace she wore for a bra but when his large palms slid around to cup her breasts and he closed his hot mouth over one nipple a bolt of electricity shot through her so powerful it nearly knocked her to her knees. She hummed at the back of her throat as he worshiped first one nipple, then the other.

When she was sure she would come just from that alone he lifted his head, "You have outstanding nipples. I'll bet they would look unbelievable with clamps tightened on them."

"C-clamps?" she stuttered.

"Uh-huh." He licked first one then the other. "Haven't you ever worn nipple clamps? Hasn't some man been so turned on by them that he just had to find the right ones to tighten on them?"

"It-it sounds like it would hurt." She wanted to be afraid but a streak of something dark and erotic flashed through her.

"It hurts good, sugar. Real good. I think you'd love it. And I'd sure love to see it."

He was kissing her again as his hands worked the snap and zipper of her slacks. Then they were gone, along with her thong. Wyatt lifted her and placed her on the bed, spread her legs wide with the knees bent, and stared at her exposed cunt. The look in his eyes made her heart race and her nerves fire.

"I'd like to take a picture of that sweet little puss," he rasped. "Keep it with me so I can pull it out and look at it any time I want."

Trouble in Cowboy Boots

The muscles in her cunt quivered and liquid trailed from her vagina. She would have been embarrassed at how wet she was if she hadn't been so completely turned on. And he'd hardly done anything yet.

Wyatt trailed the tip of one finger the length of her slit and lifted it to his mouth, licking her essence from it slowly, all the while pinning her with his gaze. His eyes never left her body as he slowly removed his clothes, toeing off his boots and dropping his jeans and shirt on top of them.

Emily sucked in a breath as she looked at his naked body. He was tall and lean and all muscle. Hair a dark shade of blond covered his chest in tiny whorls then arrowed down over his flat abdomen to create a nest of curls surrounding the most impressive erection she had ever seen. Long and thick, with a broad purple flared head, it quite literally made her mouth water.

He moved closer to the bed and she was about to ask him if he had any condoms when he dropped to his knees, lifted her legs over his shoulder and put his mouth to her cunt. He rimmed the opening with his tongue before driving it into her hot channel.

Emily's entire body shook with tiny spasms. Wyatt's tongue was an erotic torch, leaving a trail of fire every place it touched. She hitched her hips at him, urging him to penetrate more deeply. He curled his tongue—his very long, educated tongue—and the tip of it scraped her sweet spot, sending another series of ripples through her. He drank from her, holding her in place so there was no relief, no opportunity to roll away when the heat became scorching, the sensations so acute she could feel every individual nerve in her body.

The climax burst upon her with such a sudden ferocity she had no time to prepare herself for it. This was unlike anything she'd ever felt before, and she was no stranger to good sex. Or what she'd *thought* was good sex. A hurricane grabbed her, shaking her and pulling her from her foundation.

Tossing her into the air so she whirled and spun, free-falling with nothing to catch her.

And all the time Wyatt continued to probe her with his tongue and suck her essence, eating her as if she were an epicurean delicacy.

It could have been a minute or an hour, she had no idea how much time had passed, when Wyatt lifted her, ripped back the covers on the bed and placed her in the center. He bent to lift his jeans, pulled out his wallet and fished a condom from it, rolling it on with practiced efficiency.

When he moved over her she could tell from the fine tremors in his body and the way the cords in his neck stood out that his control was about to snap. And despite the fact she'd just had one gigantic orgasm, she desperately wanted him inside her. Now. Right now.

He nudged her thighs wider apart and pressed the head of his cock to the entrance of her cunt. One roll of his hips and he thrust deeply. Emily wrapped her legs around his waist, digging her heels into the small of his back to pull him in even deeper. She moved with him as he pistoned in and out, thrusting up at him as he drove deep inside her.

If her first orgasm was unbelievable, when this one broke over her it consumed her completely. She lost all sense of who she was, focused only on the spasms that shook her and the man whose cock was pulsing deep inside her. She was in the tight embrace of a fire, the heat consuming her. The contractions seemed to go forever, shaking every part of her body, and Wyatt shook just as hard with her. The muscles of his back, beneath her hands, were rigid with the intensity of his release. She screamed his name and he swallowed it with his mouth.

And then it was over, little aftershocks racing through them, then gone. Wyatt fell forward, catching himself on his forearms, dragging air into his lungs. Emily could feel the thunderous beat of his heart, rocketing in cadence with hers. She was sure she'd never be able to move again.

Trouble in Cowboy Boots

Eventually she found she could actually breathe normally and her heart wasn't going to beat itself out of her chest. Wyatt drew in a deep breath, let it out slowly and eased himself from her body.

"Right back," he mumbled.

In a minute she heard him in her bathroom, obviously disposing of the condom. Then he was back, climbing into bed next to her and pulling her against his body and wrapping his arms around her.

"You're an unexpected package of dynamite, Miss Emily Proctor," he murmured against her hair.

"Mmm," was all she could manage to respond.

"I have plans for you," he whispered, his voice deep and hoarse. "I think you're a woman who can really enjoy my kind of sex. I can't wait until tomorrow night."

His kind of sex? What did that mean?

She was too tired to try and puzzle it out. Her eyes closed and in seconds she was deeply asleep.

What the hell just happened here?

Wyatt was exhausted but his brain wouldn't shut off. Emily had lit his hormones from the moment he'd seen her in the Blue Belle Café, desperate and trying not to look it. A tumble in the sheets had definitely appealed to him, as long as she was willing and there weren't any complications. He'd make sure she understood the "rules of engagement". The kind of sex he really liked didn't appeal to a lot of women so he always tested the waters carefully. With some it worked, others just weren't interested.

Okay, well and good.

But never in his wildest dreams did he expect to be so shaken by the experience. He was completely blown away. Now he knew what the phrase "little death" meant, when people referred to the ultimate orgasm For sure he'd died and gone to heaven with Emily Proctor. He'd see how she felt tomorrow and figure out a way to see if she was interested in the games he liked to play.

God, he hoped so. The image of Emily tied to his bed, spread wide open for him, panting with lust while he fucked her six ways from Sunday, made his worn-out cock harden unexpectedly.

Down, boy!

He closed his eyes and willed sleep to come.

Chapter Three

ร

"No, no, no." Amelia Jacobs's words were chiding but her tone was soft and gentle. "Too much mixing and the biscuits come out like skeet targets."

Emily blew a strand of hair out of her eyes. Despite the big apron doubled over and wrapped around her, she was covered with a fine layer of flour. Her hair was escaping from its neat ponytail and she had biscuit dough layered on her arms up to her elbows.

Amelia had shown up promptly at five thirty, a tiny woman of indeterminate age, tanned and slender with laughter in her dark eyes, her gray-streaked brown hair twisted back into a braid. She was dressed in worn jeans and a plaid blouse, clothing Emily realized was far more appropriate than linen slacks and silk blouses. As soon as she got paid she'd need to do some shopping.

She slowed down her motions with the big wooden spoon, ignoring the puffs of flour that flew up from the bowl.

I'll never get the hang of this. What in hell ever made me think I could be a cook?

Maybe part of her problem was her mind kept drifting to Wyatt. He'd woken her when he slid from her bed at five that morning, kissing her cheek and brushing the hair back from her face.

"I need to get back to my room before Amelia shows up," he whispered. "I don't want to start any gossip."

Of course he wouldn't. God forbid someone should know he finds me attractive.

She managed to rouse herself. "What time is it?"

"Five o'clock. You'd better get up and shower. Amelia will be here at five thirty."

That had sent her bolt upright in bed. "Five thirty?"

"Yup. Up and at 'em. The guys will be wanting their breakfast."

Her brain had seemed stuck in one place. "At five thirty?"

His chuckle was soft in the darkness. "We've been cutting you slack, Auntie Em. They usually like to eat at seven."

"Seven?" She threw a pillow at him. "And don't call me Auntie Em."

He'd laughed again and ducked out of her room.

Now she looked at the clock on the stove. Six fifteen. She'd better hurry.

She looked at the batter in the bowl, then at Amelia.

"Okay." The woman nodded. "I think it's good. Let's get it in the pans and into the oven."

Amelia showed her how much dough to spoon into each biscuit cup. Emily envied the easy way she did it with just a twist of her hand, and did her best to copy her, with less than perfect results.

Amelia laughed, a tinkling sound. "Don't worry, Emily. You'll get the hang of it soon enough."

"Yeah, right. Are you planning to come here every morning until I can make something edible?"

"That will happen before you know it." Amelia's tone softened. "But I'll be here as long as you need me."

They stacked the pans in the oven, set the timer, then Emily poured coffee for both of them.

"I can't ask you to give up your free time for me like that." She shook her head. "I hope Wyatt's paying you for your time."

Amelia stirred sugar into her coffee. "Wyatt's been very good to Dan and me. We owe him a lot." She looked up at

Trouble in Cowboy Boots

Emily, mischief dancing in her eyes. "Besides, I get the feeling Wyatt Cavanaugh thinks of you as a little more than a cook. I'd be really happy to help out any woman who can bring that cowboy to his knees."

"Oh," Flustered, Emily took a swallow of coffee. "You're wrong about that. He's just helping me out because I need a job."

"Uh-huh. If you say so."

Amelia pushed back from the table. "Meanwhile, let's get the eggs scrambled, the bacon laid out and the pancake batter mixed."

"Pancakes?" Emily widened her eyes, horrified. "You mean I have to make *pancakes*?"

Amelia laughed again. "It's not water torture, Emily. Just pancakes."

"That's what you think," she muttered.

By seven o'clock she was ready to slit her throat and bleed all over the kitchen in a bid for sympathy. She felt like a walking ball of dough and there was more flour in her hair than in anything she'd fixed, but breakfast was ready to serve. She wondered where Wyatt was. He hadn't even popped his head in to check on her. Maybe it was just as well. She didn't know how to react to him after last night.

He'd been very clear about not putting her at risk for gossip, but she hadn't expected him to ignore her completely. The last two mornings he'd had coffee in the kitchen while she pulled together her pitiful excuses for meals, but today he'd been conspicuously absent.

"Go wash up," Amelia said. "They'll be trooping in here any minute."

"But—"

"The table's set and the platters are warming. Go on. You'll feel better."

What she felt like as she sluiced water over her hands and face was a bad papier-mâché project, but she repaired the damages as best she could, fixed her ponytail and braved the kitchen again. She stepped into the room just as the back door opened and the sound of noisy voices preceded the ranch hands into the house.

Hardy Wolf was first through the door, as usual, trouble dancing in his eyes and a grin that split his face.

"Why, Auntie Em! Is that real food I smell today?"

Hardy couldn't have been more than twenty-two or three but Emily wanted to tell him he wouldn't get any older if he didn't shut up. He'd started that Auntie Em business the first day and she was ready to take his head off. The only thing that kept her from biting back was her tenuous position here and her desperate need to keep the job.

"The real food's for everyone else," she smiled sweetly. "I took care to burn yours extra crisp."

"Aw, come on, Auntie Em." He slipped an arm around her waist. "Really? You took extra pains with mine?"

"Hey Hardy," one of the other hands called. "Shut up and let's see if today's food looks as good as it smells.

Amelia had somehow managed to disappear, so Emily extricated herself from the young cowboy and began pulling platters from the warming oven and carrying them to the long table. The hands ate in two shifts and Amelia had shown her how to portion out the food, keeping a second batch warm.

"Hay, Charlie, catch," Hardy said, taking a biscuit and tossing it to the man across from him.

The biscuit, lighter and fluffier than Emily had expected, broke apart in the man's hands. He and Hardy just stared at the crumbling biscuit.

"Holy shit," the older man said at last. "Where did these biscuits come from? Did the boss make a run to the Blue Belle like we been askin' him to?"

Trouble in Cowboy Boots

Emily's stomach flip flopped. Was that what they'd been doing? Begging Wyatt to bring food out to the ranch? She wondered again why he'd put up with her even for three days. Then she remembered the night before, heat warmed her cheeks and her pussy throbbed. Men would do a lot of things for sex. She'd learned that a long time ago.

Only…they hadn't had sex until last night. Had he been working up to it? Ready to toss her back out on the highway if she said no, regardless of his ethical protestations?

"Hey, Auntie Em," someone called. "How about some coffee?"

She shook herself back to reality and got busy serving. It seemed like no time before every bit of food was devoured, the men had shuffled out, looking at her strangely, and she got ready for the second shift. Everything had stayed warm in the oven without drying out, just as Amelia had told her it would. She was just putting clean plates on the table when she heard a sound behind her.

"Looks like you've got the hang of this thing."

The deep voice sent shivers skittering along her spine and the pulse in her cunt stepped up its beat. If she didn't get hold of herself she was liable to come just standing there in the kitchen. She drew in a deep breath, let it out slowly and turned around.

"Good morning, Wyatt."

If possible he looked better than he had the night before. Worn jeans clung to his long legs and a plaid work shirt was open partway to his belt, exposing the fine dark-gold hair she'd enjoyed running her fingers through the night before. He took off his hat and ran his fingers through his sun-streaked honey-brown hair, then stamped the dust from his boots before coming further into the room.

"I take it Amelia showed up all right?" he asked, a grin teasing at his mouth.

37

"You know she did." Emily opened the oven and took out a platter of pancakes. "God knows I've never made a pancake in my life."

She set the platter on a hot pad and was about to take out the bacon when Wyatt wrapped his fingers around her arm and turned her toward him.

He chuckled. "You look cute with flour on your nose."

Damn! I thought I got it all.

She reached up and swiped at the tip of her nose.

Wyatt grabbed her hand and kissed her fingers. "Leave it. I kind of like it."

"I feel like took a bath in the stuff," she muttered.

He tilted her head up and brushed his lips against her. "I'd like to strip your clothes off right now and fuck you senseless on that big table."

"Wyatt!" She could tell from the heat scorching her cheeks that she was blushing furiously. She ducked away from him. "The rest of the men will be coming in any second."

"You're right." He moved to the counter and filled a mug with coffee. "I meant what I said last night about not embarrassing you. Putting you in an uncomfortable position. But damn, it's hard to keep my hands off you."

She could feel him watching her as she carried the rest of the food to the table.

"We need to get you some jeans, cowgirl," he teased. "Those fancy Las Vegas clothes won't last very long around here."

Emily brushed her hands on her apron. "I figured when I got paid I'd ask you if someone could run me into town to get some." She frowned. "Is there actually a place in that town to buy them?"

"Boland's Feed Store. They keep a section of work clothes in there."

She raised her eyebrows. "Work clothes?"

Trouble in Cowboy Boots

"Don't worry. They've got some of the brands you're familiar with. I was thinking I'd run you into town later this afternoon. We could pick up takeout for the men at Dub's Bar-B-Que so you didn't have to stress about dinner."

"Amelia taught me how to make beef stew this morning," she said, raising her chin a little. "Tomorrow we're learning fried chicken."

Wyatt threw back his head and laughed.

"That I've gotta see."

Emily slapped him with a dish towel. "You just wait, Wyatt Cavanaugh. I'm going to learn this if it kills me."

He lowered his voice. "I've got other things I'd rather you learn. We'll talk about them tonight." He carried his mug to the table. "I think the rest of the men are here."

"Holy shit, Auntie Em!" John McDaniels, one of the older hands, was staring at the table. "Did the food fairy pay us a visit?"

"Just shut up and eat, John," Wyatt said good-naturedly. "Stand there too long and someone else will get your share."

Again Emily kept the coffee mugs filled, the maple syrup warmed and plenty of butter and preserves on the table. She did her best to ignore their comments and not be offended at their suspicious attitude about who really prepared the food. It wasn't as if she hadn't earned their disbelief. But finally every bite was gone and they'd left to go back to work.

Emily cleared the dishes from the table and stacked them in the dishwasher. She was scrubbing the pans when warm hands slid around her waist and a hot mouth brushed her beck beneath her ponytail.

"I think this is where we started last night." Wyatt's voice was heavy with desire. But then he moved away from her. "I assume you've got lunch under control. Be ready about three o'clock and we'll run into town. Maybe give you a chance to see your friends." Then his lips were back, this time at her ear.

"And after dinner I think we'll find out just exactly what you're up for, Emily Proctor."

Then he was gone, leaving her with soapy water, dirty pans, unsteady legs and a throbbing inside her like the insistent beat of a jungle drum.

* * * * *

Emily figured if she ignored the sacks of grain stacked along the wall, the abundance of ranch and farm equipment and the fact she had to change behind wooden crates of instruments, buying jeans at the feed store wasn't that much different from buying them anyplace else. And Wyatt was right—they had two of the brands she was familiar with.

Something to write in my diary about. If I ever decide to keep a diary.

She would have been satisfied with one pair, nursing them along until she got her first paycheck, but Wyatt checked her size, then pulled three more pairs from a stack and pushed her gently toward a small section with t-shirts.

"Nothing fancy," he agreed, "but serviceable for the ranch."

"But I can't afford all of this," she protested, trying to put things back.

"Call it a bonus for this morning's breakfast." He sighed. "Listen, Em. Your Vegas clothes are fine if you get into Austin or San Antonio but for Mesa Blanco and the Lazy Aces, you need to wear what everyone else does. Do us both a favor, pick out the t-shirts you like and let's get out of here."

She sorted through the shirts while Wyatt placed a feed order with Avery Boland. The cattle fed mostly on hay, he'd told her, but he supplemented it with special natural mixtures that the hands drove out to big feeding tubs in the pastures. He'd also explained that he ordered special feed for the horses to keep them fit and healthy.

40

Trouble in Cowboy Boots

"They get ridden hard," he told her, "so they need the best we can give them."

She realized how very little she actually knew about ranching. Her knowledge was limited to movies and romance novels set in the West, and for the past four days she'd been so busy trying to keep afloat in the kitchen she hadn't had time to check anything out or ask questions. Besides, she hoped her stay at the Lazy Aces would be short-lived. As soon as she and Lola and Roxie got enough cash together and got their car running they'd be off again for someplace not quite so godforsaken.

She picked t-shirts that were all dark in color, hoping they would provide some camouflage for her breasts. Not that she was all that well-endowed, especially next to Roxie and Lola, but she didn't want to give the hands the idea she might be tempting them in any way.

Wyatt had also made time for her to check in with her friends. At Chaps, Roxie was just starting her shift. Emily was amazed to see her friend smiling and relaxed, even as she did her prep work for the next wave of customers.

"I see Cliff's hanging around here." She nodded in the rancher's direction. "He keeps sliding a look at you. How's that going?"

Roxie leaned across the bar. "Kinda like Texas hold 'em. He hasn't really shown all his cards yet. But hey, at least he doesn't swat me on the ass all the time the way the high rollers did in Vegas."

"Really?" Emily's raised her eyebrows. "Funny. He looks like the typical macho asshole to me."

Roxie grinned. "Maybe there's one lurking underneath but he's keeping it carefully under wraps. By the way." She slid her gaze to Wyatt, gabbing with Cliff, and back again. "Your hot cowboy looks like he'd like to strip you naked in the middle of the bar and fuck you on that pool table if no one was around."

Heat crept up her cheeks and she fiddled with the glass of water she was drinking. "You're mistaken, Rox. I'm just the cook. And not a very good one."

Except for last night. But no way am I letting on about that.

"Uh-huh. Pull the other leg." Roxie wiped the bar. "Just watch yourself, cookie. He looks like he could be big trouble."

Emily gave a weak chuckle. "Yeah. Trouble in cowboy boots."

Lola put her ten cents worth in when they stopped at the Blue Belle. Emily was surprised to see her friend in blue jeans and a Blue Belle t-shirt, smiling as she served the few late afternoon customers before taking a minute to sit with Emily.

"I think this is the first pair of jeans you ever owned," she teased.

Lola winked. "Boland's finest."

Emily burst out laughing. "Me, too. No one would ever believe it."

Lola leaned her head closer to Emily's. "But they'd believe that cowboy has the hots for you. He's talking to my boss but eating you up with his eyes."

"I think that's just his natural look." She fiddled with the coffee cup Lola had brought her.

"Not for a second." Lola grinned. "He's so hot for you he's practically setting his chair on fire. You watch yourself, girl."

"I will. Don't worry. I can take care of myself."

"So how's the cooking going?"

Emily sighed. "I have no idea whatever made me think I knew my way around the kitchen. It's a wonder I haven't poisoned everyone by now."

Lola absently wiped the table with her cloth. "So what are you going to do? Even if he wants to drag you into his bed, I don't think Wyatt will put up with it forever."

Trouble in Cowboy Boots

Emily ducked her head. "He got his foreman's wife to come in this morning and start teaching me. Breakfast was actually good."

Lola's eyes sparkled. "You don't say. Well. Doesn't *that* put a different spin on things."

"Listen, Lola—"

"No, you listen, sweetie. That asshole who dumped you wasn't worth spit. Why don't you see what it's like with a real man?"

"But I work for him," Emily protested.

"So? We won't be here forever. Who cares if you play around with the boss as long as you don't do it in the middle of the yard?"

Emily was glad Lola couldn't see into her brain as pictures from the night before danced around. Before she could think up an answer, Wyatt was standing next to her.

"We need to get going, Emily."

She and Lola exchanged hugs as she got up to leave.

"Thanks for taking the time so I could check on my friends," she told him once they were on the way.

"I figured you'd want to see how they were for yourself." He placed a warm hand on her thigh. "Like your jeans?"

"My jeans?" She frowned. "They're fine. Why?"

"I think we should make sure they work okay. See if you can unsnap and unzip them without a problem."

Her jaw dropped. "Here? In the truck?"

"Yeah, sugar. Right her."

"Wyatt, we're driving down the highway at sixty miles an hour and there are other drivers our here."

"They don't care. Anyway, we're higher than most people so no one can see." His voice changed to a commanding tone. "Do it, Emily. Now."

Moisture flood the crotch of her thong and the tiny muscles in her cunt quivered. Fingers trembling, she popped the snap and ran the zipper down.

"Good. Now tug those jeans under your hips."

"Wyatt!" What on earth?

"Just do it, sugar. Come on. Right now."

Wondering if she'd lost her mind, Emily shifted around until her jeans were down past her butt and her bare ass touched the leather of the seat.

"What now?" she asked.

"Does it get you hot, Emily? Thinking about what I'm doing?" His hand squeezed her thigh. "Be honest, now."

"Y-Yes. A little."

"Wondering what comes next?"

"Y-Yes." She squirmed as the pulsing in her pussy increased in anticipation of what Wyatt might have in mind.

"How about this?"

His hand slid from her thigh across the warm flesh of her tummy and down inside the front of her thong. She gasped as the tip of one finger probed into the nest of her curls and rasped her clit.

"Like that?" He chuckled. "You know, I love these little curls here, but they get in my way. I think maybe tonight we'll get rid of them."

Emily had to fist her hands to keep her thoughts together as Wyatt's finger danced across her nub. "Get rid of them?"

"Oh, yeah. I could tell last night you wax, but since we don't exactly have a place around here for you to keep it up, I think we need to get your little puss completely naked. Then I can keep it that way myself."

She had never thought of completely denuding her cunt, but the thought of Wyatt shaving her himself created a fresh rush of cream.

Trouble in Cowboy Boots

Wyatt slid his finger into her slit and chuckled again. "Oh, yeah, that gets you hot. You like my finger here?"

She nodded.

"Say it, Em. Out loud."

"Yes. I do." Lord, he was getting bossy. But she had to admit it had an erotic effect on her.

"You do what?" he prompted.

"L-Like it."

"Like *what*, Emily?" He pressed his finger hard against her clit. "Tell me."

"I like your finger there."

"Where?" he prompted.

"Touching my clit. In my pussy."

There she'd said it. As soon as the words left her mouth the quivering in her pussy increased. God, she wanted his finger *there*. Inside her.

"Would you like me to fuck you with my finger? Maybe two?"

She wriggled on the seat. "Wyatt, you're driving. You want us to have a wreck?"

He laughed. "Sugar, I'm paying careful attention to my driving. I'm just glad you're not at the wheel."

He brushed her clit again then slid his finger up and down her slit. Without warning he adjusted his hand and pushed two fingers inside her. Immediately her inner muscles clamped around him. He wiggled the fingers before sliding them out.

"Oh, no." The words were out before she could stop them.

His laugh was a soft caress. "That's all you get for now, sugar."

"Wyatt!" She wanted to grab his hand and drag it back to her crotch.

45

"We're almost home. I want you on edge like that for later." He lowered his voice. "I have big plans for tonight."

She caught her breath at his words, wondering exactly what he had in mind. Before she could ask they turned in through the gate of the Lazy Aces and pulled into the parking area. Emily had barely finished pulling her jeans back into place and fastening them before Hardy and two other ranch hands hurried up to the truck to help unload the cartons of Dub's Bar-B-Que.

She had the passenger door to the cab open and started to get out but Wyatt materialized, putting his big hands on her waist and lifting her easily out and onto the ground. The look in his eyes when they locked with hers turned her already overheated body into a solid flame.

"Later," he mouthed before releasing her.

She had no idea how she kept her wits about her while she unpacked the food and fixed platters and bowls for the table. Wyatt lounged against the counter, watching her with those hazel eyes, the green and gold flecks in them burning like jeweled flames. And all the time she moved around she was acutely aware of the throbbing in her cunt and the tightening of her nipples. And a hungry need to feel Wyatt's big cock inside her.

Chapter Four

Finally, finally, dinner was over. The men had left, some to the bunkhouse, Dan to the house he and Amelia shared about a half mile from the main house, others to homes nearby. Emily didn't know if she wanted to find more things to do or rush through her chores. On the one hand she was erotically intrigued by Wyatt's hints for the evening. On the other a tiny thread of anxiety ran through her as she wondered if she'd like whatever he had in mind. What she'd do if she didn't. Worse yet, what she'd do if she did.

"No more stalling." Wyatt's voice was soft and low as he came up behind her, untied her apron and tossed it to the counter. "Everyone's gone now."

She turned slowly, his body so close to hers not even a sheet of paper would slide between them. His erection pressed against her through her jeans. He was ready, no doubt about it.

"Come on," he told her. "I got everything ready."

"Ready?"

"Yeah. Did it while you cleaned up."

As he'd done the night before, he lifted her into his arms and carried her out of the kitchen, through her little sitting room and into her bedroom. The covers were pulled way back on her bed, a large bath towel was spread over the sheet, and on the nightstand was a bowl of water, a razor and a can of shaving cream.

"Your shaving cream?" she asked, since she didn't have any.

He shook his head. "Got it this afternoon. Let's get you naked here."

She stood silently, trembling with anticipation, as he peeled off her clothes, tossed them onto a chair and arranged her on the bed with her buttocks on the side edge of the mattress. He had brought in an ottoman from someplace which he pulled over and sat down on.

"Time to get to work, sugar." He snapped his fingers. "Wait. Forgot something." He turned on the television, found a cable music channel that played soft mood music. Bending over her, he pulled her arms so they rested on the mattress over her head and linked her fingers together. Then he sat down on the ottoman. "All right, then. Here we go. And don't move. Not even a little."

Emily watched him, body thrumming with desire. He took a washcloth from the bowl, wrung the excess water from it, then draped it over her cunt. It was warm and its heat penetrated her flesh. He did this twice more before uncapping the shaving cream, shaking it, and applying it to the narrow strips of public hair she maintained. Fingertips massaged the cream into her skin. Then he picked up a safety razor from the nightstand and bent over her.

One large hand pressed against the inside of her right thigh and fingers stretched the skin at the top of her mound so it was taut. The razor glided gently over the skin, one swipe, then another. Wyatt reached over and rinsed it in the bowl, then went to work again. The music created a soothing environment in the room and Emily, surprisingly, found herself relaxing, even as she anticipated each stroke of the blade.

"This little puss is going to look so good naked," Wyatt crooned. "Maybe we'll get a little tattoo right *here*.' He touched the tip of a finger to the skin covering her public bone.

She jerked at his words. Tattoo?

"Careful," he warned. "Don't want to leave any scrapes here."

Trouble in Cowboy Boots

"A tattoo?" She wet her bottom lip. "Are you for real?"

He chuckled. "Absolutely. I think a little heart would look just great."

"Wyatt!" She had to stop herself from shrieking. "I can't let some strange man tattoo me *there*. I'd die of embarrassment."

"Right now we're only talking about it, sugar, so relax. Take a breath. I just think it would be so appetizing."

The razor clinked against the bowl, Wyatt moved his hand and in a moment a thick layer of the cool cream covered her labia and drew a line all the way down to the globes of her ass. Two fingers gently pinched the skin to draw it taut and he went to work with the razor again, first her outer lips, then very gently her inner ones.

She jumped when one finger slid only to the first knuckle into her vagina, then out. Wyatt lifted the finger to his mouth and slowly licked it.

"Someone's creaming," he said, slowly licking her juices from her skin. "I love that this is turning you on, sugar. And it is, right?"

"Yes." The word came out on a low puff of breath.

"I wonder what else would turn you on." Wyatt rinsed the razor again and stroked the damp washcloth over her now naked cunt. "Let's add a little something to this, okay?"

"W-What do you mean?"

He leaned forward and placed an open-mouthed kiss on her clit, letting his tongue flick back and forth over it before leaning back.

Already aroused from the act of shaving, of imagining the razor sliding over the skin of her pussy, she squirmed at his touch. The muscles in her belly clenched and every nerve in her body was shrieking. She was sure whatever he had in mind was only going to tease the flame higher. By now Emily was ready to beg him to fuck her.

Desiree Holt

His tongue flicked over her clit again, then he lifted her and turned her over so she was face down.

"Wyatt? What are you doing?"

"Gotta get the rest of that soft, fine hair." He arranged her on her knees, placed her head on her forearms and spread her thighs apart. "Don't move a muscle, sugar. I don't want to accidentally hurt you."

"But what are you doing?" she asked again.

"Just hold perfectly still."

He moved the washcloth along the cleft between the cheeks of her buttocks, rubbing it against the skin like a caress. One hand pressed against the base of her spine and prevented her from jerking when she heard the hiss of the shaving cream and felt its thick smoothness on the puckered skin around her anus.

"Ohmigod! You're not—"

"Just hold tight, sugar. It'll be fine."

The kiss of the razor was gentle and smooth against the tender skin as he moved it carefully over every bit of the skin around her hole. Emily held as still as she could, her bottom lip caught between her teeth. She'd never had a man touch her there so intimately. Oh, not that she hadn't indulged in anal sex. But Nick the scumbag, had mostly been interested in his own satisfaction. Even when he'd worked her so it didn't hurt, he'd never lasted long enough for her to reach her climax.

"Finish yourself off," he always gasped, throwing himself on his back like a flopping fish.

But she had the feeling no matter how things played out, Wyatt would be totally different. He bathed the area with the warm cloth again, then placed soft kisses all over her ass. She was ready to turn over onto her back again when the flat of Wyatt's hand cracked against her ass. *Smack!* A stinging blow that made her jump. What on earth—

"Hey!" She tried to move away but he pressed one hand firmly on the base of her spine, holding her in place.

Trouble in Cowboy Boots

Another blow landed, on the other cheek. And something strange happened to her that almost frightened her. Instead of incredible pain, the stinging of the blow created heat that rushed to her pussy and her nipples, arousing her in a strange new way. Wyatt drew one finger along her cunt, testing her wetness and she heard his soft laugh.

"You like that. I had a feeling you would. Let's try it again."

Still holding her firmly in place, he resumed spanking her, first one cheek of her ass then the other, until she lost count and was only aware of the burning heat consuming her and the need growing tightly inside her.

Then he stopped and she couldn't hold back the moan of disappointment that rolled from her lips.

Wyatt touched her anus, rimming it with his finger again and again.

"I'm going to fuck you here, sugar. Not tonight because you aren't ready. But I'm going to make you ready. And when I do this, you'll come like you never did before." He turned her onto her back again, eyes fixed on her naked cunt. "Beautiful. Just like I knew it would be."

He bent over her and kissed her, a hot kiss that singed her mouth, his tongue probing and tasting. He hadn't told her not to touch him now so she lifted her hands to run her fingers through his thick, silky hair. Her tongue met his, dueling with it, and she thrust hers into his mouth. He seduced her with his wicked tongue, fucking her mouth and leading her into an erotic dance.

When he stood up his face was dark with lust and hunger.

"So tell me, Emily. Have you ever been tied up before?"

Her eyes widened. She opened her mouth to answer him but no words came out.

And there was that chuckle again, like the devil's laughter.

"Let me tell you how I like my sex, Emily Proctor." As he spoke he slowly removed his clothes. "I like it rough but not so rough it's not enjoyable. I like to dominate, but only if my partner is willing to submit. Do you understand what I'm trying to tell you, sugar?"

She nodded, eyes wide, pussy fluttering.

"In the bedroom I want to be the one to call the shots, whatever they are. I want to tie you up and spank you. Fuck you with every kind of dildo. See you on your knees sucking my cock. Tease you until if you don't come you'll go crazy, and not let you come until I tell you to. Can you take that? Would that give you pleasure, Em?"

"I-I think so. I've never, um, you know…"

"Never done this?" One corner of his mouth turned up in a half-grin. "Oh, I know that sugar. And I want to tell you this takes a tremendous amount of trust." The grin disappeared. He was fully naked now and looming over her, his cock swollen, the head dark and engorged. "Truth time, Emily. We haven't known each other that long but you've had a good chance to see what kind of person I am. Think you could trust me? Like that?"

Could she? Take a step that big with a man she'd just met?

"You'd have a safe word," he went on. "Any time you want to stop all you have to do is use it. No questions asked. And Emily? You have no idea how much your submission would turn me on. It would be a gift I'd cherish. So in reality, you'd be the one in control."

He tried to stay calm while he waited for her answer. Her eyes never left his and he could almost see the questions chasing themselves through her brain. He couldn't remember the last time an attraction to a woman had been this strong, like a virtual punch to the gut. Last night had shattered him, breaking down the wall he always kept carefully erected

Trouble in Cowboy Boots

between himself and his partner. He'd learned to be physically involved, to elicit trust, without letting his emotions off the leash.

But Emily Proctor was a completely different story, and he didn't have any idea why. She was nothing like the women he'd dated. They were tall, knowledgeable, steeped in Texas life and aware of the culture of ranching. They could hold their own in an upscale restaurant or a musky barn. And they expected the same thing he did—a fulfilling relationship for whatever time it lasted. He wasn't looking for a permanent thing and he carefully chose women who felt the same way. He liked his freedom, his independence. He was far from ready to give up the banquet life offered, nor had he felt the need to.

But somehow this woman with the silky brunette hair, who looked far more fragile than she actually was, had knocked down those barriers in a heartbeat. Well, okay, in an orgasm that defied description. This whole thing had moved along at fast-forward speed. But she'd gotten to him in a way no other woman ever had. He wanted to tie her up, fuck her senseless, spank that luscious ass and then fuck her there. More. All. Everything.

She was also the only women he'd fucked in this house. He was always very careful to separate his sex life from his real life, not wanting to give any of his women the idea they could make themselves at home on the Lazy Aces. But everything about Em was different, and he wondered if he was following his cock only to find his head in a noose. Still, he had no intention of changing his mind, he wanted this woman with an unexpected fierceness.

What if she said no? How would he be able to let her stay here, temptation just beyond his reach? But he couldn't fire her. He'd already let that cat out of the bag.

Shit!

He wished she would say something already.

53

Then she nodded, slowly, and a soft "Yes" floated from her mouth.

Wyatt let his breath out in a whoosh and his heart began beating in triple time.

"Stay right here," he murmured. "I'll be right back. Do not move."

She nodded.

He yanked on his jeans and shirt and raced through the house, confident that no one would wander in accidentally and ask him what the mad dash was about. In his room he opened a locked drawer and took out the things he wanted, yanking off his t-shirt and folding it to hold everything. Then he was back in Emily's bedroom, placing everything very carefully on the nightstand and stripping off his jeans again.

He paused to take a look at Emily, stretched out on the bed, the sweet naked little cunt just calling to him. She had stayed right where she was, in the same position, a look of expectancy on her face.

Too fucking wonderful.

Reaching out he ran his hand over the pink skin.

"Sweet. Just fucking sweet."

Lifting Emily, he whisked away the towel still beneath her, tossed it aside and arranged her with her head on the pillows. As he reached for the fleece-lined leather cuffs beside the bed, he gave silent thanks that the beds in the house all had old-fashioned spindled headboards.

With great care he fastened each of the cuffs around her wrists, threading the thongs and linking them through the headboard. Emily followed everything he did with her eyes. When he had the cuffs secured, he bent his head and kissed her, first brushing his lips against hers before tracing the seam with his tongue and finally thrusting it inside. She welcomed his invasion, meeting his tongue with her own, and in that instant he knew it would be all right. That she would accept

Trouble in Cowboy Boots

everything he had to offer and meet it with her own challenges.

His blood raced with anticipation and his cock flexed with need. He knew the playtime in the truck and shaving her cunt had enhanced her arousal. Now he wanted to see how long he could tease her, how well she could follow his order not to come until he finally gave her the release she wanted. He only hoped he could control *himself* long enough.

Kneeling between her thighs, he reached for a small vibrator that was one of his favorites. All of the toys were brand new — he always restocked after a relationship ended — but he knew how stimulating this particular toy could be.

Emily was watching him, the heat in her eyes unmistakable, her face flushed with desire. God, he wanted to lick every inch of her body. He settled for kissing the insides of her thighs, just feather-light touches, tiny licks with his tongue, a ghost of a touch. He was rewarded when she quivered with need, automatically arching her hips up to him, urging him to the place she really wanted his touch.

He chuckled against her soft skin. "You want more, sugar? Let's see how you like this?"

He turned on the little vibrator and ran it in short strokes over the top of her mound, over the newly naked skin. Although he circled the clit peeping out from the folds of pink flesh he deliberately skirted it, saving it until she was begging for him to touch her *there*.

"Please," she begged, as the vibrator slid up and down her labia and rimmed the opening of her vagina.

"Please what?" He heard the huskiness in his own voice. "Tell me what you want, sugar?"

"More. You know." She tugged at the cuffs as if trying to free her hands to show him what to do.

55

Wyatt bent forward, even as he kept the little toy buzzing around on its journey, and licked each nipple, once, with the tip of his tongue.

"If you want it, you have to tell me," he urged. "I want to hear you say the words."

Signs of her internal struggle flashed across her face. Then she wet her lips, took a deep breath and said, "Put it on my clit."

"Ah." He smiled at her. "See there? That's my girl. And here's your reward."

He placed the little toy directly on her clit and exerted a slight amount of pressure. He knew the vibrations were racing through her pouty lips and into her wet channel. He knew exactly how much this would arouse her. He kept his eyes glued to her face as she trembled and bucked, trying to squeeze her legs together, riding the wave rising within her.

He slipped one finger inside her cunt and was rewarded with the wet kiss of her tender flesh and the clutching of her muscles around his touch. Her hips bucked again and the flush on her face deepened.

"Keep those beautiful eyes open," he ordered when she closed them to lose herself in sensation. "I want to watch them when you come."

No sooner had he said the words than her climax roared up through her, shaking her, hot cream bathing his finger inside her. She pushed her heels into the mattress. Lifting herself into the stimulation as she continued to convulse in the grip of the orgasm. And despite her obvious need to lose herself in the blaze of carnal heat, she kept her eyes open, locked with his. The jade green darkened to the color of moss, golden highlights dancing in them as she rode out her orgasm.

When she finally stopped shuddering she let her head fall back on the pillows and struggled to draw air into her lungs.

Wyatt turned off the vibrator, dropped it beside him and crawled up to place his lips against hers, barely touching.

Trouble in Cowboy Boots

"Wasn't that good, sugar?" he breathed into her mouth. "I love watching you come. You let it all go."

"Uh-huh," was all she could manage.

He thrust his tongue inside her mouth, licking every bit of the inner surface before lifting his head.

"Let's see how you like this." He picked up a realistic-looking dildo and rubbed it across her breasts, then dragged it down the valley between them, all the while watching her. "Lick it. Suck it into your mouth."

He placed the tip against one of her lips and obediently she snaked her tongue out to swipe across the tip. When he nudged it against her, she opened her mouth and he gave her as much in as she could take.

"That's it. That's how it will look when you suck my cock, sugar. Swirl your tongue around it. Pretend you're tasting me."

He had to pull the dildo away from her after mere seconds, afraid he would come from just watching her. And he wanted to be inside her when that happened. Memories of the wet, clutching warmth of her pussy rolled back over him from the previous night and he wanted that feeling again.

Nudging her thighs wider apart, he slid the dildo inside her channel, then pressed a little button on the bottom that set it in motion. At once Emily went wild, hunching down on the toy, riding it as if it were his cock inside her. She yanked on the cuffs, not to free herself but to give herself a pushing off point, and fucked the dildo with a wildness that sent jolts of lightning to his already aching balls.

Long before he wanted to, he worked the dildo free, reached over for a condom and used both hands to roll it onto his erection. He bent her knees back until they touched her breasts, placed his hands beneath her ass and drove into her with a fierceness that startled him. Holy hell! What was it about this woman that shredded the control he so prided himself on?

57

Then there was no more time for thinking. Her pussy closed around him like a wet fist, cries of pleasure rolled from her lips and he powered into her with hard, fast strokes. He'd wanted to take it slow this first time, but that didn't seem to be an option. He gritted his teeth, watching for signs that her climax was rising within her again. When he saw it, felt the spasms milking his cock and her body shake with the force of it, he allowed himself his release, bracing himself on his hands as he drove into her over and over and over.

He lost every sense of himself as the orgasm shook him. There was nothing but him, this woman, her hungry cunt and his cock deep inside her. At some point he realized he'd collapsed on top of her, heart racing like a wild mustang. He knew he had to be crushing her beneath his weight so he made the effort to ease up a little and rest on his forearms.

Reaching over her with one hand he released the cuffs so she could lower her arms. Then he kissed her, a deep kiss that was equal parts of lust and passion and...something else. Something he chose to ignore. Fucking Emily was better than winning the lottery and that's what he would concentrate on.

Finally he rolled carefully away from her and made it to the bathroom to dispose of the condom. He swept the toys from the bed and dropped them into her nightstand drawer, then climbed under the covers beside her. He took a moment to massage her arms, easing the strain of them being manacled over her head, before tucking her up against him and resting his chin on her hair.

"Sleep, Emily," he murmured. "Rest."

"Amelia's coming again in the morning," she said drowsily.

"I know. Close your eyes. Morning gets here far too soon."

Chapter Five

ജ

"If they call me Auntie Em one more time I'm dousing them in bacon grease," Emily grumbled as she mixed batter for pancakes.

Amelia laughed. "I'd pay good money to see that. By the way, you're mixing much smoother this morning. Did you practice last night?"

"Oh, no, I—" She looked at Amelia, who had mischief dancing in her eyes. "What?"

"I used to have that same morning after blush on my face when I was younger," Amelia teased. "And even now Dan still rings my chimes."

"Amelia!" Emily felt the heat creeping up her cheeks. "I haven't any idea what you're talking about."

Amelia's laugh was like music dancing in the air. "Okay, if that's how you want it. But I passed Wyatt as I came in this morning and he had a big shit-eating grin on his face."

Emily just shook her head. Like Wyatt, she didn't want what was happening between them to become the subject of ranch gossip. He was gone most of the day, out with the hands or working in his office in the barn, so there was little chance for anyone to see them together. She was more than grateful for that, especially after last night.

Again her cheeks warmed. She'd always had a healthy appetite for sex and even been open to new suggestions, but Wyatt was introducing her to a whole new level of sensuality. And he'd been right about one thing—giving him control actually put her in charge. The more she allowed him to take charge of the things they did, the more aroused he became and the more it heightened his orgasm. Last night his powerful body had shuddered so hard with his release she wasn't sure he'd survive.

Of course, she hadn't been sure she would, either. He took her to a plane of greater arousal, greater sensuality than she ever remembered feeling before. Wondering what he had in mind for tonight made all the nerves in her pussy ignite and sent a low rush of heat through her body.

"Better get that griddle hot," Amelia reminded her. "First shift will be here in five and you still have to scramble the eggs."

Lordy! Would she ever be able to multitask in the kitchen? She'd thought it a miracle yesterday that she got through the day without burning anything or throwing food away. Wyatt's generous offer to pick up barbecue last night had been a big help but no such luck today. Amelia had shown her how to bread chicken this morning before they started breakfast. She'd finish that after she cleaned up from the morning meal. But the work had put her a little behind.

"Here they come," Amelia warned, as boots sounded on the back porch.

Shit! I'm not ready.

Apparently no one cared, because in they came.

She spooned pancake batter onto the griddle and emptied the beaten eggs into the heated frying pan.

"You producing another good breakfast today, Auntie Em?" Hardy asked as he led the way to the tables.

"You Auntie Em me once more," she told him, "and I'll turn you into a munchkin."

"Ooh!" He widened his eyes and waved his hands. "I'm scared, guys. Real scared."

Amelia flapped a dish towel at him. "Hardy Wolf, you shut up and sit down or you won't get any breakfast at all." She pulled the biscuits from the oven and plopped them into two baskets which she carried to the table, then flipped the pancakes while Emily worked on the eggs.

Trouble in Cowboy Boots

"Lookie!" Hardy broke open a biscuit. "Flaky again. Yee haw."

"Just like you, Hardy," Emily called. After four days she was feeling more confident with the men.

"What do we use now for target practice?" someone joked.

Emily banged her wooden mixing spoon so hard on the counter it nearly shattered and gritted her teeth. She didn't have time for this bullshit. Even with Amelia's help she was barely keeping her head above water. Who knew it took so many men to run a cattle ranch? Who knew she'd pick a ranch the size of the Lazy Aces that ran ten thousand head of cattle? She wondered if slopping beer at Chaps wouldn't have been a better choice.

Breakfast was barely finished before she rolled up her sleeves and breaded the rest of the chicken the way Amelia had shown her. Holy shit, it took a lot of chicken to feed twenty men. She didn't even count herself, unsure if she'd even have an appetite by the time she finished cooking. This afternoon she'd peel potatoes and Amelia had promised to slip over and make the gravy, thank god. Gravy! Where had she gotten the mistaken impression that on ranches all they ate were things that came out of cans. She could open cans with the best of them.

Or cooked on a grill. That was her only other skill. Who knew she'd have to make *real food*?

By late afternoon she'd served lunch—this time she *did* open cans, large ones of chili—finished the prep work on the chicken and put the covered platters in the fridge, and taken out the veggies for dinner. Fixing a glass of iced tea, she carried it out to the back porch and sank gratefully into one of the rockers.

She hadn't really taken time to look at the ranch, and had seen very little of it except for the kitchen and her bedroom. Now she watched as two men worked horses in the corral with

61

a handful of calves. She'd have to ask Wyatt what that was all about. In the distance she could see cattle grazing in the pastures and half a dozen riders trotting slowly along the fences. At the open doors of the barn two men were loading hay into the bed of a dual cab pickup.

She rocked slowly as she sipped her tea, taking in the vast amount of land that stretched away from the house to a vanishing point on the horizon. So this was what the west was all about—acres of land, cattle, horses, blue skies, oak trees and some others she didn't recognize, and cowboys.

Cowboys who eat a lot.

"Taking in the sights?"

She'd been so engrossed in studying her surroundings she hadn't heard Wyatt mount the side steps to the porch until his warm voice slid over her like a velvet blanket. Her hand jerked and the iced tea sloshed over the rim.

"Sorry." He lowered his lanky frame into the rocker next to her. "Didn't mean to startle you." He took off his hat, shoveled his fingers through his hair, wiped his forehead on the sleeve of his shirt and clapped the hat back on his head. "So how's everything in the kitchen?"

Was that a smile teasing at the corners of his mouth?

Emily wiped her hand on her jeans—her *new* jeans—and took another sip of her tea.

"Everything's just fine. Fried chicken for dinner tonight."

"Oh? I'm impressed. Second day of cooking school and you're tackling a staple of the west."

"Amelia said you aren't a cook if you can't make fried chicken," she told him.

"But you aren't a cook anyway, are you, Em?" His voice was low and deep. "Exactly what are you?"

"I'm a refugee from Las Vegas, broke and homeless." She glanced over at him. "And I can book a mean convention."

Trouble in Cowboy Boots

"Well," he drawled, "that ought to be a big help in Mesa Blanco."

"Did you sit down here just to rattle my chains?" She took another swallow of iced tea, determined not to rise to his baiting.

"Yeah, kinda." He chuckled softly. "I love it that you don't back down. That you can give as good as you get. You'll have those idiots who work for me eating out of your hands before another week goes by."

"They're just interested in eating, out of my hand or anywhere else."

He rocked silently for a moment and Emily toyed with her glass.

"It's Friday. I thought maybe you'd like to try out another pair of those new jeans tonight and take them into town."

Emily had to stop her jaw from dropping. "You want to be seen in public? With me?"

"Em." The word was filled with dogged patience. "Everyone in the county knows by now you work for me. They don't expect me to keep you hidden under a rock. And they know you're alone here except for your two friends."

"I thought you said…"

"What I said was we should keep our private business private. That hasn't changed. But there's nothing that says I can't take you into town for a little socializing." He tilted his head back. "Just to set the record straight, I'm only talking about a visit to Chaps and a chance for you to see your friends. I wasn't planning to strip you naked, tie you up and fuck you on the pool table in front of the entire population of the county."

Her tea slopped onto her feet as her hand shook and her glass tilted.

Wyatt's laugh was full and rich. "Take it easy, Emily. Teasing you is too much fun."

63

"So you don't really want to take me into town. Right?"

"Of course I want to. You need to have a little fun." He leaned closer to her. "Loosen up."

Her cheeks felt as if she'd burned them. Maybe he really did plan to strip her naked in the honky-tonk. "I thought I was plenty loose last night," she muttered.

Wyatt rose from the chair. "That's for sure, sugar. So tonight we get to have fun, and then we get to play. Better close your mouth before you catch flies. And I'd say it's about time to start dinner. Lot of chicken to fry."

She didn't know if she should dump the rest of her tea on him or tell him to go to hell. Before she could do either he ambled off the porch, still chuckling to himself.

* * * * *

Emily was sure she'd never get the smell of frying grease off her skin or out of her hair, but the dinner had been a success. Nobody had thrown pieces of chicken at her, the potatoes and gravy were both smooth and the big bowls of vegetables scraped clean. When the kitchen was spotless she turned to scrubbing herself, using extra dollops of fragrant shampoo and scented shower gel. Better to smell like a ripe flower garden than a short order cook, she decided.

She stepped into a pair of the new jeans, pulled a magenta short-sleeved silk blouse out of her closet and took extra pains with her makeup and hair. She decided it was worth the effort when she saw the heated look in Wyatt's eyes as she walked into the kitchen where he waited for her.

"My, my," he drawled as his eyes raked over her. "You sure do clean up good."

"You're not so bad yourself," she commented.

He had put on clean jeans and a green plaid shirt that brought out the emerald flecks in his eyes. He'd exchanged his shit-kicker boots for a hand-tooled pair that she knew from the Vegas high rollers were custom Luccheses. A black Stetson sat

Trouble in Cowboy Boots

on his head. He looked like every bad boy she'd ever seen or dreamed about and was more dangerous than a pound of C-4 explosive.

He pushed away from the counter where he'd been leaning. "Ready?"

Emily rubbed her hands nervously on her jeans. "I guess so."

"Fun, Emily." He took her arm and led her out the back door. "Remember? We're having fun."

But she knew she'd be under scrutiny from all the people in town who knew him. His friends. Other ranchers. Whoever. It was Friday night and Chaps, being the only game in town, was sure to be crowded.

"Relax." He helped her up into the truck cab. "You'll be fine. It's much easier than Las Vegas."

A lot you know. I don't have my protective professional suits on or my Blackberry in my hand like some electronic sword.

Her other problem was that in a very short space of time she'd found herself falling for this sexy-as-sin cowboy. Not good. Obviously he had no plans for anything permanent and she was only focused on getting away from Mesa Blanco.

She sighed, wishing she didn't spend her life painting herself into a corner.

The parking area outside Chaps was jammed with pickups and SUVs. Wyatt managed to squeeze the truck into a spot at one corner of the bar, then came around to help her step down. She swallowed back her nerves as he pulled open the door to the building and she was assaulted by sound — people talking, laughing, jukebox music blaring into the crowd.

There didn't seem to be an inch of space left anywhere in the honky-tonk. People lined the serving area along one wall, clamoring for refills while the Roxie and another bartender, somehow unfazed by it all, simultaneously served the bar customers and took orders from the two waitresses. Every table and booth was filled, people were crammed onto the miniscule dance floor moving to the music blasting from the juke box, and the clink of balls signaled a pool game in progress.

Wyatt elbowed them some space at one end of the bar, grinned at Roxie and held up two fingers.

"Lone Stars, when you get a minute."

"How do you know I drink beer?" Emily found herself shouting to be heard.

Wyatt put his mouth close to her ear. "Sugar, it's the national drink of Texas. You gotta have at least one."

Nick had liked to dance, but his idea of dancing was groping to music. Now that she thought about it, his idea of everything had always been about what he wanted. What he liked. As it was with most of the men she'd dated. Years ago her college roommate had told her she had crappy taste in men. She picked them by how they looked — expensive — not by what they were. But Emily had a plan in life. Corporate success for herself and a partner of equal or greater value. Then it had all come crashing down on her head, disappearing and Nick along with it. she'd chosen Nick because she thought he'd look good on a formal Christmas card.

Well, that was what she got for being so superficial.

But Wyatt Cavanaugh was real. She just had to remember he was temporary. He wasn't looking for wife and she wasn't ready to settle down in the middle of godforsaken nowhere.

His warm breath tickled her ear and the touch of his arm across her shoulders singed her flesh. She picked up a bar napkin and fanned herself with it, hoping the rise in her temperature was due to the crowd of people in the room and not Wyatt Cavanaugh. Despite the fact that everyone in the place seemed to be focused on having a good time, she was acutely aware of many eyes on her as she and Wyatt had walked in. She wondered how many other women he'd brought here, or who of the women in the place he'd dated. Taken to bed. Whispered his special brand of sex talk.

Stop it! You're only staying around long enough to score some bucks and keep traveling, and he certainly hasn't given a hint he's looking for more than fun and games.

Roxie plunked two frosty bottles of beer down in front of them and smiled at Emily.

"Rox, I didn't know you were such a whiz at bartending," Emily commented.

"How do you think I earned my way through the School of Hard Knocks?" Then she was off to serve another customer.

"Drink up," Wyatt said, handing her one of the bottles.

Someone tapped her shoulder and she turned around to see Lola standing behind her with the sheriff, Sam Campbell.

"You look great, honey." Lola grinned. "I take it things are going okay?"

"Oh, sure." She paused to take a sip of her beer. "Wyatt's a good guy to work for."

"Uh-huh." Lola winked. "And play with, too, I'll bet."

"Lola!" Emily did her best to look indignant but couldn't quite pull it off.

"That's okay, sweetie. The sheriff is teaching me his own special brand of law enforcement."

"So you're doing okay?" Emily asked.

"I'd say so." She shrugged. "The job's a lot better than I expected. The owner's a real nice lady to work for, I'm getting to know the customers and she's letting me use the little apartment behind the restaurant."

"Any word on the car?" Lola had agreed to take the lead on that.

"Yeah, but the word isn't so good." Lola sighed. "Sam's been checking every day at the garage, and when they told him how much it would cost just to get it started and out of town I didn't have the heart to tell anyone."

"Damn."

Emily's stomach muscles cramped. She had only taken the job at the Lazy Aces because it was temporary. She not only didn't intend to spend her life cooking for a bunch of cowhands, she was sure her *thing* with Wyatt would run its course and then what?

"You don't look like life's treating you too badly." Lola winked at her. "How's the cooking going?"

"Oh, hell." Emily took a long drink of her beer. "I'll be lucky if I don't set fire to the kitchen before this is over." She lowered her voice and bent closer so Lola could hear her. "At least Wyatt took pity on me and got the foreman's wife to teach me a few things."

"Oh?" Lola arched an eyebrow. "Sounds like he might be interested in keeping you around."

"All things are possible." Wyatt's voice intruded into their conversation.

Emily jerked, embarrassed that he'd heard Lola's comments. "Um..."

He plucked the bottle from her hand. "Excuse us, Lola, if you don't mind. I think I'll try and find us a square inch of space on the dance floor."

A square inch of space was about all they got. Couples were jammed together, doing little more than moving their feet in place. Wyatt pulled her against his long, lean body, wrapped his arms around her and began swaying to the music. She could feel every inch of him against her, including his belt buckle and his thick erection.

She inhaled his scent, a heady mixture of clean laundry, soap and something woodsy. His hands were warm on her back, holding her in place. She recognized a ballad by Brad Paisley, one of her favorites, and let its sound wash over her, wishing she could freeze this one moment in time.

Trouble in Cowboy Boots

She didn't even realize the music had stopped until someone jostled them. Then she heard the sultry voice with the Texas drawl and all her senses went on alert.

"Well, hi, Wyatt. I haven't seen you out two-steppin' for a while."

Wyatt's hands tightened on her and Emily looked at the woman trying to glue herself to Wyatt's body. Tall, with a head full of dark, bouncing curls, dark eyes, and breasts that stuck out all the way back to West Texas. She'd managed to tug one of Wyatt's arms from around Emily and now had her own linked through it in obviously possessive gesture.

"Hello, Diana." He extricated his arm from her grasp and tried to move away, but the dance floor was too packed to allow room to maneuver.

Her eyes narrowed and her gaze raked Emily from head to toe. "And who's this little toy you're shuffling around? Not your usual speed, cowboy."

Wyatt's grip on Emily tightened. "Emily, meet Diana Landry. My neighbor."

Her full lips cracked in a wide smile. "Oh, honey, we're so much more than that." She winked at Emily. "Much more. Wyatt and I are…very good friends." She switched her gaze to him. "I'm home for the next couple of weeks, hot stuff, if you want to pay a neighborly visit."

Emily was stunned that the woman would be so blatantly predatory when it was obvious Wyatt was with someone else. She wondered if it would be possible for her to shrink down to miniature size and jump into Wyatt's pocket. No doubt about it. That was the only word for this woman — predatory. But she had to admit to herself that Diana Landry looked to be much more Wyatt's style than she was.

The man standing with Diana stared at all of them impassively. "Come on, Diana. Let's get another drink."

"Oh, but I—"

69

"Good idea. I think we'll do the same." The juke box had cranked over to another tune and as everyone began what passed for dancing, Wyatt grabbed Emily's hand and tugged her through the crowd, back to the end of the bar. He signaled Roxie to bring them two more beers.

Emily picked up the bottle and took a long swallow. When she set it back down she was irritated to see her hands were shaking. She'd dealt with a lot of women like Diana Landry in Las Vegas, but she'd always been the one in control. Here she was completely out of her element. She wanted to tell him she'd changed her mind about everything but this wasn't the place to discuss it. Right now she just wanted to leave.

Wyatt cupped her chin and pulled her face close enough to hear what he was saying. "You're thinking so hard I can almost hear it, even over this crowd. Ignore Diana. She isn't worth wasting one minute of your time. We're neighbors, no more. Right now I'm sorry we're even that."

Emily shook her head. "You don't owe me any explanations." Then she stopped talking. She'd have to shout to say more and she didn't want anyone around them to know their business. "I appreciate your efforts to entertain me tonight, but maybe it would be better if we just left."

Wyatt set his beer bottle down carefully on the bar and took Emily's hand. But instead of heading for the door he led her right back onto the dance floor, positioning them so they were far enough away from Diana and her date not to bump into them but close enough to be seen. He proceeded to wrap his arms around her, holding her tight to his body, every inch of them touching.

Butterflies were doing the tango in her stomach but the muscles in her pussy were fluttering, her panties were wet and her breasts ached with a painful need. Close contact with this man made her brain take flight and her body scream for more. Oh, this was so not good.

She tilted her head back as much as she could and looked up at him, "Wyatt, I think —"

Trouble in Cowboy Boots

He put his mouth right on her ear. "That's your problem, sugar. You think too much."

She would have said more but conversation in here really was impossible. Instead she just let herself lean into him, savoring the scent and feel of him. Surely he'd realized what a poor substitute she was for someone like Diana Landry and that was all right. She wondered why she had such a letdown feeling. She'd expected something like this. Maybe tomorrow she'd have one of the hands drive her into town and bunk with Roxie or Lola while she figured out what to do. But right now she'd enjoy the moment.

The song ended but Wyatt made no move to leave the dance floor. Instead he tucked her head into his shoulder and rubbed his big hands up and down her back in a public show of possessiveness until the next sound boomed out. Once, when she sneaked a sideways glance, she saw Diana at a table with three other people staring daggers at her and pressed herself even closer to the man holding her.

He made dancing as intimate as sex, insinuating one long leg between hers, so when she moved her cunt rubbed against his thigh. The thickness of his erection behind the denim of his jeans was like a branding iron burning into her. When he bent his head lower he nipped at her ear and licked at the edge of her jaw before shifting his head again.

The music changed again and one of his hands slipped up to the nape of her neck, his fingers threading through her hair and gently massaging her scalp. He moved enough to the music to allow her breasts to rub against his chest. If only they were alone and she could rip off her blouse and his shirt and feel the soft dark-gold hair on his chest against her swollen nipples.

Emily had no idea how long they danced—if what they did could be called dancing—but after a while she felt as if they were in a cocoon by themselves. The crowd and noise fell away and she was only conscious of Wyatt's body against hers, his thick cock, his warm hands, his lips and teeth taking secret nips.

By the time he led her from the dance floor her legs were wobbly and the pulse of need inside her beat insistently. Wyatt stuck some bills under their empty beer bottles then tugged her toward the door with him. He had it partially open when she heard Diana Landry's sultry voice again, right at her elbow.

"Nice seeing you, Wyatt." She trailed her fingernails along one arm. "I'll be up very late if you want to drop by."

Wyatt stopped away from her. "No, thanks, Diana. Been there, done that, and it wasn't all that great."

Diana's eyes widened, an angry flush stained her cheeks and she drew back her hand as if to slap him.

Wyatt grabbed her wrist. "You don't want to do that. Believe me." He pushed the door open and nearly dragged Emily into the parking lot. Even in the limited light from the parking lot she could see the angry flush staining his cheeks and the rigid set of his jaw.

Emily buckled herself into her seat and sat quietly as Wyatt backed the truck out of the lot, spitting gravel, and roared out onto the highway. They'd driven a good five miles before his jaw unclenched and he broke the silence.

"I'm sorry."

She turned her head and stared at him "*You're* sorry? For what?"

"For my past sins, I guess. I would have insisted Diana apologize to you but that just would have started another scene."

"Wyatt, when I was working in Las Vegas I dealt with women like Diana all the time." She snorted. "BBBM, we used to call them behind their backs."

"Huh? What does that stand for?"

Trouble in Cowboy Boots

"Big Boobs, Big Mouth." She sighed. "Predatory females with too much money and not enough manners. And hot pants for anything that caught their eye."

"That's Diana. Hands down." He'd been driving at what Emily considered an excessive speed but now he slowed down.

"Maybe she's more your type than I am," Emily ventured.

"What the hell is that supposed to mean?" She could hear the anger in his strident tone.

"She's a lot more experienced, and obviously knows what you like."

"But the pleasure is in teaching you." His voice was soft, seductive. "Aren't you having fun learning?"

She swallowed. Hard. "Yes."

"All right, then. No more of that. If I wanted Diana she's made it obvious she's there for the taking. I guess that was my style until…"

"Until what?" She wished she could see the expression on his face.

"Never mind." He sighed. "I'm just sorry we ran into her. Sorry she behaved the way she did."

She rubbed her hands on her jeans. "So tell me, Wyatt. Do you think the little performance on the dance floor had any effect on her at all?"

"I hope so." He tapped his thumb on the steering wheel. "But with her, who knows."

"Well." She rubbed her jeans again. "I have two comments to make on that. I don't think it fazed her at all. And it wasn't necessary. I wouldn't want you to be embarrassed by giving people the wrong impression about, you know."

He stopped tapping. "About *I know*? Exactly what does that mean, Emily?"

She wet her lips, suddenly sure that whatever she said would be the wrong thing. Why in hell had she ever gotten involved with this man anyway? She was better off when she was just the pretend cook trying to hang on long enough to get out of here.

"People might get the wrong idea about us. That could be difficult for you."

Swerving suddenly to the right, he pulled off onto the shoulder of the road and jammed the gearshift into Park. Releasing her seat belt with one hand, he hauled her over the console and into his lap. She had just opened her mouth to ask him what he was doing when he pressed his lips to hers and his tongue slipped into her mouth. There was no questioning his intent. He fucked her mouth with his tongue as his hand came up to cup one breast, thumb rasping over the nipple.

His other hand cupped her head, fingers threaded in her hair, pulling her head back to give him better access to her. As his mouth moved down the column of her neck to the place where the pulse beat rapidly, his hand kneaded her breast and his fingers pinched the nipple.

Emily moaned, her fingers clutching his arm to steady herself.

Then, just as suddenly, he lifted her and set her back into her seat, carefully rebuckling the belt.

"Don't presume to tell me what I worry about. I don't know if what we've got is just incredible sex or not, but I damn sure intend to find out. I'm not concerned about what this town thinks. I grew up here and they've seen all my warts. I'm sorry if I have given you that impression. My concern is how the men who work for me treat you. Period. Now." He put the truck in Drive and pulled back onto the road. "We're going home to see how you like what else I have in mind."

Chapter Six

Emily stared straight ahead, eyes fastened on Wyatt's cock which was barely two inches away from her. He was magnificently naked, standing legs spread apart, eyes blazing as he looked down at her. She was kneeling on the carpet, hands fastened behind her with the handcuffs, desire ramped up at the feeling of submission, of his dominance. Her only rational thought was, "What would vanilla Nick think about me now?"

"Open your mouth," he commanded.

Obediently she did so. He moved closer and rested the head of his cock on her bottom lip. She licked the head, tasting the salty flavor of him in the tiny bead of liquid at the slit. Swirling her tongue over the velvet softness, she pressed the tip into the slit, pleased at the hiss of his indrawn breath.

"Tilt your head back, Emily."

When she did he rocked his hips, his cock riding over her tongue and into the back of her mouth.

"Breathe," he told her. "And keep your head tilted back. I don't want to hurt you."

His hands moved to cup her head on either side and he thrust himself in and out of her mouth. She closed her lips around him, teeth barely scraping the soft flesh over steel. Wyatt shuddered every time her teeth raked the pulsing shaft, fingers tightening on her scalp. Then he began to ride her mouth in earnest.

"Look at me, Emily."

She raised her eyes, met his burning with the fire of carnal heat.

"God, you look so beautiful like that, on your knees, my cock in your mouth, hands behind your back."

His hands worked her head back and forth on his shaft. "That's it. Suck it, sugar. Just like that. Jesus." He closed his eyes, then opened them. "This is what I want, Emily. You. Here with me."

Wyatt gritted his teeth. He was afraid to say too much. Give away too much. His feelings for this woman were still so complicated he had trouble sorting them out. He only knew that the first time he fucked her the explosion had rocketed through every part of his body. Singed his mind. Last night, when he'd begun to introduce her to the kind of sex he liked, she hadn't turned away from anything. Actually embraced it all. And the pleasure he got from it was beyond anything he'd ever experienced before.

Running into Diana tonight had been a sour note. He'd been afraid it would send Emily running to her room and locking the door, unwilling to compete with the bawdiness of a woman like that. But he didn't want bawdiness. He wanted Emily, strong yet submissive, knowledgeable yet inexperienced. And with a quality he couldn't quite put his finger on.

One that scared the shit out of him.

Now as his cock moved in and out of her warm, wet mouth, her soft lips closed around it, he thought for sure he'd died and gone to paradise. He moved her head to show her the tempo he wanted and felt his balls draw up and a tingling race up his spine. For two nights he'd wanted to come in her mouth, holding himself back to climax inside her. But tonight he knew he could climax more than one time. God, with her he might go all night.

And so he gave himself over to the pleasure, letting the desire build, race through his bloodstream.

He glanced down at Emily, the sight of her on her knees before him, hands bound behind her back, lips wrapped

Trouble in Cowboy Boots

around his shaft, drove his desire even higher. He rocked his body, still using his hands to guide her, letting his pleasure build and build.

When he felt his climax hit he gripped her head hard, holding it in place, his entire body taut, muscles of his neck corded as he spurted into her mouth again and again. The splash of liquid hit her tongue and the roof of her mouth and slid down the back of her throat.

Lost in the fog of carnal satisfaction, only when the last drop of cum had been wrung from him did it occur to him that Emily — obviously untutored Emily — had swallowed every drop perfectly. She was staring up at him, eyes wide, face flushed, lips still wrapped around his now semi-hard cock.

He pulled out of her mouth, reached down and lifted her to her feet. Placing his lips on hers, he plunged his tongue into her mouth and tasted himself inside that hot, wet cavern. The sensation was so erotic he felt himself hardening again.

"Well done," he said in a soft voice, his lips still against hers. "Very well done."

She was lying on the bed on her stomach, inordinately pleased with herself that she'd given Wyatt such satisfaction. She'd learned quickly, without her hands to help her, that if she tilted her head way back she could suppress the automatic gag reflex and swallow every drop of his semen.

He'd knelt down to release her bonds, showered her face with kisses, then lifted her to the bed and arranged her to his satisfaction. Now she laid sprawled half on her knees with pillows beneath her stomach, her hands bound in front of her, a silk blindfold tight across her eyes.

The bed dipped with Wyatt's weight and he knelt between her spread thighs and she jerked when his lips trailed kisses across first one cheek of her ass, then the other. Oh! Was that a tongue tracing a line across the plump flesh?

Desiree Holt

She sensed him move back slightly and without warning his hand descended in a sharp slap on one cheek. Her cunt reacted immediately, remembering the sensations from the other spanking. Heat rushed through her and liquid trickled out to coat the lips of her pussy.

In an instant another slap landed and she moaned.

"Like that, do you?" Wyatt's voice was husky and thick with carnal need.

"Yesss." The word came out on a long breath as another slap landed.

The cheeks of her ass tingled as the spanking continued. The inner walls of her pussy fluttered, her breasts throbbed and heat engulfed her from her waist to her knees. When the next slap landed on the lips of her cunt the impact sent jolts of electricity sparking through her.

His touch was never too hard, just enough so she rode the thin edge of pleasure-pain. And wanted more. When he stopped she wiggled her ass at him, a silent invitation for more.

He placed a soft kiss on each cheek. "The idea is to know when to stop, sugar. So you'll be begging for me to do anything that will help you get to that orgasm." He leaned over her, his cock brushing against the lower curve of her ass. "Are you there yet, Em?"

"Yes, yes, yes. Do something. Please." She couldn't believe how totally aroused she was, her cunt begging for something to fill it, her nipples aching for his mouth and teeth.

He shifted his weight again and feathered his palms over the flaming skin of her buttocks. "I've got something special for you tonight. Ready to try it?"

The pulse in her womb stuttered in its beat. "Yes. Anything."

"All right, then."

She sensed movement, heard the opening and closing of a drawer, then his hands were in her ass, fingers trailing down

Trouble in Cowboy Boots

the crevice. In the next moment something cool touched the puckered skin of her anus.

"Gel," Wyatt murmured. "Relax. It's special. It will make you feel very, very good."

Emily realized in seconds what Wyatt's idea of "good" was. One of his long fingers pushed through her hole into the tight channel of her ass, carrying the gel and spreading it into the tight, hot tissues. At first it was cool and very soothing. Then a low hum of heat spread through the dark tunnel, igniting the dozens of tiny nerves there and pushing the insistent thrum of her pulse. Her pussy tingled and her clit developed an insistent ache of its own.

"W-What is that?"

"Something to help you take the butt plug I got for you."

She jerked her head back. "Butt plug?"

"Uh-huh." His hands separated the cheeks of her ass, then something soft and hard at the same time pressed against her opening. "Breathe, sugar. Take deep breaths."

Being blindfolded made every one of her other senses far more acute and receptive to stimulation. As the plug intruded slowly into her tight channel the flutter in her cunt became a rhythmic clenching, her blood felt icy-hot and her breath caught in her throat, lodged there as a giant fist of sexual hunger grabbed her.

Ohmigod!'

The sensation was unlike anything she'd ever felt before. An orgasm shimmered just beyond her reach and she mentally clawed for it.

The plug was all the way in now. Wyatt leaned over her and trailed soft kisses the length of her spine. Emily shivered and thrust her hips back up at him.

"I knew you'd like that, sugar."

His deep voice wove a cocoon around her, but she didn't want to be contained. She wanted to be...*fucked!* Oh, god, she wanted him inside her. Right along with that plug lodged in her ass. She was so highly aroused she was sure she could come if Wyatt just touched her. Every bit of her body was on high alert, begging for that stimulation that would push her over the edge.

Wyatt's hands were warm on her body, caressing her everywhere before sliding the pillows from beneath her and gently turning her over. He lifted her hands over her head and rested them on the covers there.

"Don't move them," he ordered. "Keep them right there."

"But I want to touch you," she whispered.

"I'll do all the touching for both of us." His lips brushed hers, his tongue tracing the line of the seam.

She shivered as the image of him naked imprinted itself on her mind.

He touched her only with his lips, moving them over her body teasing and tormenting her. He sucked each nipple in turn, biting each one gently then laving them with his tongue. He moved slowly down between the valley of her breasts to her navel, tracing the indentation with the tip of his tongue.

By the time he got to her still-naked cunt she was quivering with desire and hunger, gritting her teeth against the need to defy him and reach her bound hands out in an effort to feel him beneath her fingers. He nipped at the skin at the top of her mound, licking after each little bite, dragging the tip of his tongue over the tip of her clit and tugging it free from the folds of flesh that guarded it.

Emily was acutely aware of the butt plug filling every bit of her rectum, the sense of it enhancing the need clawing inside her.

Wyatt closed his hands around her ankles, lifted her legs and bent them at the knees, pushing them back toward her breasts. She could visualize herself now wide open to his erotic assault. When his tongue traced a path the length of her slit

Trouble in Cowboy Boots

before dipping into the well of her vagina, only the pressure of his hands held her in place.

Over and over he sketched her cunt with his tongue, tasting the wet flesh of her lips and plunging into the warmth of her vagina. A low moan drifted out on the air and she realized it came from her.

Wyatt's tongue had a life of its own, plunging and plundering and driving her crazy. Emily tried her best to arch her hips to him but his grip on her was too firm. He laughed softly, the sound vibrating against her hungry flesh. He would drive her right to the edge of erotic pleasure, push her until that tight coil inside her was ready to snap, then back off until she was nearly out of her mind with the need to climax.

"Please," she begged, a sob catching in her voice. "Please, Wyatt."

"Please what?" His deep voice resonated through her body. "Please let you come? Please fuck you?"

"Yes, yes, yes." She tossed her head from side to side, "All that."

"Tell me, Em, and I might do it. But you have to say the words." As he spoke in that low, thick voice his fingers rimmed her vagina and slid down to her anus to where the edge of the plug protruded.

"You know." She was getting desperate, the hunger so acute she could barely stand it.

"I'll know if you tell me." His licked the tip of her clit. "Let me hear it, Em."

"Please...let me come." She nearly screamed the words.

"You know I control it, right, sugar? Tell me you know." His voice was soft but demanding.

"I know," she nearly sobbed. "I know, I know."

"And?" he prodded.

"And what? Oh, god, please."

81

"Tell me exactly what you want me to do. That's your key to pleasure."

"Fuck me!" She was so aroused, so on edge, she would have done anything, said anything, to have him inside her. "Fuck me, Wyatt."

"With pleasure."

She heard the snap of latex, sensed him positioning himself and then he was inside her, slowly filling her, his cock pushing at the butt plug through the thin wall separating them.

"Ready for the ride?" he asked, his lips barely touching hers.

"Yes. Now. Please."

He moved in and out, slowly at first, letting her get used to the feel of the double penetration. Emily wrapped her legs around his waist, digging her heels into the base of his spine, trying to urge him to move faster. She was hot and cold at the same time, nothing existing for her except this place, this time, this man and the plundering of her body. Her release hovered just beyond her reach, tantalizing her as her body strained for it.

"Look at me," Wyatt commanded, deftly pulling off the blindfold.

She opened her eyes and looked directly into his, darkened now almost to slate, the flecks of gold and green like tiny jewels flickering there. His face was drawn tight with tension as he fucked her with a steady tempo.

"More," she cried, pressing her heels into him harder. "Please, Wyatt."

And then she couldn't speak, couldn't think, as he rolled his hips one last time and pounded into her with incredible force.

She exploded, everything disappearing but the giant spasms that rocked her body, the stars bursting in the black velvet that seemed to wrap around her, and the cock throbbing

Trouble in Cowboy Boots

inside her as Wyatt spurted again and again into the latex sheath. She screamed his name as the muscles of her cunt clenched around him and milked every last drop from him. The orgasm gripped her and shook her until it seemed to be one giant, continuous convulsion.

She didn't even realize her body had begun to relax until Wyatt reached up, deftly released her wrists and kissed her gently.

"Be right back," he murmured.

She heard him moving around in the bathroom, disposing of the condom, running water, rummaging in the cabinet. She could do no more than lie there dragging air into her lungs and waiting for her thundering heart to resume a normal beat.

Then Wyatt was back, sitting beside her, massaging her stiff arms and rubbing cream into them. Turning her over and slipping the plug from her ass. Wiping her gently with a warm cloth.

He turned her onto her back again and stroked her cheek with his fingers. "Tomorrow night we'll put the plug in and leave it there all night. Did you like it, sugar?"

She nodded.

"Words, Emily," he prompted. "Remember? I have to hear the words."

"Yes," she told him in a weak voice. "I liked it."

"Good. We're gonna work on getting that sweet ass in shape for my cock."

He climbed into bed next to her, pulled the covers over them both and tucked her body up against his. In moments he heard the even rhythm of her breathing that signaled she'd fallen asleep.

"You have definite possibilities, sugar," he murmured very softly, his lips against her hair. "I might even be able to overlook your flaws in the kitchen." He kissed the top of her head. "Better go to sleep. Long day tomorrow and maybe even a longer night."

Chapter Seven

Wyatt urged his horse into a slow trot as he moved from one section of pasture to another, his mind on other things than checking fences. But that was why he'd come out here with the men today, hopefully to distract himself. He was spending way too much time thinking about Miss Emily Proctor.

Settling down had never been high on his to-do list. He'd always figured it was something he'd do when he got too old to run around. After watching the disintegration of his parents' marriage—and subsequent multiple remarriages—he'd made a vow not to put himself in a position like that.

He'd wanted Emily from the first minute he laid on eyes on her, dragging into the Blue Belle with her friends, looking like the end of the world was at her doorstep. Hiring her as a cook had been an impulse and had worked out exactly the way he expected—she had no idea what a kitchen was used for. But she'd been a trooper about digging in and learning and the food she was turning out now was way more than edible.

Taking her to bed had been a risk. Introducing her to the kind of sex he liked even riskier. She could have run screaming into town and told Sam Campbell she'd been hired by a sex maniac. But instead she'd accepted everything not just willingly but enthusiastically. She'd gone from mild trepidation to eager anticipation and now the sex was so hot they nearly set the sheets on fire.

But in the course of teaching her the pleasures of erotic sex flavored with BDSM something had happened to him. Those things called emotions he usually kept under tight lock

Trouble in Cowboy Boots

and key were giving him fits. If he didn't watch himself he'd be asking Emily to stay permanently at the Lazy Aces. And that would be a big mistake. The minute he let his emotional guard down, made a commitment, she'd either be whining about something the way his mother had, or he'd be bitching the way his father had, or the two of them would be spending nights in other people's beds.

One of the reasons Wyatt had bought this place was to get as far away from his parents as he could and, if he was honest with himself, hide from civilization as he knew it. He'd taken all his rodeo winnings and invested it in this place and it had paid off. Now he had to make sure he didn't lose control of things.

As he thought about what he planned to send the right message to Emily—at least what he thought was the right message—a sour taste rose from his stomach to his mouth. This just wasn't his style. But a man had to protect himself, right? Even if it did probably mean giving up the best sex he'd ever had in his life.

* * * * *

Emily moved slowly around the kitchen, doing her prep work for supper, setting the table—something she'd learned to do ahead of time—and checking on the meat. She was slow cooking a roast in the oven the way Amelia had told her to do and it smelled heavenly. Who'd ever have thought she'd be able to cook anything that smelled so good? She laughed to herself.

It hardly seemed possible that she'd been at the Lazy Aces for almost three weeks. Her cooking had improved to the point she could prepare a meal herself and *almost* not burn or overcook anything. Hardy had finally stopped tossing her biscuits around at breakfast, the message from the others loud and clear that he was destroying perfectly edible food. Amelia only showed up every other day now, the lessons leaving her with containers of food to mix and heat, stir and heat or just dump into the microwave and heat. And while breakfast had a long way to go before being pronounced a gourmet feast, she could handle it by herself and get everything to the table on time. Even the double seatings didn't scare her so much anymore.

As she worked she thought about her conversation the day before with Lola and Roxie. Wyatt had started letting her take one of the ranch trucks into town Sunday afternoons to spend time with her friends. Lola's boss at the Blue Belle encouraged her to pack picnic lunches for them—one of the benefits of small town life—and they'd drive to a place by Rockbottom Creek where the county had set out picnic tables, and spent the afternoon eating and gabbing.

Just yesterday they had discussed their current situation and tried to figure out what the immediate future held for them. Money was still in scarce supply even when they pooled everything they had.

"I know we should go," Lola said, nibbling on a chocolate chip cookie, "and god knows this town could bore you to death after five minutes. But..."

"But?" Roxie prompted.

"But I don't know if I'm ready to move on yet." She brushed crumbs from her fingers. "Besides, we still have to figure out our transportation. And secondly..."

"Secondly?" Emily said.

Lola sighed. "Call me crazy but I kind of feel as if we have a time out from life here. You know, all the craziness we've lived with for so long. Vegas glitz."

"Your reluctance to examine our options wouldn't have anything to do with the wickedly sexy Sheriff Campbell, would it?" Emily wanted to know.

Lola actually blushed. "Let's just say Sam and I are finding new ways to pass the time." She looked at Roxie. "And how many times now have I seen you and Cliff in the Blue

Trouble in Cowboy Boots

Belle having a meal and looking like you were the only two people in the world?"

Roxie grinned. "We're just feeding the inner man, girls. After all, he *is* my boss."

Lola flapped a hand at her. "Big deal. Did you see anyone looking over your shoulder and waving a red flag? Besides, it's not as if we'll be here forever." She glanced over at Emily. "And what about you, missy? The last time I saw you and Mr. Cowboy Boots in Chaps you were dancing so close I wasn't sure one could breathe without the other."

Now it was Emily's turn to feel heat on her cheeks. No way would she give up the details of what was becoming an increasingly kinky form of sex with Wyatt Cavanaugh. Some nights she barely had time to shower after she straightened the kitchen and dab on some cologne before he was at her bedroom door, a predatory grin on his face, hot desire in his eyes and an erection barely restrained by his jeans. Sometimes during the day she could hardly concentrate on what she was doing as thoughts of what they did at night roamed through her mind.

The one thing the three women had agreed on was for the moment they were stuck where they were. The car wasn't really salvageable and it was taking forever to save up enough money for some kind of new wheels.

"Besides," Emily pointed out. "It's not as if we even know where we're going."

And where am *I going,* she wondered as she gave the counter a last swipe.

If anything bothered her it was the emotional feelings she was developing for Wyatt. In the end that might be what finally drove her away. He'd been very clear that he was only looking for a playmate, that she was the perfect candidate because she was temporary, and that they could enjoy themselves for whatever time she was at the Lazy Aces. She'd had her eyes on bigger and better things, but the sex was beyond anything she'd ever enjoyed so it seemed like a good deal. And he was very diligent about making sure nothing happened to cause the men to lose respect for her. For that she was grateful.

He'd taken her to Chaps a few more times, obviously not caring about who saw them dancing as if they were welded together, or who questioned his taking his cook out for the evening. On the dance floor they moved slowly to the music, having found a rhythm that fit them both, and the dancing always became a teasing prelude to afterward, when the sex would be hotter and wilder than ever. He turned her inside out, his dominant nature in the bedroom a bigger turn-on than she'd ever thought it could be. No problems there.

What happens when Wyatt gets tired of me? Will he decide Diana Landry is a better, less complicated companion? Someone more suited to his unfettered lifestyle? The woman had certainly been all over him like white on rice whenever Emily and Wyatt were in Chaps. It seemed the last few times he hadn't been quite as determined to fend her off. How could she go on working here if this thing between them—whatever it was—fell apart?

In disgust she hung up the dishtowel and her apron, poured a glass of iced tea and took it out on the back porch with her. She had finally adapted to the hours at the ranch, and now the aches in her body were from more pleasant exercise than cleaning the kitchen or standing at the stove.

But over the past few days she'd been battling with feelings that were giving her fits. As she rocked and sipped she tried to figure out what to do. She was about to head back inside for another cold drink when she heard the whine of a big truck engine coming down the drive, the spray of gravel as it stopped and the slam of a truck door. She stood up and walked to the end of the porch, curious as to who it was. Wyatt was out riding fences with his men and hadn't mentioned expecting anyone.

Trouble in Cowboy Boots

Her eyes popped when she saw Diana Landry striding toward the back porch. It wasn't so much the woman herself, although that was a shocker, as the outfit she was wearing. The shorts rode so high on her thighs they were nearly indecent. A sleeveless blouse hung open over a strapless halter that barely contained her breasts. Wild curls danced on her shoulders as she walked and her lip gloss glinted in the sun.

"Wyatt's not here," Emily said, clutching her empty glass. "He's out riding fences."

Diana gave her a knowing smile. "He'll be back. He's expecting me." She let her eyes rake over Emily from head to toe and back again. "I can't imagine how he stands having a mousy little thing like you in the house, but I guess if you stay in the kitchen it doesn't matter."

Emily stared at her, searching for just the right retort, but the sound of hoofbeats distracted her. She looked up to see Wyatt riding into the yard and pull to a stop in front of the barn.

"Here he is now," Diana smiled and headed toward the barn.

Wyatt had barely dismounted before she threw her arms around him and kissed him, pressing every inch of her body against his., rubbing against him like a sleek cat Emily waited for Wyatt to push her away but instead he kissed her back just as enthusiastically, hands reaching down to cup her ass.

Emily closed her eyes, wondering if she was going to throw up. What was he doing? What was going on here? He hadn't said a word to her about expecting Diana or having plans with her.

You're not his social secretary. Or his wife. He can do whatever he wants, remember?

She turned back into the house, unwilling to watch the unpleasant scene. In the kitchen she rinsed her glass and stuck it in the dishwasher, wishing she had the nerve to raid Wyatt's liquor cabinet. Instead she sat down at the table to look over her list for supper, hoping to distract herself.

Hoping Wyatt would come in and tell her Diana Landry had dropped dead in the yard.

Instead he poked his head in the back door and said, "See you tomorrow."

Emily's head snapped up. "You won't be here for...for dinner?" She wanted to say "for tonight" but her courage failed her.

Diana pushed him to the side and wedged herself into the doorway. "He'll be eating something much better." She gave Emily a bawdy wink. "I told him I'd come pick him up because I didn't plan for him to have the strength to drive home tomorrow." She pulled on Wyatt's belt. "Come on, cowboy. We're wasting time."

Emily sat at the table, staring at the paper in her hand, until she heard the truck engine turn over and the big vehicle pull out of the yard. It was blatantly obvious what he and Diana the Slut would be doing tonight. They couldn't have made it more obvious. Her eyes burned and she felt sick to her stomach. She'd always thought when Wyatt wanted to end this he'd at least be straight about it. Honest. That seemed like the kind of person he was. Not one who would humiliate her like this.

She would not cry over this. No man was worth it. She'd learned that painful lesson the hard way. But she certainly couldn't stay here. She'd make dinner, then get one of the hands to take her into town afterward.

God, what a mess.

She knew Roxie was at work but Lola would be in her place behind Blue Belle's, resting her feet after working the breakfast and lunch shifts. She'd just have to confess the whole thing and ask if she could share a room. She had no idea what she'd do for a job, but she'd worry about that tomorrow.

Trouble in Cowboy Boots

Pulling herself together she called Lola on the cell phone she'd held onto.

"Hey, Emily." Lola's voice was filled with curiosity. And anxiety. "You okay? Why are you calling?"

"Don't say anything," Emily begged. "Just listen, please." Digging her nails into her fingers to keep herself from falling apart, she explained her situation in terse, short sentences. "Don't ask me any questions right now, okay? Just tell me if I can bunk in with you."

"Oh, honey of course you can. But—"

"No buts. We'll talk about the problems when I get there. I'll see you after supper."

Disconnecting the call and mentally saying what the hell, she grabbed a water glass and headed for the bar in Wyatt's den. It wasn't locked. The hands knew to respect the invisible off-limits sign. Deciding that bourbon would be her medicine of choice, she poured a generous amount into the glass, carried it back into the kitchen and added a handful of ice cubes. Then, sipping slowly at the drink, she finished putting dinner together.

"Auntie Em, are you okay?" Hardy's young eyes held concern as she put the last bowl of vegetables out. "You seem kind of…funny."

"I'm fine, Hardy. Just fine. Eat before your food gets cold."

Evan Trippy, an older hand, stared at the glass she picked up from the counter. "That's a little dark for iced tea, Auntie Em. You haven't gotten into the boss's bourbon, have you?"

"Of course not." She hoped the expression on her face was indignant enough. It was ruined, however, when she tripped over her feet walking back to the counter. "I'm fine," she insisted as four of the hands leaped up to help her. "Sit down and eat."

She stood at the sink, taking small sips of her drink, while the men finished dinner in an unusual silence. Emily couldn't

91

look at them and no one apparently could figure out what to say to her. By the time the glass was empty her head was swimming and she wished for nothing more than a gun to blow a hole through both Wyatt and Diana the Slut. She rinsed the glass and refilled it, draining it in the hope the water would dilute the alcohol but all it did was make her dizzier.

When the scraping of chairs on the floor signaled the men were finished eating she turned to clear the table, but they were already handling it.

"You should go sit down, Auntie Em," Hardy said, concern etched on his face. "You don't look like you feel too good."

"I'm fine, Hardy. And I can clean up the kitchen."

But when she took the plate from Hardy's hands it slipped from her grasp and shattered on the floor. Her immediate urge was to cry but she was determined not to shed tears in front of the hands.

"Come on, Auntie Em." Evan's voice was gentle as was his touch on her elbow. "Sit down at the table and I'll get you some coffee."

Since she didn't seem any too steady on her feet she allowed herself to be led to a chair. One of the other hands brought her a mug filled with hot liquid and she wrapped her fingers around it.

"Thank you," she told him. "Evan? Do you think one of you could run me into town after dinner? My friend Lola is staying in that little apartment behind Blue Belle's."

She saw the men doing the cleanup exchange looks. Finally Evan nodded.

"Sure thing. You going to visit your friends?"

"Yes. I need a night out." She concentrated on not spilling the hot coffee as she took small swallows.

But when she came out of her bedroom lugging her suitcases both Evan and Hardy raised their eyebrows.

Trouble in Cowboy Boots

"You going somewhere, Auntie Em? I mean besides to visit Lola?"

"Yes." She set the suitcases on the floor. "Could you help me with these?"

Hardy looked at Evan then back to her. "Does the boss know about this?"

"The *boss* is otherwise occupied," she spat. "And it's none of his business."

Evan took her hands in his. "Em, if something's wrong just tell us. We'll fix it."

Emily ground her teeth together, trying to keep the room from swimming before her eyes. "I. Just. Want. To. Go. To. Town."

The cowboy shrugged. "All right, then. Hardy, put these suitcases in one of the trucks. I'll help Auntie Em outside."

"I don't need help," she protested, then proceeded to trip over her feet again.

The ride into town was thick with silence. Neither of the men apparently knew what to say and didn't want to upset her by saying the wrong thing. Emily was just as glad. Her head was still swimming, although not as bad since the coffee, and she didn't want to fall asleep.

The moment they pulled up behind Blue Belle's Lola opened the door to her apartment. Evan and Hardy set down the suitcases and stood looking at Emily.

"You gonna be okay, Auntie Em?" Hardy asked.

"What's wrong?" Lola frowned in concern. "Is she okay?"

Evan shrugged. "You'd know that better than me."

"Do you have any idea what happened?" Lola asked.

"I'm right here," Emily said through gritted teeth. "You don't need to discuss me in the third person."

"Yes, ma'am." He looked at Lola. "Want us to hang around?"

Lola shook her head. "No. I've got it from here. Thanks, guys."

"Our pleasure." They both touched the brim of their hats and moved back to the truck.

"Okay." Lola gripped Emily's arm. "Come inside and I'll fix some coffee while you tell me every ugly detail."

"Don't want coffee." Emily shook her head from side to side.

"Maybe not, girl, but that's what you need. Come on."

* * * * *

Wyatt was well on his way to being drunk and he knew it. He set the glass on the marble-topped nightstand, looking at it with disgust.

Diana leaned her naked body against his back and trailed her long red-tipped nails along his arm and down to his thigh. "You just need to relax, honey. You're all uptight. Come on. Lie back and let me make you feel good."

"Forget it," he muttered, stifling the impulse to gulp the rest of his drink. In all his thirty-eight years—at least since he'd started having sex—this wasn't a problem he'd ever been faced with. Getting it down was usually the challenge, not getting it up.

Diana slithered around to face him and straddled him, her cunt centered directly over his unfortunately soft cock, her large breasts swaying in front of his face. "How about if I tie you up this time," she grinned. "We haven't tried that yet."

"I don't think so." He placed his hands around her waist and lifted her off his body. He realized suddenly that rather than enticing him, she disgusted him, a startling revelation. He and Diana had played BDSM games several times over the past five years, both of them enjoying the edgy tension of it. Neither of them was into the complete lifestyle but the games ramped up their sexual pleasure.

Trouble in Cowboy Boots

But today Diana could have been spread-eagled on a St. Andrew's Cross with her cunt wide open to him and her nipples clamped and he didn't think his cock would pay one bit of attention. It pained him to realize that it wasn't the games that he'd come to enjoy but the woman involved. And Diana Landry was just not that woman.

All he could think of, imagine, see in his mind was Emily Proctor and that terrified him more than anything. Commitment to him was worse than a bad case of the mumps but it seemed it had snuck up on him when he wasn't looking. And the cure he'd run to get wasn't even making a dent.

"Give it a minute, Wyatt. You know I can make you feel good." Diana knelt beside him, swept her long hair out of the way, wrapped her fingers around his cock and lowered her mouth over it.

If anything it made him softer.

Trying hard not to be the asshole he knew he was, he cupped Diana's head and moved it away from him.

"Don't take this the wrong way, but I think you'd better take me home." He shifted away from her and swung his legs off the bed.

"Home?" There was no mistaking the shock in her voice. "But we practically just got here."

He stood up and began pulling on his clothes. "I know, and I can't tell you how sorry I am. But face it. This just isn't working anymore."

"You bastard!" Something cold splashed on his back and he realized she'd thrown his drink at him.

"I am that," he agreed. "I'm not being fair to you."

"It's that mousy little nobody, isn't it? That dreadful piece of nothing you took pity on."

He shrugged. "Whatever. I just need to get out of here."

"Then you can walk," she screeched at him. "You want to leave, go ahead. But I'm not giving you a ride."

95

Desiree Holt

Wyatt zipped up his fly and tucked in his shirt. "Fine. And...I'm sorry."

"Sorry?" she screamed. "You don't know what sorry is. You haven't even started being sorry."

He barely made it through the door before he heard the splintering of glass behind him. Taking the stairs two at a time he managed to make it outside before Diana did him real bodily harm. As he walked up the drive to the road he pulled out his cell and punched the number for Lazy Aces. He hoped someone was in the barn to answer.

"Yeah, boss?"

Good. It was Evan, one of the more levelheaded of the hands. "I need you to come pick me up. I'll be on the highway at the entrance to the Landry place."

"Pick you up?"

"Yes." He gritted his teeth. "Right now. And bring Emily with you."

There was a long moment of silence. "Boss, she's not here."

"Not there?" He frowned. "Did she get a ride to visit one of her friends?" After the humiliating way he'd walked out on her he wouldn't have been surprised if all three women were after him with a skinning knife.

"She's gone, Wyatt," Evan said quietly, "but not for a visit. She took her stuff with her."

Wyatt's stomach clenched and the expensive bourbon he'd slugged down threatened to surge back up into his throat. "Who took her and where did she go?"

"Me and Hardy drove her. I was afraid she'd try to walk if we didn't. We left her at her friend's place behind Blue Belle's."

"Evan, you get your ass here right now. Speed limit be damned. I need to get to town."

96

Trouble in Cowboy Boots

* * * * *

"I never should have brought her here," Lola said to Roxie, trying to push Emily's drink away from her. "She already had a snootful when she showed up."

Emily had her arms crossed on the bar, her head resting on them. "I'll have two snootfuls if I want," she mumbled.

"That's okay." Roxie reached a hand across the bar and brushed the hair away from her face. It was a quiet night so she was able to stand and talk to her friends. "She's earned it. That jack-off. Wait until I tell Cliff what his good friend has done."

"Nooo," Emily wailed. "Don't tell. Don't tell." She wanted to die of embarrassment at the thought of anyone else knowing how she'd been embarrassed. She wondered if she'd ever get the image out of her mind of a half-naked Diana plastered against Wyatt's hard body, a knowing look in her eyes.

"Sweetie, you can get as shitfaced as you want tonight," Lola said soothingly. "Tomorrow we have to examine all your options."

"I heard someone say the feed store is hiring," Roxie commented.

"She won't be working at the feed store or anyplace else," a rough voice growled.

They had all been so preoccupied none of them had noticed Wyatt and Evan enter the honky-tonk.

"Well," Roxie drawled. "If it isn't trouble in cowboy boots. Lose your way, Wyatt? I heard you were busy tonight."

"You get away from me," Emily slurred, squinting one eye at him.

"Time for you to come home, Em." He pushed her glass away and attempted to lift her off the stool.

Emily batted at him feebly but Lola planted herself in the way.

"I don't think she wants to go with you, asshole."

"Right now I think she's too drunk to know what she wants," he grated. "Come on, Em. Upsy daisy."

Emily wished he'd stop jiggling her. All the liquor was sloshing around in her stomach and threatening to make a second appearance.

"Go 'way," she muttered. "Hate you."

"Yeah, sugar." Wyatt's voice softened. "And with good reason. But we're going to fix that."

"Emily?" Lola's face was close to hers. "You want to go with this scumbag?"

"Wanna lie down."

She felt Wyatt shift positions as he nudged Lola out of the way. "I'll give her a place to lie down. Out of my way, ladies. And I mean now."

Cliff had come from the back to see what was happening. He touched Emily's face gently. "You want me to throw this guy out, Emily?"

But she'd closed her eyes again and fallen into blessed blackness.

* * * * *

Emily pried one eye open and looked around. She was lying on her stomach, naked, in a huge bed, in a room that didn't look familiar at all. She vague remembered waking up in the dark, holding her pounding head, and someone giving her aspirin. The next time she'd opened her eyes it had still been dark and the process was repeated. At some point she'd felt herself carried into a shower and gently bathed, then fed hot tea and more aspirin.

Now, thankfully, although her eyes were gritty her head no longer felt as if a sledgehammer was working at it from the inside out. But where the hell was she?

Trouble in Cowboy Boots

She rolled over, taking in the huge room, the big bed, and the naked man next to her.

Naked man?

She sat up quickly, thankful her head didn't fall off, and pulled the sheet up to her neck. Wyatt! She was in bed with Wyatt!

"We're in your room," she guessed.

He nodded. "And that's where you'll be sleeping from now on. I want everyone to know just who you belong to."

"But you're at Diana the Slut's," she said accusingly. "I saw you leave."

He laughed, a warm, low sound. "Big mistake. Besides, if I'm there I can't be here, right, sugar?"

"I left here," she pointed out.

"So you did." He reached out a hand and stroked her cheek. "And with good reason. I was what Cliff would call an inelegant bastard." His voice softened. "But it's your fault."

"My fault?" she squeaked. "How do you figure that?"

Carefully he urged her back down on the pillow. "You went and made me lose my heart to you, Auntie Em. Something I never intended to do."

He slid his arm beneath her shoulders and pulled her head against his chest. In quiet tones, caressing her arm with his long fingers, he told her the details of his parents' marriage, their divorce, their many remarriages and divorces. His escape to West Texas to find peace and a life that didn't include high maintenance females.

"Although Diana certainly fits that last category," he admitted ruefully. "My bad." He told her as briefly as possible the debacle of his attempt to use Diana to cure him of his feelings for her.

"You didn't want me," she accused. "I left."

"Something that's not going to happen again." He shifted so he could look directly at her.

99

She stared at him. "You took care of me."

"Of course I did." He brushed her hair back from her face. "You needed taking care of and I'd have to shoot anyone else who thought they'd do it."

"If I could take back last night I'd do it in a hot minute. And I can't promise you I'll be the easiest man to tame. I've had too many years of bad habits. But I swear to you I'll do my damndest. Will that be enough for you? Because I don't want to lose you, Em."

She wanted to make him squirm, to plead with her, to apologize ten times over. But the feel of his naked flesh next to hers overrode everything else.

"If you promise to be very, very good," she teased.

"Maybe *you* should spank *me*," he joked.

"Hmm. That's a thought."

He brushed his lips against her. "Are feeling okay, Em? You tied one on pretty good last night."

"Someone took really good care of me. I think I'll live."

"Do you think you're up for a little playtime? Because I'm having a hard time keeping my hands to myself. And in case you didn't notice, that isn't a hammer banging against your thigh."

Heat surged through her and any vestige of a hangover disappeared with it. "I think we can give it a shot." She grinned at him. "Maybe you should tie me up so I don't run away again."

His hazel eyes darkened to smoky gray and lights danced in the irises. "I have something special for you today, sugar. When we're done I guarantee you won't want to look at any other man."

That was already true but she wasn't about to tell him. Not yet.

"What did you have in mind?"

Trouble in Cowboy Boots

"Don't move," he ordered, rolling away from her. "Stay right where you are."

She heard him rummaging in the nightstand drawer, then he was back next to her, turning her over and sliding pillows beneath her stomach. In seconds he'd arranged her so she was on her knees bent over the pillows, her wrists bound and the rope fastened to one of the slats in the headboard.

"Blindfold, Em," he said, pressing the folded silk against her eyes. "You can feel things better when you can't see."

He was right about that. Already her pussy was wet and the inner walls of her vagina fluttered in anticipation. His hands stroked the inside of her thighs, teasing the skin, brushing lightly against the lips of her cunt, arousing her and leaving her hungry for more.

The bed dipped more as he bent down between her outspread thighs, opened her cunt lips with his fingers and proceeded to lap at it with long, slow strokes. Each pass of his tongue was like the lick of a flame, each touch of his tongue a carnal caress. She wiggled her hips trying to urge him to do more but he laughed softly, the sound vibrating against her and arousing even more.

"You in a hurry, Em? I'm ready to take my time here."

"Please." Already he had her begging. She wanted his mouth on her clit, his fingers and his cock inside her. And she wanted it *now*.

"I like it slow, sugar." He chuckled again, but his voice was hoarse and thick with his own desire. "I finally figured out you're what I need in my life so I'm not about to rush things."

"Mmmm." She tugged on her restraints as his tongue probed into her vagina then retreated.

He lapped and sucked, nibbling the wet flesh, thrusting his tongue inside her again and again until she was nearly mindless with the need to climax. Yet he kept her hovering right at the edge, every nerve in her body screaming for release.

When he stopped suddenly and moved away from her she cried out in frustration.

Wyatt smacked her ass. "Quiet. You can scream when I tell you to."

The heat of the slap radiated over the cheeks of her ass and down to her cunt, adding to her clawing hunger. When she felt the cool gel on her anus her stomach clenched in anticipation. Was he going to do it tonight? Was he finally going to fuck her in the ass?

Her breath came in gasps as he worked the gel into her dark tunnel, first with one finger, then two. Oh, god, she was so ready to feel him inside her. In her ass. Now! Oh, now!

When she felt his fingers scissor to stretch her tissues she frowned beneath the blindfold. "Wyatt?"

"Just making sure we both get the most pleasure out of this." His voice was so thick with hunger now she barely recognized it.

In the next instant ropes were wound around her ankles and tied to the short posts at the corners of the bed. She was effectively spread-eagled, her ass raised into the air and open to him for the taking.

More gel, the snap of the condom, and the head of his heavy cock pressed against the tight ring of her hole.

"Breathe, sugar," he told her. "Just like when we put the plug in, only better. Breathe with me. Come on."

She heard him inhale and did so herself, exhaling when he told her to. Inhale, exhale. Again, again. And on every exhalation he penetrated a little further, until he was in her to the hilt.

"Get ready, sugar," he told her, leaning over her and reaching one hand around to find her clit.

Trouble in Cowboy Boots

His strokes were slow at first, the friction of his fingers on her clit timed to the same rhythm. But as her body grew even hotter and her pulse began to beat like a drum he sped up the rhythm.

"Damn, Em," he ground out. "This ass is so sweet it's burning me to death I can't hold out much longer."

"Now, Wyatt," she pleaded. "Do it now."

He pounded into her, pinching and rubbing her clit, faster and harder. More, more, more.

They exploded together. Emily's entire body shook with pleasure, spasms rocking her as Wyatt shot off like a rocket inside her. She spun into the vortex of a whirlpool, focused only on the heavy cock in her ass and the clenching of her cunt over and over again. She was out of control. Screaming his name, engulfed by an orgasm more powerful than anything she'd ever felt before.

Wyatt leaned over her and gently bit her shoulder, plunging her into yet another wild climax. Again she shuddered until she thought surely her body would splinter into tiny pieces and still the tremors kept coming.

At last she collapsed, utterly drained, Wyatt a heavy presence inside her and over her.

He put his mouth next to her ear. "*Mine.*"

"Yes," she agreed weakly.

"Always," he added.

She nodded, incapable of further speech.

Then he was pulling out of her, releasing her bonds and heading for the bathroom to dispose of the condom. In seconds he was back with a warm cloth, bathing her, then rubbing her arms as he'd done all the other times. He stretched out beside her and tugged her gently against him, still stroking her and kneading her muscles.

"No more garbage about leaving." His voice was firm.

"No more Diana?" she asked.

He smacked her bottom. "Don't even bring her up."

She smiled to herself. "Then no more leaving."

"Ever," he insisted.

"Ever," she agreed, and smiled to herself. Why would she want to leave when she finally had everything she wanted right here?

TROUBLE IN A STETSON
Regina Carlysle

&

Dedication

&

This book is dedicated to all who have been told they are too pretty, too ugly, too skinny, too fat or are judged on the basis of skin color, political leanings or religious beliefs. This is also dedicated with love and affection to my daughter.

Trademarks Acknowledgement

&

The author acknowledges the trademarked status and trademark owners of the following wordmarks mentioned in this work of fiction:

Barbie: Mattel Corporation

Cadillac: General Motors Corporation

Coke: The Coca Cola Company

Stetson: John B. Stetson Company Corporation

Superman: DC Comics

Chapter One

ༀ

Lola Lamont gave her poor old pink Caddy a baleful look through the plate glass windows of Blue Belle's Café and heaved a giant sigh. Her sweet baby had pretty much bitten the dust and her current companions at the table were right, she needed to be put out of her misery. Lola and her friends, Roxie and Emily, had rolled into the tiny town of Mesa Blanco, Texas with the old monstrosity of a car gasping and wheezing like a two-pack-a-day smoker.

Refugees from Vegas, the three friends had, in a moment of madness, said *to hell with it* and loaded up for a grand adventure with only pennies in their pockets and the good sense of a trio of pigeons.

What the hell had they been thinking?

The sad truth of the matter was they hadn't been thinking at all. Roxie had lost her job as a security expert for high stakes gaming at a Vegas casino and Emily had been a victim of downsizing at the hotel where she worked. And herself? Lola sighed, still feeling the pain of it all. She had been fired from her show *Pink Flamingo Girls* for being too old. All those years of dance lessons and keeping her body in primo shape had turned to nothing just days after her thirtieth birthday. Then to make matters worse, her boyfriend Nick had dumped her days after that. Talk about a double whammy. Lola had never been one to have little pity parties for herself but she was about as blue as the décor of Mesa Blanco, Texas' only café.

They'd stumbled into the place, exhausted, stressed and dying of thirst only to be met by three of the hunkiest, rope-'em-up, tie-'em-down cowboys they'd ever seen. The place had been practically empty except for them and, gallant gents that they were, the men had treated them to soft drinks, lord love 'em. Wyatt Cavenaugh, a local rancher, had already offered Emily a job as a cook of all things. Dang woman could barely boil water. Together they'd driven off in the man's big truck. Roxie was, at the moment, caught up in a low conversation with the handsome owner of the local honky-tonk.

Tension ratcheted up a notch when the other dark, hunkalicious man moved closer to her and leaned in. The scent of him filled her head. "Want another Coke?"

Lola felt that deep, gravelly and oh-so-sexy voice roll over her body to settle in her pussy. Uh-oh. Trouble in a Stetson, for sure. Ever a sucker for a rough, smoky voice, she nodded. "You're sweet but no thanks. Sam, is it?"

He tipped his big, black Stetson, his dark eyes burning with a look she'd come to recognize from just about every man she'd ever met. Hunger. Desire. Lust. Definite interest. Ooh boy. Did she *ever* know that look. "Sam Campbell, county sheriff." His kissable lips turned up at the corners and Lola's heart thumped hard in her chest. Late afternoon sunlight beamed through the window near the table to settle on the lines of his bronzed, weathered face and glinted on dark hair that she was dying to get a better look at.

"Lola."

"Yeah, Lamont, a Vegas damsel in distress."

Arching a brow, she gave him a considering look. "And you've come riding in on your big white horse?"

"Looks like it."

"My hero. Nice to meet you." Smiling, she held out her hand which he immediately engulfed in his. The warmth of his touch was sudden and unexpected and Lola felt the loss when he finally released her.

Damn if he wasn't the sexiest man she'd seen in a long, long time and that included Nick Mantucci whom she'd thought was awfully handsome. Nick was a smooth operator

Trouble in a Stetson

who wore designer suits as if he were born to them. Not this man. Sam Campbell could've stepped out of a scene from one of those old shoot-'em-up movies she used to watch late at night when she couldn't sleep. Tall, at least six-four or five of brawn and yummy goodness, he not only wore the authority of the sheriff's badge pinned to his black shirt but carried it on his broad shoulders. The chest beneath that shirt was mounded and muscular practically making her fingers twitch with the need to touch. The man oozed testosterone and wasn't this a hell of a time to notice such a thing?

Mentally rolling her eyes at her silly turn of thoughts, she glanced away regretfully thinking, *wrong time and wrong place.* Besides, she was just done with men. Especially those who made promises they'd had no intention of keeping.

"So what are you gonna do, Miz Lola?" Sam quietly sipped his coffee.

Sighing deeply, she jabbed her straw into her now empty beverage glass, making the ice cubes rattle. "Look for a job, I figure." Feeling more tired than she'd felt in years, she leaned back in her chair and sent her gaze around the room as she tried to think. Her eyes lit on the fluorescent orange "help wanted" sign in the window. Straightening suddenly, she started to get up then remembered her manners. "Excuse me a minute, Sam."

Feeling his gaze on her back, Lola grabbed up the sign and walked up to the taciturn, gray haired woman standing behind the counter. The heels of Lola's cute high heeled sandals click clicked out a warning and the matronly lady glanced up with a frown.

"Can I help ya, miss?"

Lola set the sign on the counter. "Looks like you need help and I'd like to apply. Can you tell me who I need to talk with about a job?"

"You'd need to talk to me. I'm Belle Warren." Belle, all of five two and built like an army tank, looked her up and down

109

slowly and Lola got the feeling she didn't like what she saw. Figured. Lola was pretty much used to that reaction. "Where ya from, little missy?"

"Vegas, ma'am."

"Bull dung," she said matter-of-factly. "That ain't no city voice you've got there, girl."

Lola opened her mouth to speak when Sam walked up and set his coffee cup on the counter. "Can I get a refill, Belle?"

That got a smile from Belle as she grinned and reached for the coffee pot. "Sure thing, Sheriff." Seeming to forget Lola's presence for the moment, she finally turned back to Lola and planted her fists on ample hips. "No sirree. You've got the deep south stamped all over you. Where you from?"

Sam propped his gorgeous, denim-covered butt on the nearest stool and listened unabashedly. Though it was damn hard, Lola tried to forget about him and focused on Belle.

"I'm from a little bitty town just outside Jackson, Mississippi."

"You grew up there?"

"Yes'm. And I waited tables too. From the time I turned sixteen. I'm a really hard worker, Belle."

"Hmph. Well, we'll just see about that, I reckon. Now this ain't permanent. Got that? Merrylee Hawkins just had a baby and she'll be back for her job in about six weeks or so. That's all I've got to offer."

"Oh no, that's okay," she rushed. "I just need to make enough money to get out of town."

"Why? You have somewhere you need to go?"

Lola had to think about that.

No, she really didn't but she just couldn't see herself staying here. The sleepy town of Mesa Blanco was far too similar to the town where she grew up and she hadn't been able to leave that place fast enough. Nope. She wouldn't be

Trouble in a Stetson

staying. Finally she shook her head and sighed. "Not really. I guess I just need some time to figure things out."

"Okay then, I'll try you out for awhile, Lola."

Relief swept her and then she thought of something else. "Can I ask you a question?"

"Shoot."

"Someone mentioned something about a rooming house?"

"Staying there requires money," Belle said. She pursed her lips and then seemed to come to some kind of conclusion. "Listen here. There's no need for that. I reckon you're pretty much busted."

"You've got that right. I'm a downright pauper at this point."

"I figured. You ladies rolled in here without two plug nickels between you considering the three of you were gonna share one drink. Hell, I was prepared to contribute to the cause until Sam here, Wyatt, and Cliff jumped in to spring for the drinks. It's clear ya'll are pretty broke."

"Pitiful."

"Ain't it just." Belle shook her head. "Tell ya what. I've got a little apartment out back behind the café. I lived there when I was younger, back before I married and started a family. Over the years I've rented it out but it's empty now. It's not much but it's furnished and clean. You can stay there until you get on your feet. How's that sound?"

Lola was so overwhelmed she wiggled around in celebration and impulsively ran around the edge of the counter to give Belle a hug. Belle Warren was a sweetheart despite her gruff demeanor. Lola knew a little something about being judged on the basis of appearance. She should've known better. "Thank you. Thank you. Lordy! You won't be sorry, ma'am."

Belle stiffly patted her back. "Hell, I'm already sorry."

Sam thought his eyes were gonna flat pop out of his head.

It was Lola Lamont's celebratory jumping around that had done it.

Sweet Holy Jesus!

It had been a close call when he watched her glide across the linoleum floor wearing those spiky high heels on the ends those mile-long legs of hers. That alone had almost done him in. She was six feet tall at least, not counting the heels, and possessed the kind of luscious good looks that made men stammer and stutter and go all hard in the crotch. Sex on a long, gorgeous stick, for sure. Her eyes were big, round, and as blue as the bluebonnets that hung in framed display all over the walls of the café. She wore her thick, pale-blonde hair piled on top of her head in a mound of riotous curls that fell here and there around a beautiful oval face. A man who knew what he was doing would yank all the pins out of that mass and bury his face there.

Sipping his coffee, he thought about how that all silky looking hair would feel wrapped around his cock as she sucked him off with that pretty mouth. Damn, if her lips weren't mouth-watering. Full and pouty, they were tinted with some kind of rosy looking gloss. In fact, every bit of her was put together as if she'd been tended by a makeup artist or something. Her skin was flawless and mascara had been applied with precision to her thick lashes. Maybe a bit too much of that stuff for his taste but he couldn't argue with the outcome.

Watching Lola bounce around in utter joy was a sight to behold.

Sam nearly swallowed his tongue at the sight of her perfect boobs bouncing beneath the skin-tight tee shirt she wore. The belly baring creation emphasized the slender dip of her waist and flat tummy. Lola's rounded, apple-shaped ass nicely filled out her khaki shorts but it was her legs that really reached out and grabbed him by the Johnson.

Trouble in a Stetson

They were long, shapely perfection.

The kind of perfection any sane man would want wrapped around his waist while he rammed his cock deep. She was the kind of woman who made a man think of big, soft beds and messed up sheets. Sam felt his cock go hard behind the fly of his jeans.

She was trouble, very big trouble and might as well have *gold digger* tattooed to her mighty fine ass. He knew a little something about the breed and had suffered the broken heart to prove it. Best to stay far, far away from Lola Lamont. She might be a fine little playmate for a while but Sam knew she wasn't the kind of woman a mature man counted on for anything more than a quick fuck or two.

Lola was a hot affair kinda gal, not a forever one.

Clearing his throat, he stood causing both women to look his way. "Congratulations on landing a job, Lola. Let's head out to that heap out front and gather your luggage."

She batted her sweet baby blues and smiled. "Nah, I can get it. Don't you have work to do?"

Sam shook his head. "Nope. In case you haven't noticed it's pretty damn boring around here. I figure I have time to help a lady out."

"Ah, that whole damsel and white horse thing, right?"

He laughed. She was a funny little thing. "Yeah. Come on."

Before heading outside, they stopped at the table where Cliff and her friend, Roxy sat. Leaning down, obviously joyous, she gave Roxie a hug. "Can you believe it, Rox? I landed a job. Right here."

Roxie, a beautiful brunette, grinned brightly. "Fast work, sunshine. That's great news."

Lola frowned. "Belle offered me a little apartment behind the café. I think there's only the one bed but you're welcome to share, honey. We could be roomies."

113

"Hmm. Let me think about it. I might have something cooking soon myself. But if I need a place to sleep, I'll definitely come by, okay?"

Lola grabbed the luggage that passed for a purse and reached for her cell phone. Wiggling it a little, she smiled. "Call me if you have a problem."

"Will do."

Sam stepped out into the Texas summer heat and headed straight for the trunk of the pink caddy. Pink? He struggled not to roll his eyes. Why did this seem such a perfect car for Miss Lola Lamont? "Hand me your keys, Lola."

She dug through her bag and finally handed them over. His eyes widened at the sight of the mountain of suitcases piled inside. "These are mine," she said pointing to two enormous battered cases. He struggled, huffed a little, and wrestled them onto the pavement.

"Damn, woman! What do you have in these? Rocks?"

Lola laughed. "No silly. One bag is for my clothes and the other is for my shoes."

Shoes?

Shaking his head, he reached for a smaller case. His mom had once explained that these were called train cases and ladies used them to tote around makeup and such. It was shiny and black featuring a cartoon ponytailed woman. The name *Barbie* was scrolled beneath the picture in swirly hot pink letters.

Lola grabbed the handle with both hands and grinned. "Isn't it the cutest thing ever? Emily and Roxie gave it to me as a gag gift on my last birthday but I just love it."

Sam didn't know what to say to that. He wasn't the kind of man who smiled a lot but damn if she wasn't as cute as hell standing there grinning from ear to ear. "Come on. Let's get you stowed away."

"Hang on a minute." She lifted out another suitcase and a tote bag and hauled it into Blue Belle's. The trunk was nice and

Trouble in a Stetson

empty now so he shut it up as Lola came back outside. "Okay. I'm all set. Lead the way."

Sam gripped the heavier than hell suitcases and headed down the alley between the café and the feed store. Behind him, he heard the steady *snick snick* of Lola's heels striking the pavement. He stopped in front of the small, wood-frame apartment and, taking the key Belle had handed him earlier, slipped it into the lock. The musty smell hit them both in a blast. Plunging forward, Sam set the bags near the front door and immediately started opening windows in the small space.

"Ew."

Sam glanced over his shoulder in time to see her wrinkle her turned up nose. "Sorry about the smell."

"Oh honey, it's not your fault," she said with that slower than molasses drawl. "And beggars can't be choosers as my mama always said."

"Your mama is a smart lady."

"Was," she said quietly coming farther into the small living space. "She passed away right before I left home for Vegas. Here let me help you." Lola moved to the window on the other side of the front door and started to tug. "Damn, it's stuck. Shoot."

"Here, darlin', let me get it for you. There's no telling how long these windows have been locked up." Lola stepped back and Sam caught a whiff of the wonderfully feminine scent of her. She wore some kind of soft, subtle perfume that was as sexy as hell. He was more than a little relieved when she moved off to examine the place. The window opened with a creak allowing fresh air to blow through the small area.

"Hey! This isn't bad," she observed, turning in small circles around the room. "I've definitely lived in worse."

Hmm. Now that was interesting because this place was sure no palace. His cop's mind began to wonder about the place she'd come from and how she'd ended up in Vegas. What had eventually driven her away from Sin City and into

115

his town? A crime maybe? Sam immediately dismissed the idea. She didn't look like any criminal mastermind he'd ever seen.

A tiny kitchen sat to the left of the room and a bed and dresser occupied the far right. Smack dab in the middle was a ratty couch and an ancient television. Sam had never been in here before but he figured the open door near the bed was a bathroom. Sure enough, Lola peeked inside, flashed him a big smile and picked up her Barbie case from the bed. "I'll just put this stuff away. Sam, would you mind lugging my suitcases to the bed?"

Sam didn't argue. He picked up one of them and carried it over to the bed and set it down. Then we went for the next one. He'd almost made it when Lola screamed bloody murder.

"Lola!"

Instantly he dropped the suitcase to the floor. A loud pop sounded as the battered old suitcase flew open and silky panties flew everywhere.

"Spider, spider, spider." She staggered backward balanced on those spindly high heels until the edge of one caught on the open suitcase.

It all happened so fast, Sam barely had time to blink and then Lola was falling backward. Her arms flailed up and she somehow turned as she fell. Reacting on instinct he caught her and twisted as the force of her body hitting his propelled them both to the floor where they landed in a tangle of arms and legs. He didn't know how it happened but Lola was lying right on top of him, smashed against him like a remora.

Sam huffed out a breath then ran his hands quickly over every curve of her body. "You okay?"

"Ye-yes. Whew!"

The very next thing Sam noticed was that his hands were splayed over her sexy ass and her mouth hovered within a hairsbreadth of his lips. Her breath whispered softly against his skin. "Well, now."

Trouble in a Stetson

She squirmed a bit and the action only made things worse when her hot little pussy pressed against his suddenly throbbing cock. Lola's eyes went wide and unable to resist, Sam flexed his fingers over the firm mounds of her butt. Sensation raced over his body, his gut tightened at the feel of all that lush female flesh, and if he'd been a begging kind of man, he'd be pleading with her to put him out of his misery.

Yes, he was in big trouble here.

Her hands went up over his face as she seemed to study every angle before moving up into his hair. Sam's hat lay on the floor beside them, another victim in the fall.

"Black. Thick."

"Hmm?"

"Your hair. I was wondering about that."

"You are one dangerous woman," he whispered against her lips.

"Oh, honey. Didn't you know? Danger is my middle name."

Chapter Two

By the time a week had rolled by, Lola was getting the hang of things at Blue Belle's café. It was kind of like slipping into a pair of old, worn sneakers and realizing she'd missed the feel of them on her feet. She'd kept in constant contact with both Emily and Roxie and both of them were settled in jobs and had places to live, so she hoped that in a matter of a month or two they'd be back on their feet enough to leave this place.

Not that there was anything wrong with Mesa Blanco.

The people here were so nice, so welcoming that she really hadn't had much to complain about unless you counted the harsh about face from one tough sheriff. After that first day, he'd stopped by the café several times, swallowed down a quick cup of coffee and had politely asked if she needed anything. He'd even gone so far as to punch his private number into her cell phone.

Damn it to heck! She couldn't get him off her mind. After lying on the floor smashed right on top of him, she knew there was something sizzling and hot between them yet he'd made it more than obvious that he wasn't interested. But his hard, thick cock didn't lie. He wanted her all right. For some weird reason he wouldn't act on his desires and make a move.

Lola stepped outside her little apartment and locked up. It was her first real outing in Mesa Blanco and she didn't want to ruin her happy mood by wondering why Sam was so obviously keeping his distance. She headed down the alley until she hit the Main Street sidewalk, already missing her car which was currently residing at the local garage. The sun was just beginning to set as she walked the four blocks to Chaps

Trouble in a Stetson

where she was meeting Emily and Roxie for happy hour. Wearing her best jeans, red stilettos and a white top with little red cherries on it, she took off to the sound of the *snick snick snick* of her heels tapping out a little tune on the concrete. Due to the Texas summer heat, she'd swept her curls up carelessly. Several dipped down to brush along the back of her neck. She'd nearly made it to the honky-tonk when a big black truck marked with the sheriff's crest on the door pulled up beside her.

"Just what do you think you're doing?" Sam didn't look like a happy camper. His dark eyes, shaded beneath the brim of his Stetson, were narrowed. Yep, downright mean-looking.

Lola turned and looked at him. "You have some nerve asking me a thing like that after practically ignoring me all week. I don't like your bossy tone. Just because you are the law around here gives you no right." Lola cocked her hip and planted her fists on her hips. Damn the man! She could've sworn she heard Sam growl and then he sent his gaze over her body like a hot lick.

"What the hell are you wearing?"

"What?" Lola swept her arms out and looked down at herself. "You don't like cherries?"

"Fuck!"

Lola was sick of his mixed signals. She knew damn good and well he wanted her yet he avoided her. She sighed. "Look Sam, I'm thirty years old and I'm not about to start game-playing with you. Yeah, you're hot and all that but I'm done with men who give off mixed signals. You either want me or you don't. Obviously you don't so hit the road, buddy."

"Now, Lola —"

"I mean it, Sam. Beat it. I've got other fish to fry tonight." With that final salvo, she held her head high and walked the last half-block to the entrance of Chaps. She felt his stare on her back the entire way. Well, she'd only spoken the truth. She was all up for an affair with the handsome sheriff because, let's

119

face it, there was a definite connection but she'd be damned before she'd let him ignore her and then get all affronted just because she happened to be out on the town.

Roxie and Emily were already seated at a table in the darkened club when she arrived. Both were nursing something cold that would offer up a nice buzz. A plate of nachos sat between them.

Scowling, Lola plopped into a chair. "Hey ya'll," she said before grabbing a nacho and biting down.

"Damn, get this woman a margarita," Roxie said flatly.

"Looks like she needs one," Emily added, lifting her hand to the waitress on duty.

Lola looked at her friends, feeling that instant connection she always had with them. "How about ten? I'm sick of men I tell you. Sick, sick, sick."

"Who do you want me to kill for you, honey?" Roxie, a tall, very pretty brunette leaned back in her chair, one dark brow raised.

"The sheriff. He's got to go."

Emily, also brunette but more on the petite side of things, propped her elbows on the table. She looked ready to do battle. "I'll hold him down while Roxie smacks him in the nose. So he's being an ass, huh? What did he do? Heck, that first day in the café he couldn't take his eyes off you."

"Yeah, I know," Lola sighed and thanked the waitress for the frosty margarita she'd set down in front of her. Running her finger around the rim, she gathered up a bit of salt and stuck it in her mouth. "I swear, just looking at the man makes me shiver and then there was that thing where he caught me when I fell."

Emily's eyes went wide. "Huh? Fell?"

"Yeah, spill it," Roxie said, leaning forward in anticipation of a story. "What happened?"

Trouble in a Stetson

So Lola told them all about the spider and her fall and about how she landed right on top of Sam, owner of that big, hard cock. Emily started laughing first and then Roxie and before she knew it she was laughing too. But then she went serious. Huffing out a breath, she sipped her drink. "But ever since then he's been avoiding me like I have a disease or something and then tonight, before I walked in the door he pulls up and glares at me, questions what I'm wearing and gets all pissy. I'll never understand men."

"Avoidance," Roxie said with an air of finality. "Cliff told me that Sam's wife left him because she just didn't want to be tied to a poor county sheriff. She took off for Dallas, found herself a wealthy man and married him. I think it broke Sam's heart. He loved her or at least thought he did."

"I didn't know." Lola wondered about a woman who valued money over love. She could never be that way despite the poverty in which she grew up. Finding someone to love was more important than anything, in her estimation. To think Sam had suffered because of this woman made her heart tighten with sympathy. He was a good man despite his ornery ways, and proud. Even now, as ticked off as he made her, Lola wanted to crawl up in his lap and hang on for whatever ride he wanted to give her. Not even her ex-fiancé, Nick, had affected her this way. She wanted to know Sam and see what made him tick. "That's so sad."

Emily lifted her hand to order another round before looking her dead in the eye. "Know what I think? I think he's one scared puppy."

Lola laughed. "Scared? Of me? Hell, I don't think anything frightens that man. He's one tough hombre."

"I think you're on to something, Em," Rox chimed in. "I mean look at you, honey."

"What? What's wrong with the way I look?"

"Not a thing," Emily said, taking up the thread. "But you've gotta admit you come off pretty flashy. Maybe Sam just has the wrong idea about you. He sees that whole tits and ass combo you have going on along with everything else that goes with it. He wants you but he's scared to get involved."

Anger whipped through her. Same old story. Same sad song. "I'm sick of this shit, ladies."

Emily patted her hand. "I know you are, honey. We know how sweet you are and how smart. It just takes people awhile to realize you are a whole lot more than just another pretty face."

Lola sighed.

Several hours later she stepped from the shower, dried her hair and pulled on the cute little nightie she'd bought before leaving Vegas. The silky pink fabric felt like sheer heaven against her skin. Once upon a time she bought these things to please her fiancé but no longer. An unabashed girly-girl, she now wore the frilly, beautiful things just to please herself. After slathering on lotion that matched the perfume she always wore, she settled on the couch and flipped on the television. While a reality show about finding true love and everlasting happiness flickered over the screen, Lola thought about her conversation with her friends. Things were hopping between Emily and Roxie and the men in their lives. They didn't say much but then they hadn't needed to. Both were really distracted by the men they had met in Mesa Blanco on the day they'd rolled into town.

Hoping the boring show would help her get sleepy, she continued to stare at the screen when she heard mumbled voices.

Huh?

Suddenly alert, she straightened and stood to face her front door.

More mumbling and muted male laughter.

She might be a country hick from the Mississippi boonies but she'd lived in Vegas long enough to learn caution. Lola

Trouble in a Stetson

grabbed her cell phone and frantically began searching for Sam's number.

"Loooooola! Loooooola!"

Lola froze and then heard another laugh, louder this time. It was followed by a series of little knocks at her window. A chill raced up her spine as she pressed Sam's number. He answered on the first ring.

"Lola? What's wrong?"

How did he know something was wrong? No matter. "Sam, come quick. There are some men outside my place."

"Be right there. Don't you *move*."

She heard the anger in his voice along with that no-nonsense tone one expected from a seasoned cop. Clutching the phone to her chest, she stood there, frozen in place.

Anger riding him hard, Sam gripped the steering wheel and gunned the vehicle toward Lola's place on Main Street. He was officially off duty now but he was restless and just driving around, hoping for a way to blow off some steam when her call came in. Tracking down prowlers outside Lola's place was just the excuse he needed. The fact that Lola herself was the reason for his black mood and restlessness was pretty damn ironic.

His britches had been twisted in a bunch from the first minute he'd set eyes on the outrageous woman and he didn't know what he was going to do about it. She was not his type but damn if she didn't push all his buttons and then some. Rounding the corner, he stopped the truck and jumped out. Making his way down the alleyway, his anger dissolved somewhat. Three local teenage boys, swigging on bottles of beer were prowling around outside Lola's place. He'd known them since they were babies and knew their parents. They certainly weren't dangerous but had sure as hell crossed the line tonight.

"What the hell are you boys doing?" Sam tromped up and three bottles of beer hit the ground. One of the kids yelped but he wasn't sure who. "Got an explanation about this? It better be a good one."

"Um. Well, uh…" one began.

Well, shit.

"Do you boys want to get locked up in my jail?"

A chorus of nos sounded. Sam pulled out his cell phone and punched in his deputy's number. Within thirty minutes, the boys' scrawny asses were loaded up and being taken home to face the wrath of their parents. He wasn't excusing what they'd done, but since they'd never been in trouble before, he was willing to be lenient despite how raw he felt at this moment. Had they done anything other than scare Lola and make utter fools of themselves, he would have been much harsher.

Sam tromped up to Lola's door prepared to knock when she flung it open and leaped into his arms. Those long, luscious legs went around his waist and her arms squeezed so tightly at his neck he almost lost his breath. His hands swept the silky bit of nothing covering her back and instant lust swept him and carried him under. Stepping into the room as if he owned the place, he kicked the door shut not giving a hot damn at the moment about anything but being there for her, with her.

But if she wanted more from him tonight he wasn't fool enough to say no.

"You okay?" he whispered into the mass of her hair.

"I am now."

"Just a few local kids acting like fools. I sent them home to their parents unless you want to press charges."

"No. No charges. They just scared me." She looked up at him, her big, blue eyes suddenly at half mast and filled with easily recognizable heat. Her breath came out in rapid little

Trouble in a Stetson

pants. "You're quick. You got here so fast," she whispered breathlessly, her voice like honey and molasses.

"About to get a lot faster. I'm sick of dicking around here, darlin'." Turning he pressed her against the door and planted his lips along her neck. The sexy, classy fragrance of her curled through his system. He wanted her. Savage hunger and the need to touch her surged through his blood like aged whiskey. Sam swept his hands down her sides and arrowed straight to her ass. The firm, toned globes fit neatly into his palms and Sam stroked them as though he'd wanted to do from the very beginning. "Been wanting to do this for days and I'm not a man who's into self denial. I'm done needing you, watching you, and not letting myself take what I want."

Lola squeezed him tight and planted soft, sexy little kisses all over his face. "About damn time, cowboy. Fuck me now, Sam. Don't you know I'm dyin' for you?"

"Hell."

Lust riding him hard, he took her lips in a wild kiss that was little gentleness and all need. Sam fell into it, tasting her addictive sweetness, plying her tongue with his until her response flowed heady into his mouth. Lola was one hot bundle of woman and he suddenly knew he'd never get his fill of her. Her nipples tightened into hard little nubs that pressed the soft cotton of his tee shirt. Needing a firmer touch, he moved one hand from her ass and sent it down until the heat of her pussy practically singed him. Groaning low, breaking the savage kiss, he licked and nibbled at the slender column of her neck, feeling her sigh break over him like a song.

Sam slid his fingers past the elastic of her next-to-nothing panties and stroked them over her drenched heat. Dragging his fingers over her slit, dipping into the melting layers of her pussy, he flicked her clit with his thumb until she squirmed, a tiny frantic sound breaking from her lips. "I love the feel of your cream on my fingers, darlin'. God, you're responsive and sweet." He sent two fingers deep, hearing Lola whimper as he finger fucked her long and slow and then he ratcheted up things by pressing her clit again and then again. Lola tightened her legs around his waist and shivered against him. "Ready for my cock, honey? God, please say yes. Not a beggin' man but—"

"Yesyesyes. Sam, hurry."

A little cry left her lips when he withdrew his fingers from her juicy pussy. Reaching into the front pocket of his jeans, he found a condom and put it between his teeth. "Hang on, darlin'."

"O-okay."

Using his upper body strength, he pressed her tightly against the door for balance. The rasp of his zipper sounded loud in a silence filled with anticipation. Ripping the package open, Sam covered his heavy erection then pressed up until he'd barely crowned her vaginal opening. Holding just the head of his cock there was pure agony.

Then finally he'd had enough. Plunging upward, high and hard, he filled her pussy to maximum capacity. Lola cried out, the sound low, nearly frantic. The idea that she was as hot as he was goaded him on as he gripped her ass and began to fuck her against the door. In and out he plunged, holding on tight as sensation tore through his body at the speed of light.

So good. So good.

Tight and perfect.

Lola milked his cock, fucking him back, writhing against him as if she couldn't fuck him fast enough, hard enough. Her little cry swept the air coupling with the sounds of their bodies slamming together in the fervent need for blind orgasm. Then her cry became a wail as she pressed her head against the door, tightening her legs as if she'd never let him go. Lola went still then flew apart in his arms. Gasping his name, she flexed and squeezed. The orgasm slammed into him with the force of an eighteen wheeler hitting a brick wall. Lust swept him, completion too, powerful and sweet until with a low sound of his own, he jetted his cum into the end of the condom.

Chapter Three

Breathing hard, Sam held Lola in place against the door and wondered how she'd managed to turn him into an animal. He'd never been a man to disrespect women but he'd jumped her beautiful bones like a maniac. Drawing back, he looked straight into her eyes.

"I ought to apologize but I'll be damned if I can do it, honey. I'm not sorry. Not a goddamned bit."

Lola sent her fingers through his hair, eyes focused on his lips and damn if he didn't feel his cock twitch. It was still buried inside her.

"No apologies necessary," she whispered. "I swear, Sam, if you hadn't jumped me soon, I planned to make my own assault. Getting up close and personal has been on my mind since I first clapped eyes on you."

Sincerity rang in her voice and Sam grinned. Kissing her hard, once, twice, he finally pulled back and withdrew from her body. Not bothering to tuck anything away just yet, he took her hand and led her across the small space, straight to the side of her bed. Sam tapped the end of her nose. "Don't move."

Feeling her eyes on him, he stepped into her tiny bathroom, noting the little personal touches she'd added to the barren space. Pink fluffy towels hung along one wall and colorful bottles and tubes, makeup he figured, were in a basket near the sink. Taking care of condom disposal, he grabbed up a wash cloth and cleaned up a bit. Feeling like a voyeur in this feminine domain, he picked up a swirly cut-glass bottle and gave it a sniff. Yep. That was the scent that drove him crazy but he'd rather smell it on her skin.

When he stepped back into the room, Lola was sitting on the bed primly, her legs together, smiling at him. "I'm glad you rode in that on big white steed tonight, Sam."

He grinned. "More like a big, black truck." Stepping closer, he took in her skimpy bit of fluff she wore and damn if he didn't want to strip it right off her over-the-top luscious body.

She stood and closed the gap between them. "No matter how you got here, honey. You are mine right now and I aim to enjoy it. Take it off, Sam. I want to look at you."

"They sure grow their ladies bossy down in Mississippi, don't they?"

Lola reached for the hem of his tee shirt and he helped her by grabbing the cotton and yanking it over his head. She practically purred as she sent her palms over his belly and then up over his chest. "I learned a long time ago that a lady needs to be pushy if she wants to get anywhere in this world. Dang, Sam, you feel so fine. You're one hard man, aren't you?"

He didn't plan to answer that but then he couldn't if he'd wanted to. Lola planted her lips on his flesh and suddenly talking was the dead last thing on his mind. Her tongue tasted him slowly, lingering over his pecs as her hands trailed down his sides as if she aimed to study every inch of him. Her warm breath rushed over him and his cock did more than twitch this time, growing hard again and then her busy hands found his erection. Slowly, as if she weren't torturing him with her touch, she gripped his cock and dragged her fingers over every thick inch until finally holding his balls in the palm of her hand.

She flicked her eyes up to him, her eyes at half mast. "Mm. Sam, you are a helluva man, aren't you? Delicious." Lola teased his balls gently as sensation rocked him and then finally she released him to push his jeans from his hips. These tiny, teasing touches were killing him so he stepped back out of reach. Sam reached for the heel of one boot and yanked it off to

Trouble in a Stetson

toss aside. When he took care of the other, he shucked out of his jeans and briefs to stand naked before her.

"Ah, man," she whispered as if to herself. Her tongue swept her bottom lip as she studied him. Sam went hard as a damn stone. Lola's hot, sweet look took him in from the top of his head to his feet, stopping to linger at his chest, belly, cock and thighs as if she were memorizing each detail. Sam couldn't remember when a woman had looked at him this way. So hungry. So eager.

"Your turn," he managed. "Damn if you don't look like a present I need to unwrap."

"Who needs a bow, right?"

He wanted to smile but couldn't. His mouth went dry when he traced his thumbs under the miniscule straps holding that pink confection to her shoulders. Sliding them down, watching the silk slip perilously down to drape seductively at the ends of her breasts, Sam stepped in to claim her. Again. One careless push and the material fell downward, gathering over hips.

Lola stood there bare from the waist up.

Damn!

Her breasts were the most perfect things he'd ever seen. Reaching out he traced the pale pink nipples, loving the way they hardened instantly. Responsive.

Hell yeah.

His mouth went dry. He'd seen plenty of naked females in his thirty-four years but never one whose body seemed expressly made for sinning.

Needing to taste her, he bent and sucked one into his mouth. Sam settled his hands at her sides just below her breasts and dragged his thumbs over the sensitive flesh beneath those pale mounds. Sucking, pulling, scraping with his teeth, he hungrily ate at her nipple. Lola made a soft yet urgent sound and he switched to the other. Sam wrapped her up in his arms, insinuating his thigh between hers until he pressed against her pussy. It was drenched and hot. Manipulating, pressing his thigh against her wet flesh, he worked her over. He wanted Lola as insane with lust as himself. He'd be damned before he accepted less. Lola took the bait and writhed against his thigh, drenching the spot with her cream.

Finally Sam released her nipple and settled his lips over her heart. It was pounding hard and fast so he kissed her there as he brought his hands around to tease her belly with his fingers. Snagging the elastic of her panties, he stepped back and tugged until they fell in a tiny puddle around her bare feet.

Lust flashed through his body like lightning.

Lola's cleanly waxed cunt allowed him a tiny glimpse of her pink pussy. Juices glistened on her labia, tormenting him with the desire to ram home again, deep and hard.

"You're beautiful."

"You don't mind it?" she whispered, sudden uncertainty in her wide eyes. "I had to keep it like this because of my costumes."

He tore his gaze from the sight of her bare pussy and moved in on her. Settling his hand low to cover the moist flesh, Sam swallowed hard as raw desire burned him. He slid his fingers over her, flicked her clit tenderly, and then pressed it. "No explanation needed. Like I said, you're beautiful. Everywhere."

Lola whimpered, closing her eyes.

Sam noticed she wore no makeup tonight. Well, hell, of course she didn't. She was getting ready for bed when those little assholes started messing with her. He wondered vaguely why she bothered with all the goop. Her lashes were pale but thick, lying against her cheeks and her skin was flawless. Manipulating her pussy, he settled his lips along her long, slender throat to draw her fragrant skin between his teeth as he began to slowly finger fuck her.

Trouble in a Stetson

Lola moved to meet each stroke until finally she whispered his name.

Not needing an engraved invitation to fuck her, he grabbed her around the waist and backed her up until the mattress settled against her thighs. "Here now, honey. Let me spread you out like I want you," he said.

Once she was centered in the middle of the bed, he arranged her as if she were his own personal doll. It was a caveman kind of thing he knew and out of character for him but Sam couldn't help it. Lola made him feel savage. His cock, protesting the slowness of his actions, throbbed and ached and reached high, almost to his belly but damn, he wanted it to be good for her. He'd never been a guy to suffer performance anxiety but he wanted to measure up to the men she'd surely fucked before.

Sam knew it was lame to think such a thing. Maybe his ex had done a big number on him after all. No, he'd never be a rich man but never let it be said he couldn't make a woman scream with pleasure. Sam planned to prove his point with pretty, sexy Lola.

"Hurry, Sam," she whispered. Her legs were slightly spread and her arms were flung away from her body as if just waiting for him so that she could wrap those long limbs around him.

He shook his head. "No more condoms, darlin'. I'm sorry. This is just for you."

Her sudden smile surprised him. "You don't strike me as a one condom guy, Sam. What's up with that?" She laughed a little then sent a sexy gaze down his body to focus on his cock. That happy camper twitched in response. "See that little table over there with the godawful ugly lamp on it? Open that top drawer, honey, and we'll get you all fixed up."

Curious and not about to tell her *no* to anything she might suggest, Sam reached over and opened the drawer to find a black velvet bag with a drawstring top. He picked it up and jiggled it before lifting a brow at her. "What's this?"

"Just open it," she whispered in that soft southern voice. "I think you'll be glad you did."

Opening the bag, he dumped its contents on the bed and his eyes went wide. His libido did a little two step as electric heat pulsed wild through his veins. Sex toys, all in delicate, girly colors fell from the bag to land on the mattress. "Hell, woman, you've thought of everything," he said, grinning as he plucked a box of condoms, size large, from the pile. "You brought these with you from Vegas?"

"A smart girl doesn't leave home without them." The teasing lilt of her voice coupled with the naughty twinkle in her eyes turned him on more than anything in his entire sexual experience with women.

"I think I'm in love."

Sam was teasing but he wanted to bite his tongue for saying such a careless thing. She wasn't staying in Mesa Blanco and had made that very clear. Lola Lamont was the kind of woman who only needed a man like him for sex. That was the plain, unvarnished truth. She was rich man arm candy and not for him on any kind of permanent level. But damn it, she was here now and he aimed to enjoy her.

"Then come on over here and show me how much." Her laughter caused Sam an inward sigh of relief. Grinning at her, he pulled a condom from the box and shoved the erotic toys out of the way. "Oh, you got a purple one."

"Shit, woman! Purple?"

"But Sam, it's my favorite color."

He didn't particularly care if the rubber came in rainbow shades and had pictures of unicorns on them. Sam only knew he could safely fuck her again. Crawling between her legs on the bed, he sat back on his haunches and grinned at her. For a man who was, he knew, more dour than most, it was a

Trouble in a Stetson

surprise to meet a woman who could make him smile. He could handle some of that in his life.

"I could eat you up with a spoon, woman."

All hint of playfulness disappeared from Lola's expression as her tongue swept along her bottom lip. She brought her hands up to cup her own breasts. Diamond-hard nipples peeked from between her fingers so Sam went for them. Bending over her, he sucked first one and then the other into his mouth before dragging his lips over every inch of her body. His teeth tested the flesh of her belly as his hands gripped her thighs. Sending his thumbs on a little quest, he drew them over the sensitive inner flesh of her thighs, groaning to find her damp. Her cunt was delectable. He'd never fucked a woman who was waxed so perfectly. Sam kissed her there, finding the skin baby soft.

Beneath him, Lola went still.

Sitting back on his haunches again, he parted her legs more, further exposing her. Damn if he didn't love what he saw. Her glistening flesh was pink and dewy, soft. Drawing his fingers over her as if memorizing every sexy little layer, he opened her labia. Her little clit was swollen and so tempting. Sucking it into his mouth and making her scream suddenly became the most important thing in his world. Sam bent to her and licked her there before sending a breath over that wickedly sexy bit of flesh. Above him, Lola sighed.

Concentrating on the delicious task before him, he buried two fingers deep into her pussy. Lola's back bowed on the mattress and her long, long legs spread out a bit wider.

"Oh, Sam."

Bending low to her pussy, Sam sucked the morsel into his mouth, alternating the pressure until she was squirming and panting. Her fingers sank into his hair and gripped hard but he didn't give a shit about that. He wanted to eat her flesh, drink her cream until she flew apart.

In short, Sam wanted to be master of her universe.

133

Nipping and sucking, all the while fucking her with his fingers, Sam felt the frantic press of her bare pussy thrusting against his face and knew with each whimpering sound that Lola was quickly approaching orgasm. Digging into the task and loving every minute of it, Sam felt her go suddenly still. Moving in for the kill, he flattened his tongue and swept through those drenched layers of flesh once more before sucking gently at her clit. Lola's quick little scream swept the air as he kept it up, sending her over that erotic edge and then gently bringing her down with a slow lap of his tongue. Her pussy pulsed against his mouth and vaginal walls clamped down on his buried fingers.

When the only sound left was Lola's panting breaths, Sam reared up and covered his cock with neon purple latex. He was beyond caring what kind of candy-ass man would wear such a thing as he buried his hard penis deep. Lola moaned and so did Sam but when she wrapped those super long legs around his ass, Sam thought he'd died and gone to heaven.

Savage lust raced through his veins heading straight to his hungry cock. Each hard vaginal squeeze threatened to take off the top of his head and pulsing fingers of pleasure raced down his spine settling in his tightly drawn balls. Frantic to have her, to fuck her hard, Sam grabbed Lola's hands and settled her fingers around the rungs of the old fashioned headboard.

"Hang on, darlin'."

Lola gripped the metal and then Sam's hands did too. For what he had in mind, he needed something solid. Pressing his knees hard into the mattress, he pounded into her giving flesh. Over and over he plunged as Lola's heels dug heavily into his ass.

It was so good.

Powerful.

The woman rocked his world.

Trouble in a Stetson

The sound of their flesh meeting filled the room along with Lola's soft little cries.

"Please, Sam. Ohgodohgodohgod. Now."

Not about to let the lady down, he picked up speed and force, slamming into her like a hurricane on the Gulf Coast. He battered her until she flew apart beneath him. Sam couldn't hold on. He couldn't. Lashing her with three hard strokes, Sam felt the powerful rush wash over him as he jetted his cum into the condom, pulsing inside her with a force he'd never experienced before.

In the aftermath, Sam came down over her. He kissed her nipples, licked them gently then unwound her fingers from the rungs of the headboard. Swamped with tenderness, he kissed each one then moved his weight from her satiated body. Holding her close, drawing her against him, he kissed her temple.

"Mm," Lola whispered against his heaving chest. "Wow, Sam. I'm speechless. Do you work tomorrow?"

"Nope. I'm off. What about you?"

"Don't go in until early afternoon. That's good."

Sam looked at her, touching the long length of her back in a gentle stroke. He smiled. "Yeah, it is. Means I'm staying tonight, darlin'."

Her arms went around him as she snuggled in. "Not about to argue with that, Sam."

* * * * *

The next morning Sam awoke to the smell of bacon frying.

Now wasn't *that* new?

He reached out for Lola but already knew she wasn't there. Her side of the bed was cold so undoubtedly she'd been up for awhile. Cracking open one eye, he rolled over and looked across the room toward the kitchen. He couldn't see her but he definitely heard her. She was humming an off-key tune as bacon sizzled on the stove. Dragging his ass out of bed, he grabbed his discarded jeans and headed to Lola's bathroom, his morning wood leading the way. Quickly using her shower, he noted a damp towel tossed in a laundry hamper and figured she'd already cleaned up for the day. Stretching and groaning beneath the warm spray of water, he turned the past night over in his brain, realizing he hadn't enjoyed a sexual experience more, nor could he remember sleeping so damn good afterward.

Shower finished, he dried and shrugged into his jeans and headed toward Lola's tiny kitchen. She turned, flashing an uncertain smile, a broken half of an egg shell in each hand. "Hey, you."

Sam's tongue froze to the roof of his mouth.

Standing there without a drop of makeup and her hair drawn back into a ponytail, Lola wore a tiny, white, form-fitting tee featuring the words *Pink Flamingo Girls* in flashy hot pink letters. No bra. Sam hadn't seen anything remotely resembling this woman since he was a young guy with a collection of raunchy comics. Every line and curve of her body screamed *naughty*. Coupled with the sexy tee was a pair of skimpy pink shorts that were so miniscule as to be non-existent. A strip of bare skin showed across her soft belly between the tee and the shorts.

Sam's cock responded to the sexy domesticity of Lola Lamont, and he hardened stiff as a poker behind the fly of his jeans. "Mornin'."

Lola's smile faded as she looked down and picked up the spatula to poke at the sizzling bacon and he felt her sudden insecurity reach out and grab him. His heart tightened. He'd never imagined a woman like her would suffer an ounce of doubt about anything but it was there and real and for the first time he wondered what it might feel like to live a single day in her very beautiful skin.

It couldn't be all that easy.

Trouble in a Stetson

Eager to see her happy, he went up to her and took the spatula from her hand and set it aside. Sam cupped her cheek and had the pleasure of watching her eyes widen. "Now don't you just look as sweet as all get-out, honey." He kissed her tenderly, forcing back the savage urge to just lay her down on the floor and fuck her like a crazy man. She needed tender. She needed sweet. Lola Lamont needed a man to appreciate something other than the wicked curves of her body. "And breakfast is just what I want. I'm starved. Let's eat."

Chapter Four

Lola spooned up a bite of her low-fat yogurt, watching Sam dig into his breakfast of eggs, bacon and toast. When he'd stepped close to her little kitchen, she'd almost rushed up and grabbed him to drag his sexy ass straight back to bed but a quick blast of insecurity caught her off guard. She didn't like morning afters because a girl didn't always know what to expect. So many men in her life had given her a quick kiss and headed out the door never to be seen again and Lola knew she didn't want that with Sam.

It would hurt too much.

Boy was she ever in big trouble here.

For a woman who wanted nothing more than to get the hell out of Dodge as quickly as possible, she was suddenly thinking about Sam and how great he was in bed and how tender and gentle he could be. But savage too. Yeah, Lola liked a little bit of rough. Liked it a lot.

Hot!

The man was total eye candy and the only guy in her experience who'd practically rendered her speechless with the raw, edgy brand of sex that made her toes curl.

Sam bit into a piece of toast looking over-the-top yummy wearing nothing but his jeans and a slow sexy smile. His black hair, still damp from the shower, was brushed back from his forehead emphasizing the chiseled planes of his face. "So Lamont isn't your real name, is it?"

Lola laughed and shook her head. "You figured that out, huh? No, it's Smith but the Lola is real enough. All me. My mama named me after my great grandmother and I didn't have to change it. Belle knows the truth about that, too,

Trouble in a Stetson

considering I had a little bit of paperwork to do when she hired me."

Taking a sip of his coffee, Sam looked at her over the rolling steam from the mug. "So what took you to Vegas?"

"Umm, what didn't?" Lola sighed. "Mama and I lived in a creepy old trailer park at the edge of town. Poor white trash. I know it sounds bad but that was us. I knew from the time I was old enough to think for myself that I had to get out of there."

"Sounds tough."

Compassion burned in his dark eyes and Lola felt a lump rise in her throat as sad memories tore through her. She didn't talk about her past much. Emily and Roxie knew about her life of poverty but Lola had never been one to seek pity. She was too proud for that and knew it well. "We did okay, Sam. I mean, Mama was in really bad health while I was growing up but we were a good team."

Sam took another drink of his coffee as he regarded her steadily. "What about your dad?"

Lola laughed. "All I ever got from my daddy were good looks and long legs. Mama got the ratty old mobile home and a mountain of debt. That about sums it up. Mama said that after I was born, he got on his motorcycle, took off, and that was it."

"Looks like you managed okay."

Rolling her eyes, Lola shook her head. "Yeah right. Fired from my show and stranded without a penny to my name. Doing good all right. Despite everything that happened there it was still better than where I grew up." Appetite gone, she shoved away the half eaten container of yogurt. "I hated that place, Sam. It was awful."

"Don't like small towns?"

"Nah, it's not all small towns, just that one. The girls hated me and the boys wanted to screw me." She practically snorted. "Like *that* was gonna happen. The last thing I needed was to wind up pregnant and poor and stuck in that sorry place. Anyway, I worked my hiney off in a little café kind of like Belle's place, took care of Mama and dreamed of getting out one day."

"Why Vegas?"

She shrugged. "Why not Vegas? Hey, look at me, Sam. College was out of the question and let's face it, I'm no rocket scientist."

Sam frowned. "You're not stupid, darlin'."

"Ah, Sam. You're so sweet but don't bullshit a bullshitter. I'm common sense smart but an education was just out of the question for a girl like me."

"Now, who's talkin' bullshit."

She waved his words away. "I knew from an early age that about the only thing I had going for me were my looks and doing something in Vegas just seemed realistic, ya know? After Mama died, I sold that heap of metal and everything we had and just took off."

"How old were you?"

"Um, almost nineteen." She laughed a little. "I was scared spitless. Honest to God, I'd never been away from home before and I was alone. Pretty scary."

"I'll bet."

"Ended up waiting tables and taking dancing lessons when I could afford it. Then, I was asked to work some convention showrooms. You know, cars, electronics, and what have you." Lola gauged the responses on Sam's face but with him it was hard to tell what he was thinking. Absently she picked up her spoon and poked it into the yogurt cup. "Eventually my dancing was up to speed and I auditioned for the Pink Flamingo Girls and the rest was history."

Sam's eyes zeroed in on her chest and the letters written there. Ha. He was checking out her boobs too. Such a man! Still, flashes of what they'd done last night whipped through

140

Trouble in a Stetson

her mind and before you could say *fuck me quick,* her nipples were hard and pressing against the soft cotton.

Sam cleared his throat and looked at her, his eyes burning dark with hunger. "So you danced?"

"Pranced and strutted is more like it. There were women in the show who'd taken dance lessons all their lives. I never fooled myself for a minute. They liked the way I looked mainly but I was firmly in the *prancing* part of the show." Lola locked gazes with Sam. "Anyway, I got too old and they fired me," she whispered, sensing Sam was no longer thinking about her past but more about the here and now.

"You look just right to me," he said.

Quiet fell between them. Tension crackled in the air.

Sam pushed back from the table and stood. "Wait right here."

Lola went still as he walked across the room and stopped to fool around near the side of the unmade bed. Frowning she watched him come back but then all became clear when she noted the small packet he held in his hand. Sam set the condom on the kitchen table and unzipped his jeans. His dark eyes burning with sexual hunger and a dark, sexy intensity, he pushed them down and kicked them aside.

Heat ripped through her, damping her panties, as her pussy responded to his flagrant need for her. Sam's cock rose up, high and hard, nearly to his belly. The thick stalk captured her gaze and her mouth went instantly dry as she imagined taking him deep into her mouth. He exuded strength, passion and control and wouldn't it be nice to strip some of that from him until he fell apart under the lash of her tongue?

Sam plucked the condom from the table, keeping his eyes focused firmly on her, as he tore the package open with his teeth. He gripped his cock at the base, fisting his hand around it, moving it up and then down again in a seductive move that had her pussy creaming. Memories of the best pleasure she'd ever known ripped through her system and Lola's heartbeat speeded up in response. Anticipation had her bare toes curling against the floor.

Finally Sam sprawled in the kitchen chair, his legs spread invitingly as he continued to work his cock steadily.

"Come here, darlin'."

Drawing a breath, she stood slowly and stepped tentatively between Sam's spread legs. His eyes, dark with intensity roamed up then down her body, lingering on her beaded, puckered nipples. Sam snagged the hem of her tee shirt then drew it up over her belly. Lola's breath caught and held and before she could blink Sam's lips were on her, settling hotly on the flesh he'd exposed.

"There's not a thing wrong with you, Lola. You're beautiful. Those people in Vegas are dumbasses for firing you."

The comment came from left field, catching her off balance. Warmth curled through her as she pushed her fingers into his thick hair to hold him close. His kisses fell softly on her belly as he nipped her flesh and teased with his tongue. How would she ever leave this man? Shoving the pitiful, bittersweet thought aside, she absorbed the way he touched her, the way he made her feel.

"Oh, Sam."

"Not enough," he said. Sam drew back and lifted her tee higher until it settled over her bare breasts, framing them in soft white cotton. His eyes focused on the tightly drawn nipples. "Give 'em to me."

Lola caught her breath then lifted her right breast.

"Closer. Yeah, like that." Sam's mouth latched onto her nipple and a low whimper tore through her lips. Sucking hard, then softly, he licked the spot then used the edges of his teeth on her. It was a tender bit of rough against her breast. Lola's breath stilled then gasped out again when he moved to the other breast. "You're delicious," he murmured around her throbbing nipple.

Trouble in a Stetson

His hands went to the waist of her shorts and he pushed them down along with her panties until they settled around her ankles. Impatiently, needing his fingers on her pussy, she kicked the bits of fabric away. When Sam sent one fingertip over the crease of her cunt, she dropped her head back, sighing at the sensation but then he ratcheted things up a notch. Parting her labia, he circled, then pressed her clit with his thumb. Lola trembled and shook, forcing herself to look at Sam. His eyes were focused on her weeping pussy as he manipulated her flesh.

"Sam," she whispered. "Please."

"Yeah. Ride me, Lola. I can't wait."

Lola didn't need a second invitation. Plucking the condom from his hand, she slowly rolled it over the fat head of his cock and kept going until he was covered. He was so thick, so long. Unable to resist, she fisted her hand around his erection. Oh yeah, he was more than ready for her. Sam's jaw clenched and unclenched rhythmically as he watched her hand glide over him and she knew he was as ready as she was.

Stepping back a bit, she straddled his thighs. When she was as close as she could possibly be, Sam's body heat reached out to her and her body tingled in anticipation. Grabbing his shoulders for balance, she looked down between their bodies. Sam took his cock in his hand and Lola lowered herself until that thick head was settled at the entrance to her pussy. Swiveling her body, feeling herself open fully to him, she finally took what she wanted and slid down over him.

Sam filled her to capacity, sending pleasure rolling through her body in giant waves. Instinctively she tightened, holding him deep even as he encouraged her to move.

"Aw, sweetheart." He gripped her ass, guiding her slow movements, before finally latching onto a thrusting nipple.

Heat curled tighter than a spring in her belly as she rode him. Up. Down. She swiveled her hips again gratified when Sam groaned low and flexed his fingers on her ass. Soon the slow, seductive pace wasn't nearly enough and Lola sped up, whipping up and down over his cock. When Sam's forearm settled behind her back, she bowed her body over it and felt the rush and flow of her cream as he brushed her g-spot.

"Saaaaam."

"That's it, honey, come for me." His voice was low and rough as he plunged upward, igniting that pleasure spot until she burned.

An orgasm rolled through her, hot and wild.

Lola's pussy clutched him, milked and squeezed as every nerve ending coiled tight then flew apart. Crying out, riding him through the storm, she knew she would never get enough of his man. As the last burst of pulsing pleasure seared her, Sam came too, biting gently on her nipple, groaning against it.

Lola sank against him, her breath heavy against his shoulder as Sam slowly stroked her back. "Wow. Nice way to start the day," she managed on a gasping breath.

"Yeah. You don't have plans tonight, do you?" His hand moved down to stroke her ass.

"Uh-uh. You offering?"

"You bet I am, darlin'. I'm up for a red hot affair if you are. I'll come by tonight. That okay with you?"

* * * * *

Several days later, Lola looked up from filling a batch of salt shakers and smiled when Emily and Roxie came breezing through the front door of Blue Belle's. "Hey, ya'll. Slumming today?"

Both women walked up to the counter. Roxie grinned. "I was hungry for pie."

"We have some of that. Fresh made today. How about you, Em? You're probably ready for some good stuff right about now since you actually have to eat your own cooking these days."

Trouble in a Stetson

Emily rolled her eyes and grinned. "Rub it in, why don't you?"

When they were settled into a booth with a platter of homemade French fries and slices of lemon meringue pie, they started catching up. It was mid-afternoon and quiet as a tomb in the café. Belle had worked the morning shift and was off so the friends had the place to themselves.

Roxie forked up a bite of lemon pie and hummed a little. "Damn. This is good stuff. Don't tell me you made this."

Lola shook her head. "Hey, I'm southern, honey, I can deep fry just about anything but Belle does the pies. Aren't they yummy?"

Emily bit into a crispy French fry and moaned. "Mmm. I swear, I'm starving. Did I tell you I'm taking cooking lessons? Wyatt figured out pretty quick that I can't boil water much less cook for all those ranch hands and he took pity on me. What a guy."

"Oh, that reminds me." Lola dug into one of the pockets on the slim apron tied low on her hips. "Here ya go, Em. I copied some of Belle's easy recipes."

"Note the emphasis on *easy*?" Roxie snickered around a mouthful of pie. "I swear, Em, you're hopeless. Been worried about how long you could continue fooling him."

Lola leaned her elbows on the table and watched her best friends spar. They were so good-natured and fun. It was little wonder they were such pals.

Emily sighed. "God, I admit it. I *am* hopeless but Wyatt doesn't seem to mind."

Lola exchanged a telling look with Roxie. "Do I sense more to this story?"

Em's grin answered the question handily and then she noticed a little color rise to Roxie's cheeks as she glanced nonchalantly out the plate glass window. "Um, Rox? Why do I get the feeling Em's not the only one to have something hot and heavy in the works?"

145

"I chased. I caught and he's happy about it. 'Nuff said."

"You are such a badass, Roxie," Emily teased. "Impressive."

Lola clutched her hands beneath her chin and sighed. "My hero. Oops. Make that heroine."

Roxie laughed. "Ah, he wasn't all that hard to catch."

No surprise there.

Cliff Beckett, owner of Chaps, Mesa Blanco's honky-tonk, was a red-blooded man who had eyes in his head. Roxie was a beautiful, sexy woman. Naturally, he fell into her hands like a big, good-looking wad of putty and before all was said and done, Lola suspected Roxie would mold the hunky man to her liking.

"So what about you?" Emily said, spearing her with a look. "Are you burning up the sheets with the sheriff?"

Roxie sniffed the air. "Hmm. I think I smell smoke."

Lola sighed. "Call the fire department. Does Mesa Blanco have one? Hmm. Well, if they do, call 'em quick."

Roxie and Emily both laughed.

When she told them about the kids who'd harassed her that night after they'd met for drinks, she watched Roxie bristle. "What the hell? Are you kidding me?"

"Damn little twerps," Emily chimed in with a scowl.

"No, no, settle down. I called Sam and he came a runnin'. Took them home to their folks and I'm sure that was punishment enough for the little pervs."

"What a guy." Emily sighed.

"Isn't he just?" Lola gathered up a bit of meringue on her fork. "I swear. The man turns me inside out. Makes me wonder about leaving here. Am I crazy?"

"Probably certifiable, honey," Roxie said. "None of us plans to stay but damn if I wouldn't like a little more time here."

Trouble in a Stetson

"Me too," Emily said, her eyes taking on a faraway look. "Me too."

Lola thought about her hot nights between the sheets with Sam Campbell and had to agree.

Chapter Five

It had been a hell of a day already and Sam couldn't wait to finish it up, close it down and get back to his important business with one beautiful waitress. Lola had become a permanent fixture in his life for the past two weeks and he wasn't a man who lied to himself.

He couldn't get enough of her.

Dangerous.

Sam knew he was playing with fire and like a dumbass, he was bound to get burned. The woman would be deadly to his heart and he constantly had to remind himself of what she was.

Rich man arm candy.

A blast of shockingly cold air hit Sam the minute he and his deputy Eldon, stepped through the door of Blue Belle's. Time for a quick jolt of caffeine.

Yeah, keep lyin' to yourself, buddy.

You're here for her.

Sam saw Lola immediately as she came through the swinging doors that led to the kitchen. Balancing a big tray of blue plastic glasses, she turned and started stacking them next to a giant silver urn that was marked with a popular tea label. Smiling at the sight she presented with her hair pulled up in a big, messy pile of curls, he and Eldon planted their butts on bar stools at the counter.

When Lola turned and saw him, her smile widened. "Well, hey there. If it isn't the handsome sheriff and his super cute deputy. Hey, Eldon."

Trouble in a Stetson

Eldon, a gangly young fellow in his late twenties, turned several shades of red and shyly tipped the brim of the cowboy hat that was part of his uniform. "Ma'am."

"That's Lola to you. I'm way too young to be a ma'am. Ya, hear?"

Sam laughed. "Quit tormenting Eldon, Lola. Pretty soon you'll be messing with his head like you mess with mine."

"Is that so?" Lola cocked her hip and winked at him. *Brazen little thing.* "Imagine that. Little old me messing with your head. Can I get you guys some coffee? Just made some fresh."

"Sounds good," Sam said.

When Lola turned to fill their order, he studied her covertly from top to bottom. There was something different about her these days. Back when he'd first set eyes on her she'd been harried and pretty upset about the turn of events. She fairly oozed panic. Look at her now. Her smile was bright and easy as she worked behind the counter and her teasing manner made him happy.

What the hell was up with that?

He couldn't remember the last time he'd been truly content. Sam was no fool. He knew damn good and well that Lola was responsible for the way he was feeling these days.

"So what have you gentlemen been up to today?" Lola set two steaming mugs in front of them along with a small pitcher of cream. "Lots of crime fighting?"

"Actually, yeah," Sam said as he doctored his coffee with a splash of cream and gave it a stir. "Tough morning."

Lola's eyes went wide. She stilled. "What happened?"

"Shut down a meth lab about ten miles from here. Had some help from the state police but we got it done."

"What the hell, Sam? I thought a place like this would be pretty much crime free. Are you okay? Was there shooting involved? Oh my God!"

Regina Carlysle

Sam sat up straight, noting the fear on her face and hurried to reassure her. Hell, was she worried about him? "No, honey. Settle down now. We got them while they were still sleeping off the booze from the night before. And don't forget, I had plenty of help." When Lola visibly relaxed, he picked up his coffee, took a sip and continued. "Rural areas have lots of drug problems and it keeps us on our toes. It's just part of the job."

Eldon's phone rang then and after a brief conversation and quick goodbye, he left the café to head back to the sheriff's office. Sam was alone with Lola except for one other customer.

"Hey, Lola, can I get a refill?" This from Harry, an old timer who sat at the other end of the counter. He was pretty much a permanent fixture in the place since his retirement after years of working in the oil fields. The elderly man held out his cup. Lola seemed to collect herself and gave Harry a big smile. "Sure thing."

As she poured more coffee into his cup, Harry grinned. "I heard some gossip around town that you were one of them strippers when you worked in Vegas."

"Now, Harry, that's just not very politically correct of you. They are called exotic dancers these days but no, I danced in a show. Didn't do any exotic dancing. And where on earth did you hear such a thing?"

Harry laughed, the sound rusty and rough. "Aw, I'm just pulling your leg, Lola. Trying to get your goat."

"Consider it got, you old stinker." Lola set the coffee pot aside. "Just because I came here from Vegas doesn't mean I lived some kind of wild and crazy life. I mean, yeah, I danced in a show for close to ten years, but I'm still a country girl at heart."

Smiling, Sam shook his head. She was unflappable and so damn likable.

"What kind of get-up did they have you in, little gal?"

150

Trouble in a Stetson

"Well, pretty much close to nothing and lots of little sparkly things on my costume. Had to wear this big feathery thing on my head." Using her hands, she emphasized how high it might have been. "Heavy. Oh Lordy! Heavy. Hard to do prancing, dancing and high kicks when wearing that thing."

Harry shook his head. "Now that I would've liked to see."

"Me, too," Sam said. "Some kind of balancing act but I bet you looked great."

Grinning from ear to ear, Lola walked up and leaned her elbows on the counter and stared him straight in the eye. "Not too shabby." With a flirty, highly seductive glint in her eyes, she drew the tip of one finger down his collar and then gave it a tug so she could whisper in his ear. "Wanna see, Sheriff? I think I can still muster up a high kick or two for you. I'm very flexible."

Sam's belly tightened as her warm breath sifted across the curve of his ear and his cock twitched in response. "You offering?"

Lola pulled back then surprised him by kissing him right on the mouth. It was a short, sweet peck considering other kisses they'd shared but the touch zipped straight through his body like an electrical charge.

Yeah, he was in a hell of a lot of trouble here.

"Oh yes, I think I am. You off tonight?"

Sam nodded. "Tomorrow too."

"Hmm. As it happens, I'm not working tomorrow either."

Sam's mind conjured downright dirty images of all the things he wanted to do to that wicked body of hers. His heart rate picked up. "Sounds like a date."

A chime rang over the doorbell and Lola released him. He looked over his shoulder to see a woman hovering in the doorway. Two small kids stood behind her. Sam frowned. She wore a look of desperation that he'd learned to recognize in his years of law enforcement. Lola excused herself and walked up to the woman.

Lola spoke with her quietly and he saw her shake her head. "No, we don't really need any help right now. I'm sorry."

Though Sam strained to hear more of what was being said, Lola pitched her voice low, disguising their conversation. Within a few minutes, the woman herded her children inside and they sat together in a booth near the windows. Every bit of teasing and humor left Lola's face as she headed to the kitchen. While he nursed his coffee, he watched her come back out with platters of burgers, fries and soft drinks.

As the small family ate their meal, Lola came back behind the counter, reached into her apron and took out some money. She put it in the cash register.

"What are you doing, honey?" Sam asked, though he already knew.

Lola just shook her head. "It's my tip money. They were hungry, Sam."

That was all she said. Sam got the feeling that Lola knew exactly how it felt to be without the bare necessities. There was a hell of a lot more to her than met the eye and Sam fell just a little bit in love.

Damn it.

* * * * *

Lola was nervous. She didn't know why exactly but expectation, a feeling of premonition, practically hovered in the air. Despite her tendency to be a little soft and gooshy about things she had her practical moments. Woo woo stuff wasn't something she seriously considered. Still she wondered at the feeling of something impending. Sensing her overnight excursion might lead to something monumental, she packed her Barbie makeup case. Already she'd soaked in the bathtub until her skin was pink and glowing. She should have been

Trouble in a Stetson

relaxed but no. Something was different in Sam's voice when he'd called her earlier.

"How would you feel about staying at my place?" he asked in that slow Texas drawl. "Nothing against your apartment."

She laughed. "No offense taken. It's not much. I have to admit, I've been curious to see where you live."

Silence fell on the other end of the line. "It's not fancy. I'm not a rich man, Lola."

Well now.

Where had that comment come from? Sam already knew about her past and where she'd grown up and her tiny temporary dwelling here in Mesa Blanco was certainly no mansion. She realized there was much to learn about what made Sam tick and tonight she aimed to dig deep, assuming he would let her.

Lola snapped the lid on her shiny black case and took in her appearance in the bathroom mirror. Tonight she wore her hair down and she'd straightened it instead of letting it curl as she normally did. For what she had planned for later, she would need to pull it back and that was easier accomplished this way. Smiling a little, she carried the full case into her bedroom area and set it on the bed. Lola wore a pair of khaki shorts and a turquoise halter top made of linen along with matching sandals. A medium-sized overnight bag lay unzipped on the bed and per Sam's request, she opened a drawer and grabbed her velvet bag of sex toys. She smiled. Just thinking about what they'd do to each other with all this cool stuff made her shiver. Finding a spot for her sexy stuff, she was just closing the case when there was a knock on her door.

"Oh boy," she whispered to herself. "Here we go, Lola."

When she opened the door, she caught her breath at the sight of Sam standing there in a well-fitting pair of jeans, a form-fitting black tee and his Stetson.

He was sex on a stick.

"Hey there," she said, stepping back so he could come inside. "I swear I've never seen a man who looks better in a cowboy hat than you. Come here and give me a kiss, Sheriff."

He'd looked so solemn, so serious when she first opened the door that it was nice to coax a sexy grin from him. Sam swept the Stetson from his head, exposing his black, tousled curls and moved in on her. "Howdy, darlin'. Been thinking about this for hours," he said gruffly, as he wrapped his arm around her to draw her flush against his body. Bending to her, Sam kissed her hard, sweeping his tongue deep for a slow tasting that had her toes curling in her cute turquoise sandals.

Lola dived headfirst into the kiss, meeting him more than halfway. Tangling her tongue with his, she moved her body against the hard-as-steel muscles of his chest and didn't stop until her nipples were stiff and aching for a firmer touch. Sam pulled away slightly to focus on her face. "You ready to come to my place?"

"Yes," she managed. "Figure I'm ready for just about anything."

"Did you pack that black velvet bag?"

The rough edge of his voice streaked through her system like lightning. "Yeah."

"Good enough. Let's head out to my place."

Lola took in the dry, dusty landscape just outside the town of Mesa Blanco, remaining quiet as they drove farther away from the city limit sign. Sam was quiet too. It was hard to gauge his mood. She knew he was more serious than most people but she figured and that was understandable considering his profession. There was more though. From gossip she'd heard she knew he was divorced. Maybe he was still loved his ex-wife. Could that be it?

The thought he still might pine after his former wife bothered her.

That could only mean one thing.

Trouble in a Stetson

She was falling hard and fast for Sam Campbell.

Sam reached out and adjusted the dial on his radio until a slow country song filled the cab of his truck. "I ran onto Mike, from the garage and asked him about that heap of junk you call a car." A small smile tilted his lips.

"Really? What did he say?"

"He wondered if I could just go ahead and shoot it and put it out of its misery." Lola laughed and then Sam continued. "No, he had to special order some parts, honey. The car is pretty old. I told him I'd let you know." He slid his eyes in her direction. "You might be here a little longer than you thought. Is that a problem?"

Lola shook her head and like a coward, looked out the window at the pastureland that flew by in shades of green, gold and brown. "It should be, but it's not." The sad truth was she wasn't sure if she ever wanted to leave. But if she did, how would Sam feel about that? Maybe she didn't want to know. She'd had her heart broken enough times in this life. Lola wasn't sure she could bear it again.

Trying desperately to shake away her uncertainty, she glanced at Sam as he made a right turn and pointed to a house in the distance. "That's my place. It's not much."

Lola saw the long, tree-lined drive and a modest brick house that nestled in the midst of a thicket of cottonwoods. A neat mailbox featuring the name Campbell sat near the road at the beginning of the driveway. She smiled. "Why would you say that? I love it, Sam. It looks so homey."

He pulled up in the circle drive in front of the house and within minutes they were walking inside. "I built this after Claudia and I got married," he said. Holding her train case and bag, he smiled. "Let me put these away and then I'll give you the grand tour."

When Sam came back from his chore, he showed her around the place. She took in the design of his simple ranch-style house, the large living room filled with overstuffed but

155

practical furniture and the adjoining dining area. Near the back part of the house, the kitchen was functional and nice, featuring tiled countertops and an island with a built in grill and cooktop. Copper pots hung above the space. A small four-person kitchen table set nearby. "Nice kitchen."

Sam looked around the room as if seeing it for the first time. "My ex liked to cook."

"Oh."

He walked up to a sliding glass door that led to the spacious backyard. "I built the patio last summer."

Making herself at home, she slid the door open and stepped out. A Mexican-tile topped table that could easily seat six people sat there along with scrolled iron chairs. A large citron candle took up space in the center. "Love what you've done here, Sam. It's great."

"We'll eat out here tonight, if that's okay with you."

Nodding, Lola followed Sam back inside to complete the tour.

On one side of the house were two medium sized bedrooms connected by a nice bathroom. "I figured we might have kids one day and these would be their rooms," he said simply before taking her hand and leading her into a large den that featured a big screen television, electronics galore, and lots of comfy looking furniture.

"Ah, so this is where you spend you Sundays during the fall of the year," Lola said, grinning. "I can see it now, you and your buddies Wyatt and Cliff hanging out in here with beer and pizza during football season."

"Perceptive woman. I think I like that about you."

Instantly the dark mood she'd sensed from him seemed to evaporate. Sam took her hand and she followed him through a door on the other side of the relatively male domain and stepped with him into his bedroom. Lola immediately spotted her bags on the floor near Sam's king-sized, four-poster bed. A

Trouble in a Stetson

big plush chair was angled tidily into one corner near the bedroom's plantation-shuttered windows.

"Bathroom is over here," Sam said, and Lola walked over and took a peek inside. The man certainly liked his creature comforts and she had to agree with what he'd done. She was a sucker for a beautiful, big bathroom. Double sinks on the marbled vanity were a soft beige and a huge tub was nestled along one wall. Nearby was a glass walk-in shower. Fluffy white towels were neatly folded in a rack that sat on the ledge of the tub. With a lift of her brows, she noted at least six fat pillar candles arranged on a tray. They were unburned and she wondered if Sam had picked them up just for tonight.

Silly.

As hard as she tried, it was difficult to imagine Sam going candle shopping. He was such a guy. Still, the thought he might have gone to those lengths sent a little thrill burning through her.

"What a downright sexy room."

Sam leaned against the wall, watching her closely. "You think so?"

"Oh yes. And candles."

"I wanted to make it nice, Lola." Sam looked down at his booted feet then focused in on her again. "You're the first woman I've had here for two years."

Since the divorce.

Her heart thumped hard in her chest. Well, guess he answered a few questions there. Tears burned behind her eyes. "You did this for me?" she whispered.

"Yeah. Why don't you get settled in and I'll fire up the grill."

157

Chapter Six

Sam sat across from Lola after a meal of grilled chicken and vegetables. Nursing his beer, he watched her randomly stack up plates and silverware, fiddle with her napkin and basically look nervous. When he began this affair with her, he'd figured they were adults and having some hot, blow-your-socks-off sex was enough. She was leaving and he wasn't dumb enough to fall in love again.

Now look where he was.

His insides melted like butter every time he looked at her.

"I know all about your job, Lola," he began as he lounged back in his chair, holding the longneck bottle of beer against his belly. "But surely you left a man behind in Vegas. I mean, a woman like you wouldn't be without a man."

Lola blinked at him. Cursing his unruly tongue, he realized he'd hurt her feelings.

"Whoa! Honey, I didn't mean it like that but hell, you're beautiful. I'm sure you had to beat the men off with a stick."

She drew a deep breath and smiled brightly. "Actually I left a fiancé."

Instant rage sent him bolt upright in his chair. "What the fuck?"

Lola held up her hands and shook her head. "No, no. Dumb. I should've said former fiancé. We broke up right before I left. Actually the whole thing went down about forty-eight hours after I was fired from the show."

Sam went still. "Did you love him?"

"I thought I did," she said quietly. She drew the tip of one finger around the edge of her wine glass. "Maybe I just wanted

Trouble in a Stetson

something permanent and he was offering. I've been a rambler for so long. Logically, I knew I couldn't continue in the show forever. Young women are meant to be showgirls and my days were fading fast. I'm not stupid."

"No you're not."

"Nick and I were together for about a year. I thought he loved me. We had great plans for the future but it turned out to be a lie. He'd been seeing another woman for a while and I didn't even know. Hmm. Come to think of it, I'm probably not that smart after all."

Sam watched her for lingering signs that she might still be in love with the bastard but saw only grim, in-your-face, realization that she'd been cheated on. Still he was curious about the kind of man who'd throw away a woman like Lola.

"What did this guy do in Vegas?"

"He owed a casino."

Figures.

The guy was filthy rich, no doubt.

Emotions clouded his thoughts, not the least of them being jealousy. If he had a woman like Lola, he'd treat her like a princess. This guy was obviously too dumb for words. Yeah, he might be rich but a real man made up his mind and lived up to his promises.

As dark blanketed the land, he stood and held out his hand. "Come on. Let's get these dishes done." He grinned, hoping to chase away the clouds from her eyes. Playfully he wagged his brows at her. "You promised to show me some high-steppin'."

Lola gripped his hand, stood, and then her arms went around his neck. Leaning in, she gave him a short, sexy peck on the lips before glancing up through her thick lashes. "I promise, Sam, I can be very entertaining."

"I've already been entertained tonight more than a decent man can stand. Can't wait to see what you have coming at me."

Grinning, she stepped back and gave him a flirty, little wink. "Just you wait, Sam. You won't be disappointed."

* * * * *

Later, he held Lola in his arms as they did some dancing around the coffee table in the living room. It was a weird thing to dance with a woman who was so close to his own height. He towered over most women. Sam buried his face in her hair, breathing in the scent of her shampoo and the faint perfume she wore. "Told ya I couldn't dance worth shit, darlin'," he said, tightening his arms around her.

Lola nuzzled this throat. Her breath was warm on his flesh and his muscles tightened as his body reacted to the feel of her in his arms. "You're doin' fine, Sam. Trust me. Aw, this is so nice."

Sam had the lights dimmed as a Keith Urban song played. He let his hand drift over the long length of Lola's back and thought about how comfortable he was with her. Yeah, she would leave one day but he wasn't dumb enough to let even one minute get away from him. He aimed to enjoy her for as long as he could.

"Hey, Sam."

"Mm?"

"Speaking of dancing, are you ready for your surprise?" She looked up, humor dancing in her eyes.

"Ready for just about anything you're offering."

Lola stepped out of his arms and grabbed a fistful of his tee shirt. "Then come on. Let me show you how the big girls do it."

Now if that didn't sound as promising as hell.

Sam let himself be led into his bedroom and finally Lola pushed him into the big overstuffed chair in the corner. "Let's get you all comfy," she said as she reached down and tugged

Trouble in a Stetson

off first one boot then the other. "Ah, there. That's better. The shirt has to go, Sam."

He grinned. "Yes, ma'am." Grabbing the hem, he pulled it off and tossed it to the floor. "Anything else, Your Highness?"

"Such a smarty pants." Lola pointed a finger at him. "Don't you move. Okay?"

"Whatever you say."

Anticipation was killing him. Sam watched her reach into her small suitcase and cover his bedside lamp with a rose hued scarf. Instantly the room was drenched in color. She looked up at him and smiled. Sitting on the bed for a minute, she turned on his clock radio and moved through the channels until soft, smoky blues drifted through the room. Finally she stood.

"I'll be back in a bit, Sam. Try not to miss me too much."

"Now who's a smarty pants?"

Lola's laughter followed her into the bathroom and as the door closed with a resounding click, he got up and went to fetch his condoms. Yes, they were the right color. No neon shades for him tonight. He dropped a pile of them on the night table and carried a few over to the chair.

What the hell? Was he Superman?

Shaking his head, Sam realized that Lola made him feel like some kind of superhero and it was about time he admitted to the truth. He was falling in love with her. He might be in for a world of hurt when all was said and done but he wasn't the kind of man who could lie to himself.

By the time more than thirty minutes had passed, Sam was getting downright fidgety when he heard Lola call to him through the closed bathroom door.

"You ready for me, Sam?"

"Yeah."

Ready for whatever she had in mind, he sprawled back in the chair but then his body got a hard jolt when Lola walked into the room.

161

Fuck.

All six feet of Lola Lamont had been transformed into at least six feet five inches of sexy, sensual, showgirl. Sam was bedazzled the second she lifted her head high and with the grace of a queen walked slowly into the center of the room. Her blonde hair was slicked back dramatically from her face further emphasizing her perfect bone structure. Pink, fuzzy looking feathers had been placed into her hair in the back, looming large and outrageous.

Sam couldn't speak. The spit completely dried in his mouth.

How many pairs of fake eyelashes was she wearing? Two? Her lids were painted with heavy sparkling color and a cluster of hot pink gemstones had been applied near the corners of her eyes and near the edges of her high cheekbones. Lola's face was as pale as white china, her lips were glossy with pink color. Something glittery had been sprinkled over every inch of her mainly bare body.

Sam went instantly hard, his cock throbbing with a violent ache behind the fly of his jeans.

She had applied some kind of large patch over each of her nipples. Gemstones matching those near her eyes sparkled there and Sam adjusted his position in the chair.

Her head high, Lola moved toward him to the rhythm of the music, her body sinuous and sultry. Lifting one arm gracefully over her head, she gave him an unsmiling, unblinking stare and struck a pose that screamed *come fuck me*. He also suddenly understood why she waxed the hair from her pussy. The miniscule thong which also glittered with tiny pink stones twinkled as if taunting him. It was beyond skimpy.

Did she wear this in her show?

Lola lowered the arm she held high above her head then sinuously raised the other. Cocking her hip, she straightened one leg until the toe of one shiny pink stiletto was pointed in his direction.

Trouble in a Stetson

"So, Sam," she practically purred. "What do you think of your Pink Flamingo Girl?"

Silence fell.

When he managed to speak, he sent his gaze over the long length of her body, his blood pumping hot and heavy through his veins. "I'm speechless. I've never seen anyone like you before, Lola."

A tiny smile curled her lips as she lowered her arm, did a graceful turn and looked at him over her shoulder. Her back was completely bare with only a tiny pink string breaking the plane of her hips. Striking a provocative pose she broadened her smile.

"Part of my costume is missing though," she whispered. "I don't have my headdress. Heavy sucker. Lots of pink gems and big, billowy feathers going everywhere." Her eyes drifted over him lingering for a moment on his lips. She smiled slightly. "Stuff is missing back here, too. Normally there are several layers of pink tulle covering my butt. It would fall all the way to the floor and float behind me when I walked across the stage with the other girls."

Imagining it, Sam feasted his eyes.

Taking in the smooth curve of her ass, the length of her legs, he reached for the snap and zipper of his jeans. If he didn't get relief soon, he was in big trouble. The rasp sounded loud in the room. To hell with it. With no finesse or explanation, he pulled his cock from his jeans and fisted his hand around the base of it. "Dance for me."

From that moment on, it didn't matter what song was playing on the radio or that he was sitting here jacking off. All he cared about was watching her as she moved slowly around the room, her movements at once graceful and seductive. She shimmied. She swayed. Inching ever closer, Lola undulated, swiveling her hips and then finally she straddled him, her body only inches from his face.

163

Sam released his cock and reached for her. He wanted to lick every bit of that shiny, glittery stuff from her body and remove that naughty looking g-string from her with his teeth. He wanted to eat her pussy until she screamed his name. He needed to devour her and not stop until they were both too limp to breathe, much less move. Wild lust whipped through his body until he ached with it.

Filling his hands with her ass, Sam frowned as Lola laughed softly and teasingly backed away. "Uh-uh-uh, Sam. Not yet," she whispered, taunting him.

"Don't do this."

"Why not? Do you think you can get me that easily?"

Falling into the game, Sam scowled. "You're gonna pay for this, sweetheart."

"Jeez, ya think?" Lola spun away giving him another hot glance at her gorgeous, flawless butt. Sliding her hands down her sides, she looked at him over her shoulder and gave him a naughty wink. "What man wants an easy woman, Sam?"

"You're not easy," he growled. "Not a damn thing easy about you."

In response, Lola smiled before she spun again then did a low back bend that further emphasized her flexibility. Her body formed a perfect sensual curve and he wondered how she managed it while wearing those high, high stilettos. When she lifted to spin again, he'd had it. Just had it!

Standing abruptly, he jerked off his jeans and tossed them aside. Within two strides he had her. Sam wrapped her up in his arms, ignoring her startled squeak, and carried her back to the chair. "Think you're boss, Miz Lola? Think you can tease me like this and get away with it?"

"Sam!"

He fell back into the chair and yanked her over his lap. Her body settled warm against his thighs and belly and his cock rose up high and hard between them. No time to think about his aching cock now. He had to touch her. Sam sent his

Trouble in a Stetson

hand over her back, touching the soft flesh and gathering bits of shiny stuff on his fingers. It glittered diamond-bright on his palms. Her ass was canted provocatively over his lap and helplessly, he stroked the firm, pale globes.

"You are a bad woman for teasing me like this."

Lola went still.

Sam felt her ribs expand against his leg when she breathed.

Teasing her the way she'd tormented him, he skimmed one finger over the slender string that bisected her hip then trailed in further, sending it between the shadowy crease of her ass.

Lola sucked in a breath.

"Spread your legs. Just a little bit. Good girl." Sam moved his fingers lower, dipping them beneath the tiny scrap of shiny fabric that comprised her thong. "You're wet. But not wet enough." Sending two fingers deep into her pussy, he felt Lola stiffen. Vaginal walls squeezed tight against his probing fingers. Hell, she was tight. Wet and tight.

"Thought you could play games with me, honey?" Sam didn't expect an answer but he damn sure wanted her squirming and ready for him. He withdrew his fingers abruptly and smacked one pale ass cheek with the palm of his hand.

"Sam!"

He spanked her again, harder this time and finally, Lola started to writhe. Over and over he smacked her gorgeous ass until it was warm and pink, the color mingling with the sparkles she'd powdered all over her body. Lola was breathing hard and wanting to test her, he dipped his fingers back into her cunt. "You're drenched, darlin'. God, I love the feel of your cream on my fingers." Pumping into her repeatedly, he felt her giving flesh go hotter than a flame, and he didn't stop until his hands were wet and glistening.

"Stand up now, darlin'."

Lola got to her feet and looked at him, none too steady on her feet. Sam reached for her, filling his hands with her warm ass and drew her close until she stood between the spread of his thighs. With an economy of motion, he snagged her thong and drew it down her legs. "Step out."

Lola complied and Sam looked his fill at her pussy. It was shiny and plump from his attentions and her clit peeking out at him was rosy red. Angling his head, he dragged his tongue over the morsel, flicked it, sucked it. Lola responded instantly by sinking her fingers into his hair and widening her stance.

"Sam!"

"You're one delicious woman," he whispered in a voice gone rough. "Gonna eat you out, Lola."

"Yes."

Sam slid his tongue over her slit gathering her cream on it. The scent of her perfume and the silky powder she'd applied to her body curled through his head, instilling a powerful hunger deep in his belly. Growling against the tender flesh, he stiffened his tongue to prod her opening then drew up again to suck her clit. Lola quivered beneath his hands, her kittenish whimpers burning him like fire. Finally, she cried out as orgasm carried her over the edge. Sam gentled his grip on her ass changing the touch to a soft stroking. Lola slumped over him and he held her like that for a moment.

When she finally managed to stand, he joined her. Sick of dicking around, he picked her up and carried her to his bed.

Trouble in a Stetson

Chapter Seven

Lola was still gasping for breath when Sam managed to draw down the covers and place her in the center of his big bed. She probably looked goofy as hell lying there wearing her stage makeup, glitter and feathers but at this point, she didn't really care. She just wanted more of what Sam had to offer. He loomed near the side of the bed, dark and gloriously hard. Lust marked the planes and angles of his face as his hungry gaze swept her body. Maybe for the first time in her life, she was totally speechless with desire.

"Don't move an inch," he said.

Lola watched him walk into his closet and return with several pairs of handcuffs and some ties. Her eyes went wide. Sam gave her a slightly evil grin that had frantic fingers of expectation zipping over her body. "Um, Sam..."

"Hush. You've played with me enough tonight. It's my turn." The handcuffs were real, not the pink fuzzy kind that she had in her black velvet "bag o' tricks". Sam dropped them with a clatter onto the end table. He wasted no time in binding her hands together over her head, snapping on a cuff and attaching the other end to the headboard. "Too tight?"

"No," she whispered, amazed at how the semi-helpless feeling ratcheted up her desire. Fresh cream drenched her pussy. Sensitive nerve endings pounded out a beat in her body. She wanted Sam and damn it, she wanted him now but he was the guy currently calling all the shots. He gave her a single hot, hungry look and grabbed up a handful of steel cuffs before heading to the foot of the bed.

"Better take these off but I hate to," he said. "These are *some* sexy shoes, honey."

Lola looked at Sam, watching as he unhooked her shoes and tossed them to the floor. He grabbed one ankle, snapped on the cuff with a quiet snick then attached it to a post on the footboard. Realizing she would be spread-eagle on the bed inched her tension level up a notch. When he'd finished with the other ankle, Sam climbed onto the mattress with her clutching the black bag full of sex toys in one big fist. Sitting on his haunches between her spread thighs, he sent his gaze over every inch of her body. "Now I have you just where I want you. You comfortable?"

"Um. Yeah, I'm okay. Whew."

A slow smile stretched his beautiful lips as he set the bag on her belly and prowled through the contents. Lola closed her eyes and listened to the sounds of Sam rummaging through the bag.

"Ah, here we go." Lola opened her eyes in time to see Sam hold up a satiny blindfold. "You okay with this?"

"Whatever you want, Sam."

"I like hearing that. Okay, hold still." He leaned forward and before she could blink, he tied the black cloth over her eyes, plunging her world into darkness. Lying there, anticipation singing through her veins, she heard a whir of sound and then it shut off. She knew he was looking at her. She felt it like an invisible caress and then his hands were on her thighs, stroking over the tops of them, his thumbs moving lightly on the insides. Lola stilled at the aching pleasure of his touch. "You're so beautiful. Your skin is as soft as the velvet of that sexy little bag of yours."

Sam transferred his touch completely to her inner thighs. She knew she was wet there but couldn't care as his fingers plied her flesh then began to stroke her pussy. Sensitized from the oral sex, she caught her breath, as he spread her labia and began to circle her clit slowly.

"Sam, please. More."

Trouble in a Stetson

His laughter was dark and infinitely sexy. With the darkness enveloping her, every stroke, every touch was intensified. Lola jerked a little when his lips found her clit again and briefly he sucked her. The low whir sounded again.

Did he have her vibrator or the clit stimulator?

Ah yes.

Lola felt the cool press of rounded metal on her clit and cried out softly. "God!"

"Hang on, honey. Tell me if I press too hard." He kept the buzz going on her clit then she heard a little snick and the buzzing intensified. As if she weren't already dying here, Sam had increased the speed. Pleasure ripped through her pussy causing her back to arch on the bed. She yanked at the cuffs anchored to the bed and a blast of cool air swept across her belly as the air conditioner kicked on. Her nipples, beneath the tight-fitting, glittery body ornaments, pulsed in tandem with her pounding heartbeat.

The stimulator did its work as she writhed on the bed. And then suddenly the sound stopped. Another whirring noise, this one louder, buzzed through the air. She gasped when Sam sent the vibrator deep. She wanted to bend her legs so she could move more freely but then it didn't matter. Sam sucked her clit as he pushed and rotated the vibrator in her pussy and Lola screamed as another orgasm grabbed her and pulled her under.

"Samsamsam." She jerked against the restraints needing desperately to touch this man who'd given her so much pleasure. When she finally stopped gasping his name, she lay still against the warm sheets and wondered what he would do next. The question was answered as she felt the velvety stroke of the head of his cock brush her lips.

"Suck it, Lola." Sam's voice was raw, edgy with unspent lust. Lola swept her tongue along the crest, drawing a single drop of moisture onto it. Exploring the contours, the shape, the feel of him was so erotic she felt her body seize up again as

169

sensual pleasure curled deep in her belly. She opened her mouth over him and with a groan Sam slid deeper. She wanted to hold his cock and feel every ridge and bump with her hands but it was impossible. Her mouth would have to do.

Pulling hard, she closed her eyes behind the satin cloth, loving the hoarse, rough sound that burst from Sam's lips. Alternating the action between hard and harder, light and lighter, she sensed Sam's struggle when he finally jerked free from her sucking mouth. "Fuck!"

Sam lay between her thighs and probed her with his hard cock. "Condom," he gasped and she felt his weight move slightly, heard a tearing sound. "Damn it to hell, I can't wait."

"Do it, Sam! Fuck me hard."

Without further delay, Sam thrust deep into her waiting pussy. The feel of finally having him inside was almost too much. She wanted to wrap her legs around his ass to hold him close but no. That wasn't happening. All she could do was lie there helplessly as Sam pounded hard in and out of her body. Impossibly turned on, she writhed beneath him, meeting his thrusts as much as the handcuffs would allow. She felt ravished. Taken. Fucked. Her mind whirled with sensation as he hit every erotic point of her pussy and love mingled and stayed, merging with physical pleasure until Lola didn't know where one thing stopped and the other started. His mouth went to her nipple and she heard him cuss.

"How are these attached?"

"Suction cups."

"What the fuck?"

"Get them wet, Sam. Then they'll come off and you can suck my nipples. I need it so bad! So bad. Come on. Do it."

Lola was desperate but she went still as his lips swept around the pink pasties. Stabbing around the edges with his tongue, he nipped the spot and Lola clamped down hard on his cock. The edges of his teeth nipped harder and she wanted it. Yes, she wanted it. His tongue dampened around her nipple

Trouble in a Stetson

then moved beneath until with a soft pop, the pasty came loose and fell away. Instantly his mouth engulfed the throbbing, stiff flesh and he sucked her hard. Fucking her with slow intensity as he lavished attention on her nipple was almost more than she could bear. "Other nipple," she whispered, shocked at the frantic sound of her voice.

Sam released her nipple with a slight popping sound and moved to the other breast. Dear God! How much could one woman stand? Beside herself with pleasure, tears leaked from her eyes but Sam would never see. Every touch was electrifying, hot, lush. She wanted to weep hard and long as pleasure carried her up and away and then she felt the other pasty fall away.

Sam took her breasts in his hands and pushed them together, sucking one, then the other nipple as he thrust his cock deep into her pussy.

"Can't hold on much longer. Come for me, sweet thing." Sam rotated his pelvis against her clit and that was it for her. Sensation raced over her flesh, curled tightly deep in her belly before expanding into a force of pleasure she'd never experienced before. Crying out she fell over the edge and into an ocean of orgasmic release and as Sam followed her there, he caught her in his arms.

Peace flowed over her like butter and she knew she'd just done the unthinkable.

She had fallen in love.

* * * * *

Lola wasn't given to depression and lord knows she'd had plenty of reasons to be depressed in the past. Heck, she was known for her sunny disposition but it was nowhere to be found today. She sat curled up on her couch starting at the television and wondered how she'd gotten herself into this mess. She'd thought with every inch of her heart and mind

171

that she'd loved Nick Mantucci but it was a pale, ghostly thing compared to what she felt for Sam.

Could she stay here? Could she reshape her life by staying in this small town and if she did, would Sam even want that? She knew he'd been hurt. He was a man who felt things deeply. He might not want the love that she was now so willing to give him. If she confessed her feelings, was she prepared to have that love thrown back in her face? There were just so many questions to which she had no answers.

Suddenly a series of playfully timed knocks sounded at her door. "Coming," she hollered, getting to her feet. Barefoot she jogged to the door and flung it open to see Emily and Roxie filling up the space. Roxie carried two paper bags that bore the logo of the local grocery store and Emily balanced in her arms, not only a blender, but yet another paper sack. "We're invading," Em said, pushing past her through the door.

Roxie followed close behind. "Yeah, time for some girl stuff."

Both women headed to the kitchen and started unloading the booty. "What's all this?"

Bags of chips, dips, chocolate, marshmallows and other gastronomic delights were pulled from the bags and placed willy-nilly on the counter. Roxie pushed back her dark hair and grinned. "We were just talking about needing a break from men and figure we'd pop over and plan us a nice little slumber party."

"Ooh. Fun!" Lola smiled broadly. "Just what I need."

"Me, too," Em chimed in. She plugged the blender in and pulled a bottle of tequila and margarita mix from the bag. "Hmm. Margaritas might be the one thing I won't screw up."

Roxie snickered. "Yeah, don't have to actually cook those, ya know?"

Lola needed this. She really did. But suddenly her smile faded. "Shoot! I have a date with Sam at Chaps tonight."

Trouble in a Stetson

"Then make it a no sex date, hon." Emily shook her head. "The man has you whipped. It'll do him good to be without you for one night. Wyatt pitched a fit when I told him he wasn't getting a thing tonight."

"No sex? Oh no."

Roxie grinned wickedly. "Yeah, he'll just appreciate you more later. I told Cliff it was ladies night. You should've seen the look on his face. Plumb pitiful."

The three of them laughed and together unpacked the goodies. "Okay, here's what we'll do," Lola said as she piled the junk food into a corner for later. "We'll all go hang out at Chaps, do some dancing, kiss the fellas goodnight and hole up here for some feminine bonding. We'll pig out and watch our asses expand."

In the meantime, they grabbed soft drinks from the fridge and lounged around in Lola's shabby little living room. "I'm glad you guys showed up," she admitted. "I've been feeling downright blue today."

Emily narrowed her eyes. "Why honey? Over Sam? What did he do?"

Lola shook her head, as love for her overprotective friends poured through her. "Nothing. The night I spent as his place was like I said. Wonderful. Hot. Wow."

"Then what's with the sad stuff?" Roxie leaned forward a little, focused on her. "Spill it."

Sighing she closed her eyes. "I've fallen for him, ladies. Why did I let myself do that?"

"We don't have any choice who we fall in love with, honey." Emily reached for one hand and Roxie grabbed the other.

"That's right, Lola. At least Sam isn't like that dickhead, Nick," Roxie added. "From what I know of Sam, he's a man of character."

"I know he is. I'm just—" Her cell phone rang mid sentence and Lola reached for it. "Hello?"

"It's Nick, Lola. How are you?"

Speak of the devil.

Lola's eyes went big and she mouthed Nick's name to Emily and Roxie. They both scowled. "I'm okay, Nick. What do you need?"

"Why so gruff?"

Lola rolled her eyes. "Why do you think? You have to admit our last meeting didn't go all that well. Let's see if I have it right. 'It's over, Lola. I've met someone else so get lost. And by the way, give me back that engagement ring.'"

"It wasn't quite as bad as that. You're such a drama queen."

"Don't call me names, shithead."

Roxie tried her grab her phone. Her face was red and Lola knew the signs that Rox was moving in to pitch a big hissy fit. Emily practically snarled. She waved a hand at them both hoping they'd calm down. Everyone might think she needed someone to fight her battles for her but they were dead wrong about that. Temper rose up. She could handle her former fiancé. "You made your feelings known and now I'll tell you mine. There are men out here in the world who know a little bit about honesty and integrity. You could learn some lessons from them, Nick. I'm glad we're done. Now don't call me anymore."

"No. No wait. Don't hang up." She heard Nick draw a deep breath and release it. Good she had him pissed. She felt better now. "Listen, I was in the safe the other day and found a bunch of your personal papers. I need to send them to you. Can you at least tell me where you are?"

"I don't want to tell you where I am, Nick!"

"Listen, this is important stuff, honey."

"Don't call me honey. I'm not your anything, mister."

"I know. I know. Shit! Come on, Lola. You need your birth certificate and all this stuff. Just tell me where you are

Trouble in a Stetson

and I'll get it in the mail to you. I promise I won't bother you again."

Lola blew out a breath. Emily was shaking her head and Roxie said, "Don't do it, Lola!"

Knowing she really didn't have much choice she rattled off the address of Blue Belle's Café. That was innocuous enough. Right?

Roxie stood up and leaned over her the second she hung up. "What the hell were you thinking?"

"Yeah, honey. The man is dirt, scum. I still remember how much you cried when he dumped you."

"Me, too," she said. "But he has some of my stuff and there's no telling when the car will be fixed and we'll be out of here."

The very idea of leaving brought a wave of tears to her eyes. This was all too much. For such a laid back, cheerful woman, she was a mess.

"Aw, Lola, I'm sorry," Roxie said as she sat beside her and put an arm around her. "I shouldn't have yelled at you."

Emily scooted closer and did the same. "Me, too. You've been through too much. Hell, we all have."

"You didn't yell," Lola sniffed. "Not too much. Oh guys, it's not Nick. It's Sam. I'm so in love with him and I'm so scared."

Em patted her shoulder. "Let's not think about it now. If nothing else, we've learned that life can certainly throw out some curve balls."

"Yeah," Rox whispered. "Got that right. Best thing to do is slow down, sit back and wait to see what happens."

Chapter Eight

Hours later, Lola twirled on Chaps' dance floor with Sam. His arms were around her and every now and then he would rest his face against her head in a tender way that threatened to undo her. Could it be that he was feeling as she did? There was definitely something between them. Sex with Sam was off the charts, but that wasn't the thing. There was comfort there. Caring. Affection. But did Sam's wounds run too deep for him to see past it and realize that Lola loved him?

Shortly after Nick's call, the girls had headed off with promises to meet up here at Chaps around eight. Afterward, they would all come to her little place to paint some toenails or something. True to their words, they'd all arrived with their guys and the three couples were currently sharing a table in the honky-tonk.

"Quiet here tonight," Sam said, as he moved with her to an old Patsy Cline song. His hand swept her back as he nuzzled her temple. It was true. Rather than wall-to-wall people there was only a crowd of around one hundred tonight. "Maybe they are waiting for Saturday night when there will be a live band."

When Lola looked up, he brazenly kissed her. Damn, how was a woman supposed to resist this? "I'm glad. I find I'm not in the mood for a huge crowd."

His arms tightened around her. "You sure you don't want to come to my place tonight?"

Lola laughed. "Nice try. You guys look totally done in at the idea there will be no sex for ya'll tonight. No, I'm spending time with Em and Rox and that's the end of it. Why don't you go and do something manly? You know, you, Wyatt and Cliff

Trouble in a Stetson

could go shoot at tin cans or something. Pee in the woods. Drink beer and talk sports. Jeez. You guys are *whupped*."

Sam laughed and spun her into a low dip. At the end of the song, he kissed her again, lifted her in the air and spun her around. Lola felt so wonderful, so happy and free, she squealed a bit. When he lowered her, a grin on his handsome face, she wrapped her arms around him, uncaring of the curious glances sent their way. By the time they made it back to the table, Cliff had asked the waitress for another round of drinks. One of the nice things about hanging out with a bar owner was the promptness of the service. Couldn't beat it with a stick.

Sam waited for Lola to take her seat but instead she looked up at him with a smile. "Think I'll hit the ladies room. I'll be back in a bit."

"Okay. See you in a few minutes."

When Lola glanced at Roxie and Emily to see if they wanted to come too, she noticed they were knee-deep in the middle of a story so she headed off without them. There was a short line when she got to the ladies room so she opened the small purse she carried and reapplied a little lipstick. It was a given that when a girl got kissed, lipstick disappeared in a hurry. Finally she took care of her business and walked into the darkened hallway to rejoin everyone when a man stepped from the shadows.

"Hey, sweetheart."

"Nick!" Lola couldn't believe it. Why in the hell was he here? "I should never have given you my address. Roxie and Emily were right about that. How did you get here so fast? Better yet, *why* are you here?"

Nick Mantucci looked as handsome as ever with his black hair and dark, swarthy skin. His expensive shirt was impeccably tailored as were the pleated trousers he wore. He was the kind of guy who would sneer at a place like Chaps. He went for elegance and class all the way. It was a wonder he

177

ever hooked up with a poor little nobody from the sticks like herself.

He moved closer, hemming her along the wall, bringing the scent of his expensive cologne with him. "I'll admit I played a trick on you, honey. I flew to Dallas and rented a car as soon as I got a bead on you."

Lola didn't understand. Not a bit. Shaking her head, she looked at him. "Why? I don't get it. We're over."

"No, we're not. Not as far as I'm concerned. Breaking things off was a huge mistake."

"No, it wasn't. You were right. Things between us would've never worked. Heck, Nick, there are a million girls in Vegas just like me. We're a dime a dozen."

"You're wrong. There's nobody like you, Lola. I figured it out soon enough and I want you back."

This couldn't be happening. Things were over between them. It had only taken one night with Sam Campbell to make her realize how misguided she'd been about everything. She wasn't the woman Nick needed. She belonged to Sam.

"Nick, go back to Vegas and find another showgirl."

"We still have it, Lola. Let me prove it to you."

Before she could blink, much less move Nick was on her, kissing her as if he'd drink her very breath. Futilely she pushed at his shoulders but the man wasn't budging. Why had she ever thought his kisses totally swoonworthy? They were nothing compared to what she felt with Sam.

"Well now. I hate to break this up."

Sam!

Lola jerked her face away and saw Sam standing there like a damn statue in the middle of the hallway. "Sam. Sam this isn't—"

"Who the fuck are you?" Sam glared at Nick, shook his head and then smiled bitterly. "No, don't answer that. Even a dumb rube like me can see you are the fiancé."

Trouble in a Stetson

"Ex-fiancé," Lola whispered. But Sam wasn't listening.

He speared her with an icy glance. "Didn't figure you to be the kind of woman to play a man for a fool, Lola. Thought you were as honest as the day is long. Guess I was wrong about that. Go on with your rich man, honey. I'm sure the two of you deserve each other."

And just like that he was gone.

Lola blinked as her eyes burned from tears. She turned her anger, hurt and frustration on Nick who simply looked at her as if he'd never seen her before. "Maybe this is for the best," he said.

"Fuck you, Nick. Why did you have to turn up now and ruin my life? Again. Or was once not enough for you? How could you hate me so much as to ruin the happiness I've found here in Mesa Blanco?"

"Are you involved with this man?"

Lola thought back to all the times Nick had laughed at her, poked fun at her accent and teased her about being "blonde and dumb". She rolled her eyes and shook her head at him as if he were a six-year-old. "Duh. How long did it take you to figure it out, Nick? Look who's dumb now."

She left him standing slack-mouthed in the hallway but then the tears began to fall. There was no way Sam would believe her considering he, no doubt, believed all the trash talk about women in her profession. She shouldn't love him after this blatant distrust but damn it, she did. Gasping for breath, she rounded the corner and came face to face with Roxie and Emily.

"What the hell?" Roxie grabbed one arm and Emily took the other.

"Is Nick here? Sam said—" Emily stopped and stared as Nick brushed past them making a hasty exit through the front door of Chaps. "Shit! He *is* here!"

Choked, her throat clogged with tears, Lola looked at them. "Get me outta here," she whispered. "Please."

There was no more talk, no questions as they herded her through the door. Honestly, she didn't remember much of the four block walk to her place. She only knew that Roxie was cussing a blue streak and Emily kept stopping to mop her face with some tissues she had in her purse. Mascara ran into Lola's eyes practically blinding her. But finally, finally they made it to her place.

Roughly thirty minutes later, Lola had stripped out of her jeans and shirt and donned a pair of plaid cotton boy shorts and a tank top. Face washed clean of all make-up she sat on the floor of her living room and was working on her second margarita. The girls had gathered up big plastic bowls and filled them with assorted goodies and a box of expensive chocolates lay open on the floor. Lola munched a crème filled candy as she sipped on her drink. "Ew. Chocolate and margaritas. It's gross together but I just can't give a rip right now."

Emily popped a marshmallow that squished with gooey goodness between her teeth. "Don't think about it. Margarita and chocolate does a body gooood."

Roxie snickered as she lifted a half empty pitcher of the drink in question and topped off all three glasses. "Ah, nectar of the gods." She sat back, crossed her legs and sighed. "I can't believe that dick Nick showed up all the way from Vegas." She dug into a bag of cheesy doodles and crunched on two or three of them. "Hey, that rhymes. That dick Nick. What d'ya know?"

Lola rolled her eyes. She was tired of bawling like a baby. Her eyes stung, her throat was raw. It wasn't the first time she'd been hurt by a damn man and it wouldn't be the last.

Emily focused on her. "I'm so mad at Sam. I can't believe he wouldn't even listen."

"It was like I was invisible. He just couldn't see me. He only saw Nick."

Trouble in a Stetson

Roxie shook her head. "Typical. Show me a man who'll actually do what I say and believe me at all times and I'll show you the guy worth marrying."

"Here here," Emily said lifting her glass. "And since we can't figure them out and most likely won't even get close to that tonight, I suggest we drink up."

* * * * *

Sam sat with Cliff and Wyatt in Cliff's office at Chaps. Slumped into a chair, his Stetson pulled low over his eyes, he thought briefly of getting the hell out of there but then Cliff opened a drawer to set a bottle of well-aged whiskey on the desk.

What the hell.

Mentally shrugging, he figured now was as good a time as any to get blistering drunk. Cliff reached behind him to his credenza and snagged three squat glasses which he promptly filled with bourbon. "Looks like we could all use one of these."

"Got that right," Wyatt said, as he lounged back in another of Cliff's office chairs. "Been a long night already. You okay, buddy?"

Sam grunted. "I've been better." He downed half his whiskey in one swallow and removed his hat. The ankle of his left leg was propped on the knee of his right so he settled the hat on the toe of his boot. Sam thought about that casino-owning, rich asshole with his hands all over his Lola and wanted to spit. He downed the rest of the whiskey and held out his glass for a refill.

Cliff complied. "Better take it easy with that, Sheriff. It's like a rattlesnake. The stuff will bite you in the ass if you aren't careful."

"Don't lecture me," he snapped. Sam drew a deep breath and shook his head. "Sorry. I'm an ass."

"No argument there," Wyatt drawled. "Did you even talk to Lola?"

"What was there to talk about? I saw her in a liplock with her ex fiancé. Hell, he might never have been an ex at all. Maybe her whole damn story was a lie."

"Not a lie, Sam," Cliff said quietly. "Roxie told me the whole story."

"I heard the same from Emily," Wyatt added. "Listen, you've always been the most rational man we know. Why don't you talk to her? Get her side of the story."

"Hell no—"

A sharp rap sounded at the door before Nick Mantucci walked inside. Sam bristled and got to his feet. Wyatt and Cliff stood too but it was Wyatt who spoke. "Whoa, Sam. Settle down now."

"What can we do for you, mister?" Cliff said.

"I need to talk with this guy. Sam, is it? I asked around and someone told me where to find you."

Sam wasn't about to give the man the benefit of standing for whatever he had to say. He sat back in his chair and picked up the refilled glass of whiskey. "What do you need?" When the man didn't answer immediately, Sam shot him a look. "Spill it, asshole. What do you want?"

Rage was killing him. Hurt and disappointment shook him. How could he have been so wrong about Lola?

Nick Mantucci shoved his hands in the pockets of his expensive britches. "Um, look, I owe you an apology. I think you got the wrong idea."

"Oh yeah. About what?"

"About me and Lola. I treated her really badly in Vegas before she left but it didn't take me long to realize that I loved her and wanted her back."

"So?"

Nick walked toward him and took the chair that Wyatt had abandoned. "I tricked her. I told her I had some of her important papers and managed to get her address. I showed

Trouble in a Stetson

up here thinking that she'd be so glad to see me she'd tell me she loved me and fall back in my arms. Didn't happen that way. You didn't see her pulling me to her. You saw her pushing me away."

Silence fell between the men. Sam cleared his throat. "Why are you telling me this?"

Nick's face was solemn when he finally spoke. "You didn't see the look on her face when you walked away without giving her a chance to explain. I did. You might as well have jabbed a knife in her heart. In all the years I've known Lola I've never seen that look on her face. She never loved me. At least not like that." Nick stood and looked down at him. "This is the way I see it. I treated her like shit the entire time we were together. I cheated on her. I treated her like she was a stupid doll who couldn't think for herself. It wasn't until I lost her that I realized that she's one in a million. She's sweet and funny. She's beautiful and kind. I threw her away like garbage. Lola didn't deserve that. That's all I'm going to say on the matter. I knew the minute she looked at you that I'd lost her forever."

With that, Nick Mantucci turned and left the room.

Rocked by emotion, Sam sat there like he'd been sucker punched. "What the hell have I done? I've lost her."

Cliff bent down and picked up the Stetson that had fallen to the floor and handed it over. "Not yet you haven't."

Wyatt gave him a calm and steady look. "Go get her, Sam. Maybe it's not too late."

Sam raced from the club and fired up his truck, hoping against hope that he hadn't ruined things with Lola.

Damn it! He loved her. Everything Nick had said about her was true. She was sweet, funny, beautiful and kind. Shit! He was such a fucking ass! Gunning the truck he pulled up near the entrance to the alley leading to Lola's place. She seemed perfectly happy in that awful dump. Why had he

183

insisted on believing her some kind of gold-digger? He was a fool. That was why.

Tromping through the alley, eager to apologize and even grovel if need be, he lifted his hand to knock when he heard the sounds of female voices. He knew Roxie and Emily were with her for their infernal "girls night". Sam went still, caught his breath and turned the knob.

Unlocked.

Figured.

Opening the door, he stepped inside. "Lola I need to talk to you."

Three pairs of startled eyes looked up at him from their position on the floor. Emily and Roxie jumped to their feet but he only had eyes for Lola. Devoid of makeup, her eyes were swollen and her face was blotchy from tears. He'd never seen her look more beautiful. She slowly stood to glare at him.

But then out of left field, Sam felt himself under attack.

A wad of marshmallows hit him in the face and he stared, open mouthed at sweet little Emily, who yelled like a banshee. "You rat! You scum! Asshole!" She tossed another handful of marshmallows and then Roxie was yelling at him too.

"You frickin' creep! I ought to kick your butt." Roxie dug into a bag and flung cheesy doodles at his head. The yellow mess rained down on him but it didn't satisfy Roxie's need for vengeance. "You made Lola *cry*! Shame on you!" Roxie went for a bigger impact and waved the cheesy doodle bag until they fell everywhere. They hit him in the mouth, his eyes. Crap.

"Yeah, shame, shame," Emily flung more marshmallows until she was pitching them at him with both hands. "Bastard!"

"Stop it! Stop it! Okay, I am. I'm an asshole. The biggest creep alive." Sam fisted his hands at his sides and looked at both of them. It dawned on him how lucky Lola was to have them in her life. Their pretty faces were fiery red with anger.

Trouble in a Stetson

Flags of bright color burned on Lola's cheeks too. "Damn it, Lola. I love you."

Emily and Roxie halted mid-attack and gazed at each other. "We're getting out of here, honey. Right now," Em stated with finality.

Roxie slipped into her boots and gave her a lopsided grin. "Yeah, we'll come back tomorrow and clean this mess up."

"Forget the mess," Lola whispered.

"Yeah. Just leave and don't come back until we call you," Sam added. Roxie sauntered out the door and as Emily turned to close it, he looked at her. "Thank you for being her friends."

Emily grinned. "Don't mention it."

Silence fell when the door snicked shut. Lola looked at him over the battleground littered with junk food and her bottom lip quivered. Damn, he'd hurt her so badly. He could see it on her face and in her beautiful blue eyes. Uncaring about the crap on the floor, he went to her and filled his fist with her messy blonde ponytail. "I love you."

"Sam." She shook her head. "I thought—"

"I was wrong about everything and damn me for jumping to conclusions. It's been so long since I trusted a woman, any woman. But hell honey, you came into my life and you were so good. Honest. I just had to believe, finally, there was someone in this world who would love me for me. Just the way I am."

Tears poured down Lola's face. "Hey, I kind of know how you feel about that, Sam. It's been that way for me my whole life, ya know? Nothing happened with Nick. He just kissed me. I tried to push him—"

"Shh. I know." Sam wrapped her up in his arms. She was trembling and he hated himself all over again. "I got the wrong idea about things. I know better now. Here's the deal, I saw that man with his hands and his mouth all over you and I just went a little crazy. I've felt like you were mine for quite a while now."

Her nose had been buried in his chest but now she looked up at him. "You have?"

"Yeah, I have. I'm in love with you, Lola. I love everything about you. I respect you. And I want you forever. Stay. Stay here with me. Okay?"

"Okay, Sam. Okay. I love you too. I'll do anything for you, honey. Heck, you can even shoot my car if you wanna."

Sam kissed her as the cracks in his heart filled with the kind of love that would last him the rest of his life. He had his sweet little showgirl and that was enough.

TROUBLE IN CHAPS
Ciana Stone

Trademarks Acknowledgement

The author acknowledges the trademarked status and trademark owners of the following wordmarks mentioned in this work of fiction:

Hallmark: Hallmark Licensing, Inc.

Left 4 Dead: Valve Corporation

Xbox: Microsoft Corporation

Chapter One

Roxie watched her friend Lola leave the café. This day had to go down in the record books as one of the worst. It wasn't bad enough that the 1966 Cadillac they'd left Vegas in had broken down. It'd broken down in Texas. Mesa Blanco, Texas, to be precise.

Roxie thought Bumfuck, Texas, would have been more apt. With a population that boasted of just over three thousand residents, according to the sign at the edge of town, the likelihood of finding a job that would not only enable her to pay for a place to stay but save enough to fix the car was remote.

"So, what'd you do in Vegas, Roxie?"

The deep, male voice from across the table had visions of something other than a job dancing in Roxie's head. Something along the lines of sweat-slicked skin, tangled sheets and low grunts of pleasure.

"This and that," she responded, turning her attention to the man seated across from her, Cliff Beckett.

Tall and lean, Cliff had the kind of build that made her mouth water. She forced aside the erotic images that sprang to mind and lifted her near-empty soda glass to jiggle the ice cubes.

"Ever work in a bar?"

One eyebrow arched. "You offering me a job, Mr. Beckett?"

"Cliff."

Roxie resisted the urge to shift in her seat. The way he was looking at her made it hard to keep her mind on business. "Well?" she asked.

"Depends."

"On?"

"How are you at tending bar?"

"I've mixed a drink or two."

"Most of my customers fall into the beer category."

She smiled in spite of herself. "Then I've twisted a few caps."

"Waited tables?"

"Once or twice."

"Dealt with rowdy fellas who've maybe had one too many on a Friday night?"

That prompted a laugh. "Honey, I lived in Vegas."

Cliff chuckled. "Which brings me back to my original question. What exactly did you do in Vegas? Showgirl, dancer?"

Roxie laughed. "No, that's Lola's thing."

"And yours was...?"

"Security."

That wasn't an answer Cliff expected. Roxie looked more like the beauties that can be found on a stage in Vegas. Busty, built and legs that made a man fantasize about what it would feel like to have them wrapped around him.

"Security?"

"Yep."

"As in bouncer?"

"Yeah, I did that. Did most all of it but for the last few years I worked the high-stakes games."

Cliff knew what she meant. When there was a lot on the table, most casinos had specialists watching. Not just from

Trouble in Chaps

cameras but on the floor. Most people would never recognize the specialists. They dressed like everyone else and often sat in on the games.

And were the most lethal people in the world to play against because their "specialty" was spotting cheats. They knew all the tricks and most of them were banned from gambling.

"Well, I don't have much of a call for that at Chaps. But I can offer you a job if you're interested."

"How much do you pay?"

"You don't beat around the bush, do you, Roxie?"

"What's the point? How much?"

"Minimum wage plus tips."

She surprised him again when she stood. "Thanks, anyway. I think I'll see if there isn't something else available that pays a bit better."

"Ten an hour plus tips." The words were out of his mouth before he realized it. Why was that? Sure, Roxie was one hot babe that he'd purely love to get between the sheets, but attractive women were a dime a dozen. Why did he suddenly have an itch to have her around? And why the hell was he offering her nearly eight dollars more an hour than minimum wage?

She sat back down. "How much does it cost for a room at that place...what was it?"

"Mrs. Chester's Boarding House."

"Yeah, how much?"

"She'd probably cut you a deal. Hundred a week without meals and laundry services."

Roxie mentally calculated. At sixteen hundred a month base salary, minus four hundred for rent, she had twelve hundred left plus whatever tips she made. And if Chaps was like most other bars in America, her tips could easily match her base pay.

Then there was food. From the prices on the menu at the Blue Belle Café, it'd cost at least a hundred a week for food. That brought her to eight hundred, plus what she made in tips. She could put more into the car fund than what it would take to live. And the car repairs were liable to be expensive. Chances were the parts would be hard to find, which would drive the price up. She wasn't all that experienced in auto repair, but she was guessing it would cost them somewhere in the neighborhood of three to four thousand to get the land yacht back on the road. If she wanted to get the heck out of Dodge—or Mesa Blanco—as quickly as possible, she was going to need to earn a lot more than ten dollars an hour.

"Twenty-five an hour," she finally said, meeting his eyes.

Cliff snorted. "I can hire three gals for that price."

"Not three with my experience."

"Fifteen an hour."

"Twenty."

Cliff smiled at her, a lazy, knowing smile she'd seen more than once. It was the smile of a gambler who was holding a pat hand. Funny thing was that she'd never seen that smile look quite so sexy, or had it affect her with a sudden tightening of her nipples and warmth that spread down straight into her crotch.

"Three to closing, Wednesday through Saturday."

Roxie couldn't believe he'd agreed. They both knew that the offer was about nine hundred percent more than he was required to pay. But she wasn't about to look a gift horse in the mouth.

"What time's closing?"

"Two a.m. Hour for dinner and fifteen minute break every two hours. You get one meal per shift and all the water and soft drinks you can hold but no alcohol unless you pay — half price for employees."

Trouble in Chaps

She considered it for a brief moment. With that pay and if the repairs on the car weren't too much, she'd be bidding farewell to Mesa Blanco inside a month.

"Done. When do I start?"

"Tonight's as good as any."

"Okay. Thanks, Mr. Beckett."

"Cliff."

"Not as long as I work for you."

The message was all too clear. Hands off. Cliff felt a grin rising on his face. He loved a challenge and Roxie Ellis just might prove to be a very stimulating one. "Have it your way. I'll expect you by five. That should give you time to get settled and changed."

"Into what?"

"You got any cut-off jeans?"

"I have a pair I can cut."

"That'll do. I'll have a Chaps t-shirt sent over to the boarding house for you."

She stood and offered her hand. "Thanks. I'll see you at five."

Cliff rose and took her hand. "Don't disappoint me, Roxie."

She met his eyes with a sassy expression that had heat starting to simmer in his belly. "Not in my vocabulary, Mr. Beckett."

With that, she pulled her hand from his, turned and left without a backward glance. Cliff reclaimed his seat, staring thoughtfully at the door. He'd have to call his guy and get the scoop on Roxie Ellis. There was more to her story than just a woman who'd thrown in the towel on a whim and high-tailed it out of Vegas. And he was going to find out what it was.

Chapter Two

Roxie turned in front of the mirror. When Cliff said he'd have a shirt sent to her, she'd assumed it would be a standard t-shirt. Not a spaghetti-strapped, tight, white, cropped-off top that showed as much as it covered.

There was no way to put a bra under it. Well, maybe a strapless one, which she didn't own. And forget borrowing one from Lola, who probably had a dozen. Roxie would have to invest in extra socks to fill Lola's cups.

At least the wording on the front of the shirt covered her breasts, obscuring her nipples. *Do it in Chaps* was stamped boldly in red.

Cheesy, but cute, she thought. And now her official work uniform. Damn, why the hell did she leave Las Vegas?

That thought caused a tightening of her jaw and brought a hard glint to her eyes. Not even Lola and Emily knew the real reason she agreed to leave with them. It wasn't something she was willing to share with anyone. Besides, what was done was done and right now she had to focus on making enough to have the car fixed so she could leave this two-horse town and get on with her life.

As she brushed her hair, her thoughts turned to her new job and her new boss. She'd always made a point not to get involved with people she worked with. It caused too many complications when it didn't work out. And in Roxie's experience, relationships never really worked out.

Cliff Beckett was going to make it hard to stick to her rule. The man was lethal. And it wasn't just his dark hair that was a shade too long to be fashionable, eyes the color of storm clouds and a face that would not be easy to forget. Maybe that

Trouble in Chaps

gambler's air about him. That air that said the bigger the stakes and the more he had on the line, the better he liked it.

There was an intensity to him that the good-old-boy façade couldn't cover. And that was lethal. At least for her. Which spelled trouble with a capital T. Bottom line? She had to keep her hands off Cliff Beckett. Regardless of how much she'd like to dive into the tantalizing pool of temptation, she had to steer clear.

With her resolve firm, she headed out the door for her first night of work.

"Want another hit?"

Cliff turned his attention away from the schedule on the bar in front of him to look up at the waitress, Diane, behind the bar. She held a carafe of coffee. "Yeah, thanks."

"So the new girl starts tonight?"

"Yep." Cliff hid a smile. Mesa Blanco was a small town and it didn't take high-speed cable, smart phones or the internet for news spread faster than wild fire. By now, half the people in town knew Roxie and her friends had broken down. Probably knew that Emily was on Wyatt's ranch, that Lola had been hired at the Blue Belle and that Chaps was getting a new waitress.

He'd lay odds that tonight's crowd would be bigger than normal just out of curiosity. It was the way of small towns. Not much happened out of the ordinary and when something did, everyone was curious.

"Shit, there go my tips." Diane muttered, her eyes turned toward the door.

Cliff turned his eye to follow the direction of her eyes and a spear of heat spiked through him. Roxie.

Christ on a crutch. What she did for a tank top and cut-off jeans was a sin. A tempting, dead-sexy sin. The tank top was tight enough to have been painted on, accenting her full breasts and exposing her from mid-torso to the top of the low-riding jeans that had been cut off short enough to make a man hope he'd see her bend over.

Over-the-knee black leather boots showcased thighs that brought images best left for wet dreams to mind.

"Mr. Beckett," she said as she stopped beside him.

"Roxie."

"Where do you want me?"

The sudden swell of erection at her words had several suggestions spring to mind. In his bed, on the bar, the floor, bent across a table. There was a multitude of places he'd like to have her.

"Why don't you start behind the bar?"

"Will do." She turned her attention to Diane. "Hi, I'm Roxie."

"Diane."

"Nice to meet you. You mind showing me the ropes?"

Diane cut her eyes at Cliff then back to Roxie. "Sure. Come on back."

Cliff couldn't help but watch as Roxie turned. Oh, damn. The way the denim hugged her ass was criminal. He better keep her behind the bar. Sure as shit, there'd be more than one fella who tried to get his hands on that.

A surge of jealously shocked him. What the hell? Was he experiencing some kind of alpha male thing? He didn't even know the woman and already he was dealing with an uncomfortable hard-on and jealousy over the idea of another man's hands on her.

He gave it some thought as he watched Diane go over things with her. Roxie got to him and he knew himself well enough to know that he'd never be satisfied until he had her. And being a gambler, the challenge of winning her had appeal.

A smile came to his face. Winning Roxie was now the goal. But the key was making her come to him. And she would. He just had to figure out the right buttons to push.

Trouble in Chaps

Yes, he was definitely going to have Roxie. Looked as if it was going to be an interesting time in Mesa Blanco after all.

Roxie could feel Cliff's eyes on her. It wasn't an altogether unpleasant sensation. In fact, quite the opposite. But she was determined to ignore it. She had ignored it for almost a week and it was starting to wear her down.

She was keeping herself awake at night imagining the damn man's hands on her and hers on him. She either needed to get laid or find a damn sex toy store because she was close to a meltdown.

By eight o'clock the place was packed and she'd popped so many beer tops she resolved to scout out the local stores tomorrow and find a nice, thick, silver ring for her thumb. That was a trick she'd learned long ago. Wearing a thumb ring helped you pop a beer top without an opener and saved you from ending up with blisters.

"Hon, why don't you take a break," Diane said as Roxie rang up another sale. "Slip on back to the office and put your feet up for a few."

"Thanks." Roxie gave her a smile. She grabbed a bottle of water from the cooler and headed through the kitchen behind the bar to the office. Thankfully, it was empty.

The moment she closed the door, the din of noise dampened. She took a long drink of water and leaned back against the door.

"How's it going?"

The sound of Cliff's voice had her springing away from the door. "Sorry. I didn't know you were here. Diane told me it was okay to take a break in here."

"Fine by me. That's what I'm doing."

"What?"

"Taking a break."

"From?"

He chuckled and ignored the question. "You seem to have caught on to things. Diane says you're raking in the tips."

"It's not rocket science," she replied, stemming the urge to back away as he rose from his seat at the desk and approached.

"That it's not."

She waited for him to say more but he simply leaned one shoulder against the wall and regarded her with that slow sexy smile. "Customers like you."

"Or the beer." She wasn't stupid. She'd been hit on and flirted with before tonight. And knew how to give just enough flirt in return to ensure a good tip but not leave the impression that she was available.

Cliff's smile widened. "Honey, they can get that beer all they want. You, on the other hand—you're a temptation they haven't tasted."

"And aren't likely to." She met his eyes to show him that she was not kidding.

"I wouldn't fire you for it, sugar."

"It wouldn't matter—if I saw anything I was interested in."

He moved a little closer. "So you haven't seen anything that interests you?"

She knew what he was asking. And knew she should meet his eyes and lie through her teeth. But her brain didn't seem to be working right at the moment. The close proximity of his lean, muscular body had her hormones spiking. She could smell the clean scent of soap and man, feel the heat coming off him.

"Nothing I'm going to act on."

"Oh? And just for the sake of argument, if you were inclined to act, just what would be the subject of your interest?"

Trouble in Chaps

"I think we both know the answer to that." The moment the words were out of her mouth, she knew it was a mistake. First rule of gambling—never give your opponent anything to use against you.

Cliff's smile faded, to be replaced with a look that had her wanting things she knew she had to stay away from.

He leaned a little closer. "You want to fill me in on why acting on this interest would be a bad thing?"

"I already told you. Not as long as I work for you." Roxie edged away a few inches then mentally cursed herself for showing weakness. "I don't mix business and pleasure."

"Yeah, I remember."

"I guess I'll get back to work." She turned to leave, eager to escape the feelings his nearness inspired.

"Hold on."

She paused.

"We've got a bit of a problem, Roxie."

"With what?"

"This."

He had her pressed against the door and his lips on hers before she could protest. She could have pushed him way. Should have. But damn he felt good, the long, lean length of him pressed against her, the taste of him. She gave in and returned the kiss, grabbing his hips to pull him more firmly against her.

Then reason returned and with it, anger. Not at him. At herself. She pushed him away.

"It isn't going to happen. I already told you."

"Yeah, I know, not as long as you work for me."

"Right."

"Easy enough. You're fired."

"No!" She pressed both hands against his chest as he moved in on her. "No."

199

Cliff stopped, planting both hands on the door on either side of her and boxing her in. "Why? We both want it."

"Sometimes that old saying is true, Mr. Beckett. The wanting is better than the having."

"I'd be willing to bet that isn't the case here, darling."

"Maybe not, but I need a job more than an orgasm."

He didn't respond for several moments. "I tend to disagree."

"Then we'll have to agree to disagree, won't we?"

"Maybe. Maybe not. How 'bout we have ourselves a little wager?"

"What kind of wager?"

"That if you spend time with me outside of work, inside of three weeks you'll change your mind and ask me to take you to bed."

Roxie barked a laugh. "That's so not going to happen."

He smiled. "Put your money where your mouth is."

"Got no money, as you well know."

"Fine. If I win, you agree to stay for six months. Working for me and sharing my bed."

"And if I win?"

"I pay you six month's salary, fix your car and wish you good luck as you leave Mesa Blanco in your dust."

Roxie considered it. "Six months regular bartender's pay or six months at the same rate you pay me now?"

His mouth twitched as if he were fighting back a smile. "Your rate."

"Define 'spend time with'."

"You know, sugar, dinner at my place, maybe some dancing on your nights off and necking on the couch."

"Necking?" Damn, why did her pulse spike at the idea?

"Well hell, Roxie, you scared you can't resist me?"

Trouble in Chaps

"Not on your best day, Beckett." God was going to get her if she didn't quit lying, but she wasn't about to let him know that resisting him was requiring effort.

"Then do we have a deal?"

Three weeks, she thought. All she had to do was hold out three weeks. She could do that. Couldn't she? She might need to find that sex toy store pretty quick, but she could do it. Only twenty-one days and then she could say *adios* to Mesa Blanco and get on with her life.

"Deal." She stuck out her right hand.

"I think we can do better than that." He claimed her in a kiss that had her blood humming and her toes threatening to curl. When he pulled back, his smile was cocky. "You're going down, Roxie."

Roxie felt the gambler within rise to the challenge. She leaned in toward him, pressing her breasts against him as her right hand moved down to cup the erection that strained against the leg of his jeans. "You wish."

Cliff laughed and moved away. Yep, he was definitely going to win this bet. Roxie might not warm his bed tonight, but soon she would. He would see to it.

201

Chapter Three

Roxie's pulse did a quick two-step when Cliff opened the front door of his house. Dressed in soft, faded jeans and a white dress shirt open at the neck, with sleeves rolled up his forearms, he looked good enough to eat.

"I see you found the place."

"Thanks for the loan of your truck."

"My pleasure, darlin'."

She almost rolled her eyes. He was laying on the Texas accent a bit thick and she knew he'd had his truck left in town for her to drive because it suited him to do so. Roxie had been around gamblers all her life and recognized when someone was setting her up to take a fall.

Not that she intended to fall for Cliff Beckett. She was just here, on her day off, because it was part of the bet.

"Come on in." He stepped aside for her to enter.

She smiled in amusement as his eyes raked over her. Her outfit obviously wasn't what he'd expected, but the look in his eyes when they met hers told her quite clearly that he liked what he saw.

Good. She'd chosen her outfit with care. A gypsy skirt that rode low on her hips, a tank top that stopped just short of her navel and an old, soft denim shirt with the sleeves rolled up and the bottom tied just above her waist. She wore her hair loose and opted for a pair of sandals to complete her outfit.

He smiled at her. "Nice outfit, but not too good for riding"

She returned the smile. She might be set on spurning his advances, but that didn't mean she couldn't play a little

Trouble in Chaps

herself. She liked the way he looked at her. Liked knowing that he wanted her. And liked being able to turn him down and cross one more day off the calendar that she was closer to leaving Mesa Blanco.

"Depends on the kind of riding you had in mind."

The look he gave her was heated enough to ignite a fire in her belly. He took her by the wrist and pulled her into his arms. Roxie fought to resist the pull, to ignore the fact that everything inside her was shouting for her to just let go and give in. To enjoy the sinful temptation his eyes promised and the delicious feel of his hard body against hers.

But that wouldn't get her back on the road so just before his lips met hers, she raised her hand and covered his lips with her fingers.

He didn't release her, but did straighten, letting one of his hands drift down her back to slide across the swell of her ass. She stepped back, forcing him to drop his hands.

"So, what kinda riding is it gonna be today, Roxie?"

"Hmmm, don't know that I'm much interested in riding today, Cliff."

His eyebrows rose a moment before his smile. "Cliff? Does that mean the rules have changed?"

She smiled and reached up to trace her fingers along the side of his face. "Let me think on that a minute."

Even as she acted, she knew she was treading dangerous ground. Playing with Cliff Beckett was definitely like handling fire. Fire that could spread in an instant. But she couldn't resist.

She stood up on her tiptoes and slowly brushed her lips across his. He made no move to take control of the moment, which pleased her. Her tongue snaked out and his lips parted to allow her access. It was a slow, long kiss with nothing of their bodies touching except their lips. Finally, just before she ended the kiss she leaned in, grazing his chest with her breasts.

When she moved back, he reached for her but she stepped back, leaning against the door.

"Well?" he asked.

She cocked her head slightly to one side. "Sorry, Beckett."

"Your eyes tell a different tale, sugar. A kiss that makes promises. Very hot and wet promises."

Unfortunately, hot and wet was just how she felt. Were it not for the bet, she'd be on him like white on rice. But losing wasn't an option and all she could do was bluff her way through the moment.

"I like it hot."

He moved too fast for her to evade and pulled her to him. "Then you're gonna love this, sugar."

His mouth crushed down on hers, one hand fisting in her hair and the other moving up to cup one breast. It was like a bolt of electricity. Every nerve ending in her body went into high gear, sensation screaming through her from his touch. When his thumb tracked over her nipple, she fought to stifle a groan and was only partially successful.

He lifted away from the kiss, a cocky smile on his face. "You are so going down."

His tease brought her back to the game, allowing her to establish some measure of control over her traitorous body that was screaming for her to rip his clothes off and fuck his brains out there on in the vestibule. She stepped away and circled him.

"Not on you. And since we know we're not doing *that,* what else you have for entertainment around here?"

She moved into the den, taking a look around. Cliff sure had a nice place. Clearly he wasn't hurting for money. And that was curious. Sure, Chaps did a good business, but she didn't see a small town bar providing the capital for this kind of house and certainly not for the furnishings it contained. He had to be into something else to afford all this.

Trouble in Chaps

She walked over to the massive entertainment center that dominated one wall. Who the heck needed a television that big? Apparently, he did. When she spotted an Xbox console in one of the glass cabinets to the side, she smiled. *Ah ha, a gamer.*

"What kind of games do you have?"

Cliff nearly groaned. The last thing on his mind was playing video games. What was on his mind was touching and tasting every inch of her. But like his granddaddy always said, "You can hog that ice cream cone fast or lick it slow and savor the taste as long as possible." That was a pretty smart old fella, as far as Cliff was concerned. So he gave in. Prolonging the anticipating and taking it slowly only made the having that much sweeter.

"In the cabinet beneath. Take your pick." He took a seat on the couch and watched as she knelt down and opened the cabinet.

Gypsy. That was the first thing that came to mind when he looked at her. With the colorful shirt hanging low on her hips and its irregular hem giving glimpses of bare legs and her hair loose and flowing down her back, he could imagine her in a Gypsy camp, dancing around a fire and tempting every man in sight.

She selected a game and put it in the console then turned to him. "Where do you keep your controllers?"

"Drawer to the left."

Roxie took two controllers from the drawer, kicked off her sandals and took a seat on the sofa beside him, hiking her skirt up then tucking it between her legs as she arranged herself, Indian fashion.

The complaint that rose to his lips died as an idea came to Cliff. "What'd you pick?"

"Left 4 Dead."

"One or two."

205

"One. I have a thing for Francis."

Cliff chucked. Why didn't that surprise him? Of course, Roxie would go for the character who looked like a big muscular biker and had a hair-trigger temper and a bad attitude.

He reached for the remote and turned on the television. "So, we teaming up or playing versus?"

"Versus."

Cliff nodded. "You play much?"

"When I can."

"Enough to put a wager on the outcome of the game?"

He could see hesitation on her face. "It's okay, if you're not up to it then…"

Oh, he had her. He could tell from the way her jaw tightened and her eyes narrowed that she couldn't back down.

"What're the stakes?"

He let the moment draw out, running his eyes over her. Damn if he didn't like what he saw. Like the way her tank top clung to her breasts. And those big hazel eyes going a shade darker when they met his. He most decidedly liked what he saw.

She rolled her eyes at him. "Come on, Beckett. What're the stakes?"

"I win, we spend the rest of the day in bed."

"Nope. That cancels our original bet."

"I didn't say I'd get in you, baby. How 'bout this? I win and you get naked with me in bed and everything but that is on the table."

"Define everything."

"Tasting, touching—anything two people can do except actual intercourse."

"And if I win?"

"Name it."

Trouble in Chaps

"You fix the Caddy and chip in two grand, cash, so Lola, Emily and I can get outta this town."

Shit. That wasn't what he'd hoped for. He wasn't ready for Roxie to leave. Was she that certain she could win? Bigger question, could he beat her?

The gambler inside decided for him. "Done."

Now came the moment. He could almost hear the wheels turning in her brain. Could she take him? Seeing the uncertainty in her eyes bolstered his confidence.

She gave him a smile that spoke of determination. "Maybe I should call Emily and Lola and tell them to start packing."

"Maybe you should wait till tomorrow and tell them about how I drove you damn near crazy with my hands and mouth."

She smirked. "Get your game on, stud. You're about to go down in flames."

Cliff started the game, hoping she was wrong.

Two hours later, Cliff was starting to worry that she was right. She was good. They were in a dead tie. As the next match loaded on the console, he turned to look at her.

She watched the screen, unaware that he was watching her instead of the television. He liked the way her brows drew together slightly as she studied the available weapons and made selection. Not to mention the sexy way she pursed her lips. Damn if this woman wasn't a breathing hard-on.

"This is it," she said.

He looked at the screen. "I've heard that before."

She cocked her head to one side as she studied the screen. "You won't survive this one. I've got your number, Beckett."

He hoped not, but just in case, maybe he'd better try to turn his game up a notch. This match, he was playing a zombie and she was playing a human survivor. If she was smart enough to keep out of areas where she had no room to maneuver and got a good bead on him, she just might survive. Or worse, she might get the drop on him and take him out.

And if she took him out, that took her out. Of town.

"Get ready to get naked, Roxie."

She cut him a sassy smile and then turned her attention back to the game. "You're such a flirt. Okay, here we go."

A stab of something akin to anxiety lanced through her. They'd battled for hours, evenly matched, neither of them able to get more than one match on the other. Now suddenly her character was trapped in an alley with zombies coming at her from both directions.

Gritting her teeth, she fought harder. She couldn't lose. This was her chance to get out of town.

That thought brought another. Just why was she so eager to leave? She had nowhere to go and no one to go to. Was she running toward something or away from something?

That was what undid her, because suddenly it all caved in on her. The truth was she was running away. Away from Cliff Beckett and the feelings he inspired. Not just the lust. That was a horse she could ride. There was something else. Something more. Something about him that said it would be all too easy to lose herself in him.

And that scared her. She'd sworn off love a long time ago, sworn never to let herself become lost in a man. It only brought pain.

Distracted, she lost focus and made a fatal error. His character, a special zombie called a Hunter, pounced. "Come on, come on, help me out!" she nearly screamed at the artificial intelligence characters who fought alongside her. If one of them didn't shoot the hunter off her, she was a goner.

Seconds ticked by, her life force clicking down steadily until those fatal words appeared on the screen. "You Are Dead."

Trouble in Chaps

"Noooo!" *Oh shit, oh shit, oh shit.* It was all she could think. She'd lost.

She turned to look at Cliff and when their eyes met all the air in the room seemed to have been sucked out. Locked in the desire in his eyes, she could only stare.

"Looks like I'm not the only one going down, today, sugar."

It took all the control she could muster to tear away from his eyes. It wasn't going to take much more for her to fall victim to him and she couldn't allow that to happen. She had to play it cool. "God almighty, you're cocky. But I'm curious. Do you always go to such lengths to win?"

"I go after what I want."

"Yeah, that's obvious." She added a little snort for effect, hoping she appeared completely unaffected by his nearness. "But the question was, are you always so determined?"

"Only when the situation calls for it."

She shook her head. "Okay and I'm supposed to translate that...how? That you feel a *hankering* for a new diversion and I look like a likely candidate?"

The frown that appeared on his face surprised her. He reached out to take her hand and tug on it so that she angled to face him.

"Listen up, Roxie. I'm only going to say this once. I don't meet many women who intrigue me. But you do. So while I do have a hankering for you, it's not just a conquest. It's more a discovery. Discovering what's beneath the surface. And sugar, I'm just as interested in pleasuring you as myself."

Nothing could have surprised her more. Had she gotten him completely wrong, assuming he was just another guy looking for a quick slap-and-tickle who would immediately move on to the next candidate?

"Why? "

Ciana Stone

"Because you're all mystery and fire. You're bold but wary and you bluff like a champion. You don't trust easy and you keep a tight rein on what's inside. You're smart, strong and ..."

"And?"

A slight flush rose on his face along with a grin. "And thinking of you keeps me awake at night."

"Well...well, I'm flattered. But don't confuse me with the fantasies, Beckett. Reality rarely lives up to fantasy."

He pulled her closer, reaching up to run one hand through her long hair. "I know the difference between fantasy and reality, honey. Just like I know there's one hell of a fire burning beneath that cool exterior."

"And yeah, I play to win. Now that I have, I sure as hell hope you're not gonna welsh on the debt, 'cause you can bank on it that if you let me, I'll take you places you've never been before."

"Promises, promises." She tried to tease but was largely unsuccessful. At the moment she was feeling completely overwhelmed.

He shook his head. "Iron-clad guarantee."

For a few moments they just sat there. She searched his eyes and, uncharacteristic to her nature, took the bait. Hook, line and sinker.

Cliff watched her eyes, waiting for her response. Was he about to get shot down? He hoped not. Something inside him said that she just might be the woman who could match him. Not just in verbal sparring, brains and talent, but in passion. That concerned him a bit. When had it become about more than just sex?

Then she gave him a sexy smile and his mind went blank to everything but his hunger for her. "Well, hell, Beckett. When you put it like that..."

Trouble in Chaps

Before he knew it, she'd grabbed his shirt in both hands and ripped it open. Buttons popped free, flying this way and that as she bared his chest. He had time to do little more than smile before her mouth was on his chest and her fingers were working on the button of his jeans.

Eagerly, he pulled her to him, claiming her in a kiss. Her hands abandoned their task of unfastening his belt to snake up around his neck, fisting in his hair, and she returned the kiss with unbridled passion.

Passion hot as a five-alarm fire. And the blaze had burned south of the belt way too quickly for comfort.

He wasn't accustomed to instant heat, the kind that made you lose your mind and revert into a primitive man with only a single thought—to get in and stoke hard. But that's where he was and it gave him considerable discomfort knowing that he'd stick to the terms of the deal and not push for that.

Still locked in the kiss he pressed her back onto the sofa, his hands tugging at the rolled waist of her skirt. She raised her hips, allowing him to slide the skirt down her legs.

He ran his hands down her sides, traveling over the curves, feeling the reaction when her thighs tightened. Damn, she felt good. Firm muscle beneath the soft skin. The return journey was every bit as good, moving up her sides to take hold of her tank top and pull it up over her head.

Her hands loosened in his hair when he tore away from the kiss to let his lips roam down the length of her neck to the hollow of her throat where her pulse hammered against his tongue through the soft skin.

Good Lord, thank you for women, he thought when he reached her breasts. Soft, round mounds that filled his hands, topped by a perfect pair of dusky nipples that screamed to be licked, sucked, bitten.

Roxie's fingers fisted in his hair when he flicked his tongue across the taut nub of one perfect nipple then sucked it into his mouth. His dick jumped in excitement when she arched up, pressing against his mouth with a small exhalation of pleasure.

That sound stirred a side of him he wasn't ready to reveal. The side that few people knew. Secreted away within was a man who needed to dominate. To know that his woman was his to pleasure at his leisure, to propel her to the edge of madness with wanting then stop her from crossing so that he could carry her toward release time and again until at last she achieved pleasure beyond her dreams.

As he abandoned her luscious breasts, he couldn't help but wonder if Roxie would be able to handle that. His mouth traveled down her body toward the lacy triangle that covered her sex. Seductive, uninhibited and strong, she got to him in a way no other woman ever had. But was she strong enough to submit?

When his mouth covered that small patch of lace, she bucked up against him, her fingers tightening almost painfully in his hair.

"Oh, god. Damn. Beckett, wait."

That was the last thing he hoped to hear. She pushed him away and he sat back on his heels. Roxie moved onto her knees, running both hands along the tops of his shoulders to his neck.

"Sorry, Beckett, but my fuse is a little short. Need to slow it down a notch."

Thank god. She wasn't backing out, just slowing down. He could do that. Maybe. Now that he had a look at her, kneeling naked and flushed in front of him, her hair spilling around her shoulders in a wild riot of waves, it was hard for his brain to retain control. His little head was screaming for him to toss her back on the couch and bury himself inside her.

Cliff's smile brought a flood of relief. Roxie hadn't lied. If he'd done so much as move his lips against her clit, she'd have exploded like a bottle rocket on the Fourth of July.

Trouble in Chaps

And once that happened she wasn't sure she'd be able to stop herself from taking things to the next level. She needed a moment to get control.

After a few moments, she leaned closer, brushing her breasts against his chest and shivering at the tingle that danced over her skin when his hands moved to play over her back and down to her ass. She hoped it wasn't obvious how eager her lips were for his when he caught them in a searing kiss.

And oh, my god, could the man kiss. Long and deep, just the right amount of pressure and tongue technique.

It had been a long time since a kiss had affected her so profoundly. She sank into the feeling, her body acting on its own accord to settle more firmly against him. The feel of his firm chest against her breasts, rising in quickening breaths was an impetus to press closer. The muscles of his abdomen tightened in time with the deepening of the kiss in what seemed an echo of the own tension mounting inside her.

His hands moved along her sides lightly, working around to her back. She'd heard women talk about a touch leaving a wake of fire but until now had chalked it up to exaggeration.

Those strong hands moved lower, cupping her ass to pull her tighter against the erection trapped between their bodies and her mind lost the ability to reason. Roxie wound her fingers in his hair, devouring him with a kiss that had the wonderful result of a groan coming from deep in his throat.

She flinched as she realized how much she wanted him, how much she wanted to forget silly bets and old fears. And with realization came the return of that annoying inner voice. The one frantically trying to remind her how unwise it was to fall victim to the sensuous temptation Cliff offered.

She almost managed to reign in her lust when his hands moved lower, pulling off her underwear to bare her ass. Feather-light strokes down the crease of her ass to her sex had her moaning before she could stop herself.

Ciana Stone

She knew Cliff was a man she didn't dare lower her defenses to. At least not emotionally. She had to keep a tight rein on her needs and emotions and just play the game, she told herself. No involvement, just some physical pleasure. That's all it was.

That was a game she'd played most of her life. She could do it now. Had to. Cliff Beckett was nothing more than a momentary diversion. She just had to take control and not let it go. As long as she controlled things, she was safe.

Determined to make that real, she moved out of the kiss and lowered herself down inch by inch, her lips and tongue enjoying the feel and taste of him as her hands worked to unzip his pants and slide them down his lean hips.

Damn. Everything really is bigger in Texas, she thought as she wrapped both hands around his shaft.

When she began to stroke, she heard him groan slightly. His body tensed and his hands tangled in her hair. Slowly she stroked, increasing the strength of her grip a little at a time and watching him close his eyes and lean his head back. God almighty, he was sexy. She'd love to have lapped at the bead of precum that sparkled at the tip of his cock, but not even someone as sexy as Cliff could make her throw that much caution to the wind.

Instead, she ran her thumb over the bead, circling the head with its slickness. In doing so, she discovered one of his hot buttons. Obviously, the head of his cock was quite sensitive because his hands tightened in her hair and his cock jumped.

She continued until he groaned and pulled back. "Now it's my turn to plead a short fuse."

"Nothing short about your fuse," she countered with a smile as he stood and stepped out of his pants.

She lay back on the sofa, watching and admiring. "I wish I had a camera."

214

Trouble in Chaps

He chuckled and lay down, covering her body with his, nuzzling her neck and earlobe. "Darlin', this ain't no spectator sport."

"But I know women who'd pay to see," she teased.

He rose up, his hands on either side of her, arms braced. "Thank you, sugar, but the real beauty is lying here under me."

Roxie snorted. She hadn't been fishing for a compliment. "You got me naked, cowboy," she said, running her hands up his strong body. "I don't need compliments."

His smile faded. "This isn't sugar coating, honey."

She shook her head in dismissal and let her hands drift down to the point where their bodies met, rubbing at the head of his cock pressed against the length of her belly. She had to turn the conversation. Now wasn't the time to allow feelings to come into play.

"I have an idea."

"Yeah?"

"Um hmm. What about a nice hot shower?"

Cliff was on his feet, pulling her up. "I have a better idea."

He tugged her to follow him down the hall and into the bathroom. They stopped in front of the wall sized mirror over the long, marble vanity. Cliff positioned her in front of him.

"Watch."

Roxie met his eyes in the mirror's reflection. "Watch what?"

"This," he said and moved her hair to one side to nuzzle her neck.

Something shot through her. Something hot and erotic. It wasn't so much his words but the way he spoke them. He was almost commanding but in such a sexual way that there was

215

no sting from the issuance. She remained silent, unsure of what she would say even if she chose to respond.

His lips traveled up her neck to nip on her ear while his hands moved around her body to cup her breasts. His thumbs moved over her hard nipples, creating pulses of sensation that had her struggling not to wiggle. It felt too good. She couldn't help it. She wiggled her ass against him and leaned her head back, closing her eyes.

Cliff almost let it pass, but wanting something bad enough sometimes had a way of provoking bold moves even when those moves might be unwise. This might be one of those times, but his need was strong and this would be a test to determine if she could learn to be the woman that could fulfill those needs.

"Don't close your eyes. I want you to see what I do to you."

She opened her eyes and met his in the reflection. He saw anxiety in them, but also a certain defiance, a need to prove she would not back down from a challenge.

"Put your hands on the vanity and spread your legs."

She complied, bending forward slightly with her hands on the polished surface of the vanity, her legs shoulder width apart. The position served to spread her ass, to expose her anus and pussy, something the tiny thong couldn't hide.

He ran his hand over her ass, up the cleft and over to the thin elastic strap of her thong. One tug and it gave way. He tossed it aside, smiling at her in the mirror. She cocked one eyebrow at him and gave him a little half smile that sent a sizzle through him hot enough to melt titanium.

He lifted his left hand to her breast, toying with the nipple, rolling it between thumb and finger. Her eyes left his to watch his hand. With his right hand he lightly trailed down her back and over her anus to cup her sex.

Trouble in Chaps

She gasped as his fingers parted her lips, working aside the hood of her clit. Her lips parted slightly in a soundless gasp.

"I want you to stand on the balls of your feet, slightly bend your legs and arch your back. Open up for me."

Bingo. He saw her eyes go dark. A thrill shot through him as she complied, the position spreading her wider. Rubbing his thumb down her sex, he penetrated her. She gasped and pressed back into his hand, her hands curling on the marble vanity as if to dig into the polished surface.

He stroked inside her, each stroke causing his fingers to rub across her clit.

She began thrusting back against his hand and he withdrew. "No, don't stop," she begged.

Damn, he liked the sound of that. This time he used his fingers, alternating between stroking inside her and rubbing her clit.

She started to tremble and he stopped. "Don't," her voice was a rough plea. "Do it. Now. Please."

Cliff understood. This wasn't the time to draw things out. She needed to come. He started again. It wasn't long before she moaned and he felt her pussy start to contract.

"I... damn... oh." Her last syllable was drawn out and breathy as she shuddered in climax.

Her neck arched, head tilting back and body trembling, lowering so that her forearms were pressed on the dresser. And the whole time her eyes were glued to his.

It excited him. Intoxicated him. And shook him.

Before that last realization could fully hit home, she blew out her breath and turned to face him. "Damn that felt good. And to be honest, right now I'd love to go down on you. But I'm not that much of a risk taker."

"I'd give you my word I'm clean but somehow I don't think that'd be enough."

"Sorry," she said and reached out to fist his cock. "Tempting as it is, I tend to err on the side of caution. However, I can think of other things we could do with this bad boy."

Cliff couldn't help but grin. Roxie's straight-forward approach was refreshing. He pulled her to him, claiming her lips.

Roxie kept her hand wrapped around his shaft, working her free hand around him to grab his ass. Holy shit, if he didn't have a fine ass. Actually he was fine everywhere. *Slow down, girl.* The orgasm he'd just given her had her primed and ready. She had to tread carefully or she'd let this go too far.

As if sensing her thoughts he started moving backward, still locked in the kiss. When he fell back on the bed, it broke the kiss. She fell on top of him, laughing.

He lay back and she straddled his legs and slid up, trapping his cock between them and rocking back and forth on it. And if the feel wasn't enough to make a strong woman weak, just looking at him was enough to have her wanting to toss caution to the wind. He looked so, so sexy lying there, those grey eyes of his darkened to the color of a thundercloud. She'd have to be damn careful. It would be way too easy to fall for him.

"Darlin', you ever heard the term ride the wild bull?" He interrupted her thoughts.

She laughed and tossed her hair. "Darlin', I've heard most everything but there ain't gonna be any riding today."

"Can't fault a man for trying," he said and pulled her down into a kiss. Damn if he couldn't turn her mouth into one of the most erogenous zones on her body. The way his tongue caressed, explored and teased, then plundered as the heat increased, teeth nipping and hands moving to hold her face immobile.

Trouble in Chaps

It had her squirming against his cock, which was trapped between them and pulsing against her belly. Her sex had a pulse of its own happening. No, make that a throb. As if sensing her need, he released her from the kiss. She sat up, perched on her knees and reached between them to take his hard cock in hand and rub it against the wet opening of her sex.

That was a mistake. She wanted to sink down on that glorious shaft of hardness so much it was almost an ache. Instead, she rocked back, fisting him with one hand and running the tip the index finger of her free hand around the engorged head.

Stroking slowly at first then increasing the tempo, she watched his body tense.

"Best slow down, sugar or…"

No way was she going to slow down. Watching him, the way his eyes darkened to near twilight, the ripple of tension that washed down his body and the way his hands tightened on her thighs let her know she was about to shove him over the edge. And she wanted to do that.

"Roxie." His voice was part warning and part plea.

"Cliff," she breathed his name.

His eyes locked on hers and stayed there as she stroked him to release. Roxie saw hunger in those depths, a need she understood all too well. She knew this was a poor substitute for what he really wanted. Just as she knew that he'd take this, for now, because the need was too great to be ignored. And yet, even in the need so clear in his eyes, she saw something else. Something that had a part of her that had been locked down for a long time trying to break free.

If only she could break down those walls. Cliff made her long for things that went beyond physical gratification. But she knew that was not something she could have, no matter how much she wanted it. What she could have was this. And it would have to do.

219

For a few minutes there was only the sound of their breath, their eyes still locked. Then she smiled and swung her leg over to climb off him. "I need to clean up."

She hurried to the bathroom and started the water in the sink. When she looked up at her reflection in the mirror, she froze in the act of washing her hands. The eyes that looked back at her were her own, but there was something different in them. Something that made her heart race with fear.

Cliff Beckett had gotten to her. Somehow, he'd opened a crack in that wall she so carefully maintained and crept in.

She had to get out of there. Now.

Finishing up quickly, she hurried back through the bedroom, refusing to look at him as he lay on the bed. She ran to the den where she made short order of dressing. Cliff walked in, naked as the day he was born, as she was pulling on her tank top.

"Is there a problem?"

"I have to go."

"Why?"

"Just do."

She slid on her sandals, snatched up her denim shirt and headed for the door.

"Roxie, hold on!" Cliff moved in behind her, putting a hand to the door as she tried to open it.

She whirled, pressing back against the door to keep as much distance between them as possible.

"What just happened?" he asked, concern and confusion clear in his eyes.

"Just let me go, Beckett."

"You reneging on our deal?"

God, he fought dirty. She'd never gone back on a bet in her life. But she couldn't stay here. Couldn't let him touch her again.

Trouble in Chaps

"No, but I need to leave now."

"Can you tell me why?"

"No, I can't."

He searched her eyes for a long moment then moved back. "Okay."

"Thank you." Relief flooded through her, along with gratitude. She threw on her shirt, turned and ran, never stopping until she was in the truck. Then she paused and looked toward the house. Cliff stood in the doorway. Every fiber of her screamed for her to get out of the truck and go back to him.

Every fear she'd ever experienced shouted of the danger of such action.

Fear won. With a sob, she started the truck and pulled away. Dear god, what had she gotten herself into?

Chapter Four

Roxie was pulling her hair back in a ponytail when she heard a knock at the door. Barefoot and dressed in cut-off shorts and a t-shirt, she ran to the door.

Lola and Emily grinned at her, their arms laden with bags from the local market and overnight bags. It was girls' night and they'd agreed to crash at Roxie's room.

"I hope that's not mojito makings," Roxie said with a grin, peeking in the top of one of the bags in Lola's arms as her friends entered.

Emily groaned. "God, no. Last time nearly killed me."

Lola laughed. "Wimps."

Roxie took a bag from her and set it on the small table beneath the window. "Just toss your stuff anywhere."

Lola eyed the bed. "We're all gonna sleep in that little thing?"

"Don't worry, you'll be too toasted to care," Emily quipped and pulled out a fifth of tequila. "Roxie, where do we get ice?"

"Got an ice chest in the bathroom."

Roxie was lucky to have scored a room at Mrs. Chester's boarding house that had its own bath. She could tolerate having only a bedroom to call her own space, but sharing a bathroom was where she drew the line.

Emily pulled an electric blender from her overnight bag. "Where can I plug this in?"

"There's an outlet in the bathroom and a drop cord under the sink. I think it'll reach the dresser if you want to put the blender there," Roxie said over her shoulder as she and Lola

Trouble in Chaps

unloaded the rest of the bags. Chips, chocolate, cheese, crackers and a couple of fat subs that had to have come from the diner.

"So, anything new?" Lola asked in a tone that sounded decidedly sly. Roxie busied herself arranging things on the table rather than look at her friend. She had no doubt there was gossip about her and Cliff but felt a bit uneasy about it. She still hadn't told her friends about her bet with Cliff and didn't know that she would.

As far as they were concerned, she was just having fun with the man while she was in town.

"What've you heard?" she asked.

"Nothing. Just asking."

"No, you weren't." Roxie looked up at Lola. "I know you. You've heard something, so spill."

"Well… Sam did mention that you'd been spending quite a bit of time with Cliff. At his place."

"Oh. Yeah, I guess so."

"And?"

"And is he half as good as he looks like he'd be?" Emily asked, returning with a blender full of ice.

Roxie shrugged. They knew her to be a woman who didn't form attachments and viewed sex as something casual. She hooked up with men from time to time, but never seriously. It was always just a "for sex and fun" arrangement. It was no surprise that they'd assume she'd had sex with him.

That was the way it should be with Cliff. *Should* being the operative word. Roxie wished she could see Cliff in that light, but something about him got to her and she was pretty sure that if she did ever have sex with him, she wasn't going to want to stop at a casual one-nighter.

And that scared her.

"Come on," Lola encouraged.

"Let's just say that the man has moves."

223

"Oh, details!" Emily said.

Roxie moved to the bed and flopped down on her back, staring at the ceiling.

"Uh-oh," Emily murmured.

"Drinks, we need drinks," Lola directed.

Emily got busy fixing a pitcher of drinks and filling three plastic cups. She and Lola climbed on the bed with Roxie. "Okay, let's have it," Emily ordered.

Roxie sighed, took a big swig of the drink and grimaced. "Damn, a little heavy-handed on the tequila there, Em."

Emily chuckled. "So?"

"So," Roxie paused. "I sort of have this little bet going with Beckett."

"Bet?" Lola looked alarmed. "Honey, you think that's wise? I mean, you haven't gone near gambling in—"

"It's not that kind of bet. Well, not exactly."

"Just what kind of bet is it, exactly?" Emily asked.

Roxie quickly outlined the details of the wager. By the time she was finished, it was time for a new round of drinks. Lola blew out her breath. "That's kinda... hot."

"Hot doesn't even come close," Roxie admitted, as she got up to refill their cups. "The man has mad skills."

"And you've got how much longer to hold out?" Emily asked.

"Two weeks. Well, thirteen days to be exact."

"So, if I was a betting gal, who would I put my money on?"

Roxie shook her head. "Damn if I know. The man gets to me in a big way."

"Question is, do you get to him?" Lola asked quietly.

Emily and Roxie both looked at her. "She's got that look," Emily commented.

Roxie giggled. "I feel a Lolaism coming on."

Trouble in Chaps

Lola flipped her off good naturedly and they all laughed. "Okay," Roxie said. "Let's have it. I know you've got something cooking in that blonde-covered brain."

"Just thinking," Lola replied. "I mean, sure you're gonna have to suffer some sleep loss, but no reason you can't have fun with it."

Roxie felt like a terrier, the way her ears perked up. "I'm listening."

"Well, hell. You *are* a woman, Rox. And you've teased your fair share of men. Why not ramp up the temptation a little?"

Roxie felt a smile taking shape on her face. "Hmmm, I like it. Grab those chips, Em. We've got some strategizing to do."

They dragged the table over to the bed. Two hours later, they were all slightly drunk and had come up with several plans, all of which had sent them into giggle fits as they contemplated the outcome.

Roxie shoved a pillow behind her back as she leaned against the headboard. "Maybe if I concentrate on giving him a case of blue balls it'll take my mind off what I'm *not* getting. And," she added, "it'll get us out of this dustbowl and back on the road with a nice little cushion."

The light-hearted mood suddenly vanished. Emily looked away and Lola got off the bed, saying she had to take a bathroom break.

Roxie suddenly realized she'd not stopped to consider her friend's feelings when she made the bet with Cliff. She'd just assumed they were as eager to leave Mesa Blanco as she was. That didn't seem to be the case.

Could it be that Emily and Lola were falling for Wyatt and Sam? That thought brought a sinking feeling to Roxie's gut. What if her friends decided they didn't want to leave? What would she do?

Roxie reminded herself that she'd been alone most of her life. She could do it again. Problem was, she didn't want to.

Emily and Lola were all the family she had and she couldn't imagine not having them around.

That's not going to happen, she told herself. They had a plan. All she had to do was win the bet with Beckett and they'd hightail it out of Mesa Blanco and on to wherever the wind blew them.

And one day they'd tell stories and laugh about their adventure. They'd remember the people they met and giggle about the hot guys they left behind. Roxie couldn't let herself believe any other way.

Lola came out of the bathroom and climbed on the bed next to Roxie. "I know you're eager to leave, Rox, but you might as well have some fun while you're here."

"Are you having fun?" Roxie asked.

Lola smiled and stretched. "Did I tell you what Sam and I did the other night?"

All at once, the atmosphere lightened. Crowding together in the small bed, they snuggled under the warm blanket as Lola began her tale. And for the moment, everything was fine in Roxie's world.

Cliff finished reading the report his investigator had sent and tossed the pages onto the coffee table. There was definitely more to Roxie Ellis than met the eye. He felt a twinge of guilt over having her checked out but quickly dismissed it. Despite outward appearances, he was, by nature, a cautious man. He always had people checked out. Not only did it save him from potential problems, it gave him the edge he needed—in both business and gambling.

Not that Roxie legitimately fell into either category. Well, maybe gambling. Loosely speaking. He was in the middle of the most erotic bet he'd ever made in his life. And he did intend to win.

He'd expected Roxie to have at least one skeleton in her closet. Most people did. What he hadn't expected was to

Trouble in Chaps

discover that she'd been blackballed from every casino in Vegas. Seems Roxie fell into not only the world-class gambler category, but was also one of the best cheats in the gambling world.

Good enough that it had nearly cost her jail time. The only reason she had escaped serving time was that the charges against her couldn't be proven. No one could figure out how she'd rigged the game of five card draw that cost four very high-profile players millions of dollars.

Nor could anyone figure out where the money had disappeared to after the win. Cliff thought about it. How did someone dispose of or hide several million dollars? She'd paid the required taxes on the money so she was square with the IRS, but her life had not changed at all. No fancy cars, penthouse apartments, or extravagant purchases. If she had that kind of money, why was she so broke on paper and where the hell was the money? All his investigator had been able to determine is that the funds were deposited, taxes paid, then what remained withdrawn.

What the hell? Had she stuck it under her mattress? Buried it in a backyard somewhere? It just didn't add up.

The report had certainly revealed some interesting information, but it'd also brought more questions. Roxie was quite the mystery and Cliff was a true sucker for mysteries.

He pushed himself up off the couch and wandered into the kitchen. He'd been up since before dawn and it was closing in on nine in the morning. Time for something to eat.

After a quick look in the refrigerator, he headed for the shower. Might as well head over to the café where there was real food before he made a trip to the market. Besides, if what he heard was true, Roxie and her friends had holed up at her room in the boarding house last night for another of their girls' nights. Chances were they'd be making an appearance at the café before long.

227

Not that he was trying to arrange a chance meeting with Roxie. Not at all. At least that's what he kept telling himself as he hurried to shower and dress.

Less than an hour later he was sitting at a table in the café with Sam, the town sheriff. "So how're things going with Roxie?" Sam asked over the top of his coffee cup.

"Interesting."

"Meaning?"

Cliff hesitated a moment. Sam was one of his closest friends but was also the sheriff. He wasn't sure revealing information about Roxie's past to the law was a good idea.

"Meaning she's not quite what I expected."

"Seems like none of those gals are."

Cliff grinned. "So I hear. Matter of fact I hear you and Legs are getting pretty hot and heavy."

"Legs?"

Cliff shrugged. "Hey, I'm a guy. I have eyes. And she *does* have legs, man."

Sam smiled. "That she does."

"And?"

"And that's all I'm prepared to say at the moment."

Cliff laughed. "That's what I like about you Sam, such a blabber-mouth."

They both chuckled and turned their attention to the breakfast plates the waitress delivered.

Halfway through the meal the door opened and in walked Roxie, Lola and Emily. Cliff had his back to the door and wouldn't have known who'd entered except for the look on Sam's face.

Damn. The man was in love. Cliff wondered if Sam realized he'd fallen for Lola. He turned in his chair and suddenly it seemed the temperature in the café rose ten degrees.

Trouble in Chaps

Roxie was wearing a pair of sweatshorts that hung low on her hips, a running top that stopped just short of her navel and sneakers. Her hair was pulled back in a ponytail, her face scrubbed free of makeup, and still she looked like something out of a wet dream.

Her eyes met his and Cliff knew. Something had changed. So far, she'd been holding her own in the bet, but the moments when she seemed to be having fun with it were not as frequent as he'd like. She was intensely determined to win. Intensely determined to leave Mesa Blanco.

And if he was honest, the bet was more about keeping her there than the sex. Sure, he wanted her. Painfully. But the idea of her leaving brought another kind of pain, a kind he wasn't familiar with and wasn't sure he could handle.

Her mouth lifted in a sexy smirk that had his blood racing. She sauntered over to a table with her friends and took a seat with her back to him. Cliff turned back around, watching Sam, whose face was split with a smile. No doubt for the lovely Lola.

"Well, I better hit the road," Cliff announced. "Got some things to take care of."

Sam nodded as Cliff stood. "Catch you later."

"Yeah, later." Cliff went to the counter, paid for breakfast then headed for the door, making sure to pass by Roxie's table. "Ladies," he nodded and smiled.

Emily and Lola wished him a good day. Roxie just sat there with that fox in the chicken coop smile on her face. Cliff returned the smile, but once outside blew out his breath. He'd lay money she had something cooking. He could almost see it in her eyes.

But what?

He shrugged off the question and headed for his truck. Sooner or later, the answer to that and hopefully many other questions would come to light. Until then, he was going to give some thought on how to up his odds in the bet.

229

Chapter Five

Saturday nights usually pulled a full house at Chaps, but this Saturday the place was slammed. Standing room only. Roxie had been on her feet for three straight hours, waiting tables, and it was getting busier by the moment.

She delivered a round of drinks to one table and stepped up to another, one occupied by four rodeo cowboys in town for the night on their way home. They'd been drinking steadily for two hours and with each drink, one of them got a bit louder and more obnoxious. She wondered if it wasn't about time to cut him off, but figured she'd keep an eye on him and let Beckett know if he got out of hand.

"Another round, boys?"

"Ain't no boys here, sweet thang," the obnoxious one boasted loudly and made a grab for her hand.

Roxie dodged his attempt and moved a step away. "Slow down there, cowboy. You know the rules. You can look but you can't touch."

"Ta hell with that." He stood and started for her. "You been teasing me all night, baby, and damned if I'm in the waiting mood. Get your sweet ass over here and give Danny boy a taste."

"Not gonna happen," she retorted, backing away.

"Oh it's gonna happen."

Roxie set her tray down on the table beside her, ignoring the curious looks and comments from the people seated there. She kept her eyes on the drunk, Danny.

"You need to sit back down."

"Rather have you sit on my face."

Trouble in Chaps

She grimaced and reached for one of the empty beer bottles on the tray as Danny moved in on her. "You really need to step back," she warned.

He laughed and grabbed her arm. Just as he started to yank her close, she raised the bottle and swung. And met with empty air. Danny boy was being pulled back like an elastic band that had been stretched to its limits and released.

Beckett had hold of him. And from the look on Beckett's face, the man was soon to be toast. Roxie started after him as he pulled the drunk along toward the door. "Beckett!"

Her call caused him to pause and when he did, the drunk took a swing. The blow clipped Cliff on the side on his chin and did little more than snap his head to one side before he retaliated.

One punch and the drunk was flailing backwards, arms waving and spit flying. Two seconds later, he hit the floor. Two seconds of stunned silence filled the bar then the drunk's friends jumped up and headed toward Cliff.

Roxie hurled the bottle in her hand, catching one of the men in the side of the head. He stumbled into a table, arms out, reaching for support and managed to overturn the table, spilling beer on two women. Their companions took exception to that and went for the man.

Meanwhile, the remaining two cowboys were closing in on Cliff. Roxie broke out into a run, headed straight for them, but before she could reach them all hell broke loose. The men were attacked by patrons of the bar.

It was ten seconds of mayhem before a boom caused everyone to freeze. The sheriff, Sam, stood in the middle of the room, his gun raised toward the ceiling.

"Time for everyone to settle down."

Roxie's eyes sought out Lola, who sat beaming at Sam. Roxie couldn't say she blamed her. He was quite a sight. Like something out of an old western. His stance clearly said "Don't fuck with me," and his eyes gleamed with what might be anticipation that someone would.

He marched over to the two drunks still standing. "Think you better come with me, boys."

Cliff hauled the man he'd punched to his feet and had a firm grip on his arm. Roxie ran over to him but he ignored her and shoved the man toward the door. She started to follow but a big hand wrapped around her arm and stayed her. Roxie whirled and looked up into Wyatt's face.

"We got this," he said quietly.

"Fine."

Wyatt released her and joined Beckett, stopping long enough to pick up the last unconscious man from the floor. Wyatt slung the man over his shoulder like a sack of seed and followed Cliff outside.

Roxie turned and almost ran over Emily. "Are you okay?" Emily asked.

"Yeah, fine."

"Oh? Then why are you biting my head off?"

"Because… because I had it under control."

Lola appeared beside her. "Wasn't that something? The way Cliff grabbed that guy and pulled him off you and the way Sam just took over and…"

"And Wyatt heaving that guy over his should like it was nothing," Emily added.

"Yeah, a real Hallmark moment," Roxie groused. Yes, it had been something to see, but she didn't want to be impressed with the way Cliff had rushed to her defense.

"What crawled up your ass?" Lola asked.

"I didn't need any help!"

Lola looked from her to Emily and Emily rolled her eyes. "Yeah, we know you're a big bad-ass, Rox, and could have kicked the guy's butt, but this *is* Cliff's bar and he was trying to protect you."

Trouble in Chaps

"I don't need his protection!"

"Well maybe he didn't know that," Lola offered.

"Whatever." Roxie didn't want to listen to reason. She knew Cliff was within his rights to act as he did and it was his place to make sure things didn't get out of hand.

But damn it all, she didn't want to remember the sudden thrill of seeing fury blaze in his eyes at having the man touch her. Didn't want to get that hot little knot of excitement at seeing him be the alpha male and go all macho.

She didn't want anything to make her want him more. And the only way to keep from thinking about those things was to be mad. So she hung on to the mad like a lifeline even though she knew it was unreasonable.

"I have to get back to work."

Before Emily or Lola could respond, she stomped over to the bar. Two seconds later a hand closed around her arm. She jerked around a split second before Beckett started pulling her away from the bar.

"Come on."

"I'm working," she said as she jerked free.

"In the office. Now."

Something in his eyes had her biting down on the urge to argue. She tossed her hair and marched through the kitchen to the back of the building where his office was located. He entered behind her and slammed the door.

"What the hell were you thinking?" His voice was loud and angry enough to have her hackles rise.

"Excuse me?" She arched her eyebrows haughtily.

"You heard me. Why didn't you call me if that guy was giving you trouble?"

"It wasn't anything I couldn't handle."

"With a beer bottle? What were you planning to do? Come upside his head with it?"

233

Ciana Stone

"If necessary."

"Smart, real smart." The mocking tone of his voice jacked her anger higher.

"Fuck you, Beckett!"

He grinned at her and it wasn't a friendly sort of expression. More like a predator closing in on its prey. "You don't want to start up with me, sugar."

Roxie snorted. "Oh, now I'm scared."

Cliff crossed his arms over his chest and stared at her. "What's your problem?"

"You!"

"Me? All I did was protect what's mine."

That one word sent a bolt of something purely female and entirely terrifying through her. But she wasn't about to succumb to either. "I'm not yours!"

"The bar is. And if you'd hit him you could've been charged with assault."

"It would've been self defense!"

"Maybe. But you were itching to do it."

"I did not."

"Yes, you did." His voice softened as he regarded here. "You've been spoiling for a fight and that poor jackass seemed like a likely target."

"That's bullshit. I have not been spoiling for a fight."

"Oh yeah, you have."

"Fuck you." There was no way in hell she'd ever admit he was right. It wasn't that she was spoiling for a fight, it was more that she felt as if a pressure cooker that was about to blow. Cliff had gotten to her on more than one level and the stress was starting to take its toll.

"You making that a formal offer, honey?" His tone was teasing, but there was nothing of a jest in his eyes.

Trouble in Chaps

Roxie went for the door knob, but Cliff grabbed her wrist. "Let go of me," she warned.

"Or?"

Roxie hissed and raised her hand to hit him, only to have him catch her fist before it made contact. She tore free and backed away, stopping only when her backside bumped into his desk.

Cliff stalked over to her, putting his hands on the desk on either side of her.

"Or?" he asked again.

"Move, Beckett."

"Or?" The heat was back in his eyes.

"Or we're gonna have a big problem."

"Oh we already have a problem, Roxie.

"Do we?" Her eyes met his and held. "And what might that be?"

"This."

At the same moment the word came from his lips, he reached behind her with his left arm and pulled her against him. Her breath came out in a small rush a moment before his lips closed on hers.

Her mind screamed for her to push him away. This was not a good idea. Not safe. But her treacherous body betrayed her. As Cliff's arm tightened around her, she pressed into him, not only accepting the kiss but returning it.

It was a lusty battle of tongues and teeth, hands gripping and roving, bodies straining into one another. Cliff growled in protest when she pushed back from him.

"Don't stop now, honey."

She shook her head and blew out her breath. She couldn't play this game. Not with him. It was too costly and she couldn't take the strain of it. "Look, Beckett, I need to be straight with you."

235

He cocked his head slightly to one side. "I'm listening."

"Okay, so here's the deal." She took a breath and steeled herself. "You affect me like a drug and right now there's nothing I want more than to get you out of those clothes and inside me. But—"

She raised both hands and pressed them against his chest when he moved to pull her back to him. "But—I work for you and as much as I want you, having you is going to complicate my life in a way I can't handle. And before you say anything, this has nothing to do with our bet."

"No problem. You're fired."

"But—" She kept the pressure on his chest, looking up at him. She couldn't tell if he meant it. What she could tell was that he wanted her. Whatever it was between them wasn't cooling off. It got hotter every day and chances were the only way to put out that fire was to give in to it.

And if she was honest, it was what she wanted. Sure, it'd mean she'd be stuck in Mesa Blanco longer than she planned, but like Emily had reminded her just the day before, it wasn't as if any of them had anywhere to go.

Besides, she was tired of battling it. "What the fuck."

With that, she fisted his shirt in both hands and yanked him to her. And in that moment civility vanished.

There was nothing gentle in his lips as they staked a claim on hers. Teeth nipped and tongues clashed. Breath came hard and fast. Cliff gave no care to the damage to her clothing as he tugged and tore anything that barred him hands from her flesh. His hand moved between her legs to the wetness that clearly spelled her desire.

She was no less impatient as she stripped his shirt off then started on his jeans. By the time his Levis were bunched around his knees, he was past the point of caring about anything except sinking deep inside the liquid silk between

Trouble in Chaps

her legs that was becoming more wet with each stroke of his fingers.

Roxie tore free from his mouth as his fingers stroked inside her faster. Her fingers dug into the top of his shoulders, her breath a series of pants. She was so close.

"Let it go, baby."

His lusty croon was all that was needed to send her tumbling over the edge. Her sex clenched to the accompaniment of a low throaty moan she made no attempt to silence.

"In me," she panted before the climax could subside.

The smile he flashed her was all the time it took for him to lift her up, supporting her with his hands firm on her ass. Roxie wound her legs around him and in one fluid motion, he slid inside.

A quick "ahh" went along with the momentary flash of pain. It'd been a while since she'd had a man and it took her body a few seconds to begin to adjust to the sensation of being so full.

A few seconds was all she allowed. Hanging onto his shoulders, she bucked against him, the motion driving him deeper. Cliff's breath hissed, his eyes locked onto hers and everything around them vanished.

She couldn't explain it any other way. Not that it mattered. All that mattered was the feel of him inside her and the hard, driving rhythm of his body. How perfect it would have been if this were more than just physical. She hated that weak part of herself that longed for more and reminded herself that this was all she could ever have.

Roxie shoved aside thoughts of what she could not have and focused on the moment. If this was all there was, then she was not going to waste a moment of it. She met him stroke for stroke, feeling sensation build to the point of madness.

"Now," she groaned. "Please. Now, now now."

Almost before the last two words were out of her mouth, an orgasm ripped through her. Not blossomed, flowered, or flowed. Nothing so tame could describe it. It ripped. Raw and primal, its force had her throwing back her head and screaming.

On and on, one wave after another pounded her. She welcomed it, wanted it and gave herself completely to it. When at last he slowed his pace, she lifted her head to look at him and was met with a look hot enough to have her tightening around him in anticipation.

Cliff worked his feet out of his boots with her still wound around him, then stepped out of his jeans and carried her into the other side of the room. Roxie hung on as he sat down on the couch, the position impaling her fully on his erection.

She grinned and urged him onto his back. The moment he was supine, she braced her hands on his chest and started a rhythm of her own. Slow at first then faster as his eyes darkened and his hands tightened on her thighs.

It was unwise and possibly unsafe but that was something she'd deal with if the need arose. Now there was only him and the tension building inside both of them. She felt him getting close; saw it in his eyes, and that shoved her over the edge. A freefall of overwhelming sensation claimed her as she rode out the storm. When at last reason returned she lay down on him, feeling the rapid beat of his heart and the sweat damp skin hot against her own.

Cliff's arms circled her, holding her tight despite the heat, his lips gently pressing against her forehead. For several minutes neither of them moved.

Finally, Roxie sat up, slinging her hair back over her shoulders. Cliff looked up at her, his hands moving to trace along the underside of her breasts. "So, I guess you no longer have a problem?"

He shook his head. "More than I started with."

Trouble in Chaps

"More?" She ran her hands over the swell of his chest and down his abdomen to the point their bodies met. The tip of his penis peeked from beneath her, swelling to full erection before she even touched it.

"Much more."

"Well, then I guess we're going to have to work on that, aren't we?"

His response was to pull her down to him. Just before their lips met, he smiled. "Oh yeah, we're gonna work real hard on it."

"Yeah?" She grinned, enjoying the easy banter.

"Yep. I've got you now."

Something akin to the kind of adrenaline rush you get when sudden fear strikes, bolted through her and the fever of lust vanished. This was a mistake. A huge mistake. She couldn't have him thinking this meant she'd stick around. She couldn't even let herself contemplate the idea. As appealing as it was, staying was not an option. She had to get back on the road, away from here.

Away from him.

Roxie tore free from his arms and scrambled off the couch.

"What're you doing?" Cliff was clearly puzzled at the abrupt change.

"Leaving." Her cut-off jeans were intact and she slid them on. Her tank top was ruined, both straps torn, so she snatched up his discarded shirt and quickly put it on.

"Why?" He sat up.

Roxie couldn't answer. What could she possibly say? That she was running because he made her want things that she couldn't have? She grabbed her boots and fled, taking the back entrance and escaping into the alley behind the bar. From there it was a short run to her room at the boarding house. She locked her door and flung herself down on the bed.

239

She'd made a terrible mistake and didn't know how to undo it. Sure, she could probably get a bus ticket out of town and escape the area, but how was she going to escape the feelings Cliff inspired? How was she going to forget his taste and touch and the way he made her feel?

How was she ever going to stop wanting him? And how was she going to explain to her friends why she had to leave Mesa Blanco as soon as possible?

Tears started to flow as she contemplated the mess she'd gotten herself in and, for the first in a long time, she gave into them and cried. For what had led her here and what would drive her away.

Pounding at the door interrupted her sobs. "Roxie! Open the door!"

It was Cliff.

"I mean it! Open it or I'll break it down! Roxie!"

And wake the entire boarding house. She scrambled off the bed and opened the door a crack. "Go away, Beckett."

His response was to shove the door open, stalk inside and slam it behind him.

It wasn't until he'd slammed the door that he got a good look at her and when he did, all his indignation fled. Her eyes and nose were red and tears still wet her cheeks.

"Aw, honey." He grabbed her and wrapped his arms around her.

"Don't," she sobbed against his chest.

"Don't what?" He worked one hand up to tangle in her hair, keeping her head firm against his chest as he kissed the top of her head.

"Don't be nice to me." Her words were broken by sobs. "Don't be a good guy, Beckett."

That surprised him enough to have him pull back and hold her at arm's length. "What's going on, Roxie?"

Trouble in Chaps

She shook her head and looked away. "Just leave, okay? This isn't going to work."

"What isn't going to work?"

"You and me. Me working for you, us…us… you know."

"You mean the bet? Forget the bet. I want to know what's going on with you. Why'd you run?"

Her eyes met his then she looked away. "Can't we just leave it at this isn't going to work?"

"No."

"Why?"

That one word shook him. Right down to his boots. He didn't know her, not really. And sure, he was attracted to her, but attraction was a fleeting thing and always died. At least in his life. So why?

The answer was as shocking as the question and not one he wanted to own up to. As much as he'd like to deny it, somehow he'd fallen for her. The idea of her not being in his life gave him a rush of anxiety.

His knees went weak. Literally. He leaned back against the door, feeling something hot rushing through his body, making his breath quicken and his skin dampen with sudden perspiration.

God help him, he was in love with her. What was he supposed to do? He'd never felt anything like this. It was uncharted territory and scary as hell.

"I need you to stay." He couldn't admit his feelings, couldn't tell her that he loved her. It was hard enough admitting it to himself.

"Why?"

Damn her, she wasn't going to let him off the hook. "Like it or not, we've started something here, Roxie. And we need to at least give it a chance to see where it'll go."

The sob that tore loose from her had him instinctively pulling her close again. "Damn, honey, don't cry."

241

Ciana Stone

She shook her head, keeping her face averted. "It can't go anywhere, Beckett. It can't."

"Because you don't want it to go anywhere." Anger, fueled by rejection, reared its head. He was a fool, thinking his feelings were mirrored, that she felt something for him.

"No." She pulled away and faced him.

Roxie saw the pain and anger in his eyes and the realization hit her like a loaded dump truck. Cliff really cared for her. That unhinged her, robbed her of her resolve to end things without discussion or confession.

"I'm not who you think I am, Beckett. I've...I've done things."

"Like rig a poker game and cheat a bunch of high-rollers out of millions?"

It was like a knife to her gut. His words cut deep and carried with them a rush of fear that had her wanting to take flight. *How the hell had he found out? And was that all he knew?*

She took a step back, needing to put space between them, needing to think. But Beckett wasn't of a mind to allow it. He took hold of her wrist and stayed her motion.

"Roxie, I'm not going to hurt you and I'm not going to pass judgment. I just want to know what happened to make you so damned scared to trust anyone."

"Beckett...Cliff, please. Let this go. If you care for me, then let it go. Let me go. There can't be anything between us. Ever."

"You want me."

"Yes," she admitted. "I do."

"Sexually."

"Yes."

"And that's it?"

242

Trouble in Chaps

Roxie thought about looking him in the eyes and telling a lie, but something inside wouldn't permit that. As much as she didn't want to, she'd fallen in love with him and she couldn't lie. She could walk away because she had to but not until she'd told him the truth. She saw that now. Only how was she going to speak of something she'd keep buried for so long, something that had altered the course of her life?

"Roxie?"

She braved a look at him and tears welled in her eyes. Brushing them aside with one hand, she took a deep breath. Time to face the music.

"No, Cliff. That's not it. Not by a long shot. I love you. I hate it, but I do."

"Roxie."

"No." She pulled free as he squeezed her hand. "Don't. Don't say anything. Please. You wanted the truth and you deserve that."

She paused. Wanting to speak the truth and doing it were as different as night and day. Once she spoke, she couldn't take it back. Once the next words were spoken there would be so many more words to follow, so much explaining to do.

Could she trust him to understand? Fear that he would not had her mouth dry and her body tense. She could lose him in the next two seconds.

And you never had him anyway if he can't accept and understand, a little voice spoke in her head. Damn that voice anyway. Why did it always have to be right?

"Roxie?"

She met his eyes and sucked in a breath. "I'm married."

Of all the things he'd expected to hear, those words were not on the list. "You're what?"

"Married."

"No you're not."

243

Ciana Stone

"Yes. I am."

"No. You were born Roxanne Marie Ellis and…"

"I never took his name."

Cliff let her hand drop. For a few moments they just stared at one another. Finally, he shook his head and walked past her to take a seat on the bed. "I had you investigated, Roxie. Nothing came up about a husband. Just a rigged card game and millions of dollars that vanished."

This couldn't be real. She wasn't being honest. But why? A sinking feel took hold in his gut. Was this her way of brushing him off? But why say she loved him if she was going to drop a bomb like this?

"It didn't vanish," she replied. "And the game wasn't rigged."

"That's not what I hear."

"You're getting the tale of the losers, Cliff. Men who'd cheat their own mothers to win. You think they're going to admit that I cleaned them out fair and square?"

He hadn't considered that. He should have. Particularly considering the men she'd bested. He'd played with them and not a one of them was above a little dirty dealing.

"Okay, so you beat them. What happened to the money?"

He saw the tears well in her eyes and the way her throat worked convulsively as she fought back emotion. "It's being used to take care of my husband."

There was that word again. Husband. He hated the sound of it. Jealously wasn't an emotion he was familiar with or knew how to cope with. He'd not really experienced it in force until now and he wished he could make it go away because it was making his gut burn and his fists long to pound something.

Part of him wanted to get up a leave. Escape the torment. But he had to know the truth. "What do you mean?"

Roxie blew out her breath and took a seat on the bed, curling her legs up Indian style beneath her.

244

Trouble in Chaps

"When I was thirteen my dad died. We struggled along for a couple of years and then my mom remarried. Charlie Rose."

The derision in her voice clearly spelled her dislike of the man. "What a piece of work. Mean and crooked as a snake. He promised her the moon and all he did was steal what little she had.

"By the time I was sixteen he'd mortgaged the farm so deep we couldn't pay it off. We lost it and my mother couldn't handle it."

Roxie paused, twirling the hair hanging over her shoulder in what Cliff read as a nervous action. The pause was so long he started to wonder if she was going to say more.

Her voice was soft and filled with sadness when she spoke again. "The day the farm foreclosed, she walked into the barn, stuck my dad's gun in her mouth and blew her brains out."

He wanted to reach out to her in that moment. Take her into his arms and comfort her, or at least the child inside her that had been so traumatized and had lost so much. But he couldn't. Couldn't make a move toward her until he knew it all.

"I left that day," she continued, looking toward the window instead of at him. "Me and Danny Morris. He'd been my best friend since we were five and he loved me. I told him I had to leave so he went with me."

A ghost of a smile flitted across her face. "As corny and cliché as it sounds, we survived for two years by the kindness of people who ran a traveling carnival. They took us in with no questions asked and made us part of their family."

Roxie closed her eyes for a moment then turned her head to look at him. He could see the emotional toll the confession was having on her. Tears welled in her eyes and she blinked them away.

"That's where I learned to play cards. And to cheat. I was good at it. Even without cheating. Danny wasn't, but he wanted to be. By the time I was eighteen, he was addicted and spent damn near everything we earned gambling.

"And that's the year we arrived in Vegas."

Roxie paused, trying not to let emotions tied to the past stop her from telling Cliff the truth. But how was she supposed to sum up all of the fears, frustrations, love and desperation she experienced in a few short sentences? She didn't know how to make Cliff understand what it had been like, having only Danny in her life. A boy she'd known almost her entire life and someone she felt responsible for, who wanted so badly to please her yet couldn't defeat the demons he battled.

She couldn't tell him of the days she went without food, or a roof over her head. Or the number of times Danny had stolen what little they'd managed to earn, gambled it away, then cried in her arms over having disappointed her.

"And?" he prompted.

Roxie blew out a breath. "To make a long story short, I found work and over the years managed to claw my way up from waitressing to dealing. I took classes to get my high school diploma and enrolled in college classes.

"And Danny kept gambling. Spending everything we had."

"Why didn't you leave?"

How could she possibly make him understand the love she had for Danny when she'd never fully figured it out for herself?

"He was my best friend. He left his family and his home for me, Cliff. And he stood by me, no matter what. I couldn't abandon him."

Cliff didn't want to acknowledge the respect he had for her, for standing by Danny. Hell, he didn't even want the man

Trouble in Chaps

to exist. But that was jealously working on him and he had to shove it aside. Everyone had a past. What mattered was the now.

"So what happened?"

Roxie climbed off the bed and walked to the window, staring out. "Danny begged me to get him into a high stakes game. He'd had a run of luck and scored 50K. I tried to talk him out of it, but he was so sure he was on a winning streak. He said it was his last game. He wanted to change. He was going to give up gambling, get an education and make something of himself. Make me proud."

She leaned her forehead against the glass, her voice almost too soft to be audible. "So, I did it. And Danny won. He walked away with a quarter of a million dollars."

Roxie straightened and turned to face Cliff, tears streaming down her face. "Because he cheated. Of course, two others at that table were cheating as well. I saw them. It was a crooked game all around. I should have stopped it, but I didn't."

"One of the players was a mean piece of work. He couldn't stand losing, so he couldn't let it go that Danny had won. And maybe he figured out Danny had cheated. I don't know. Less than a week after the game, Danny was attacked coming out of a casino."

She walked over and took a seat on the bed. "He survived, in a manner of speaking. He's in a permanent care facility in Nevada.

"I took what was left of his win and had him put there. What was left of his brain is enough to keep him conscious, but not functional. He's like a newborn. He feels pain and hunger, knows the comfort of a full belly and a touch but not much else."

"So that's what happened to the money you won?"

She nodded. "I didn't cheat, Cliff. I just did the only thing I could do to get the money to make sure he'd be taken care of.

I never told Lola or Emily. I met them later—after all that. You're the only one who knows."

She fell silent. Cliff's mind was in a whirl. Part of him wanted to pull her into his arms and erase the haunted look in her eyes. Another part wanted to smash something. She belonged to another man.

Then light split through the dark thoughts. "You said you love me."

"Yes, but I'm married."

"Only on paper."

"Cliff, I'm responsible for Danny. There's no one else. I have to—"

As much as he hated himself for it, he couldn't stop the words from pouring out of his mouth. "You've already made sure he'll be taken care of, Roxie. What more is there for you to do? You think you should spend your life alone because of it?"

She was quiet for a long time. "I should've stopped him. Should have made him quit gambling. Not gotten him in that game. It's my fault, Cliff. I don't deserve to be happy when I've destroyed his life."

That confession compelled him to act without thought. He pulled her to him, wrapping his arms around her. "Oh, honey, that's not true. You were a scared kid who did everything you could. It wasn't your fault."

"But he loved me," she whispered brokenly. "He depended on me and I let him down."

Cliff felt her body shake with the force of her sobs and held her as she cried. He'd been so caught up in his own desires that he wasn't really taking Roxie's feelings into consideration. Thinking about what she'd been through and what she'd sacrificed certainly spoke to the kind of woman she was, her loyalty and dedication.

Trouble in Chaps

It also spoke to the depth of her love. That clawed at him, twisted him up in knots. He didn't want her to love Danny, didn't want her to feel that depth of emotion for anyone but him. He wanted her all for himself.

What kind of self-centered jerk did that make him? Or did it make him a jerk? Was it wrong to want the woman he loved to be all his? To give as much of herself as he was willing to give?

Which raised a question. Just how much was he willing to give to hold her love? For the first in a long time, Cliff was faced with proving what kind of man he really was. He thought about it long and hard as she cried, searching himself.

When the sobs became sniffles, he pushed her back gently to look into her red-rimmed and swollen eyes. What he was about to say could lose him the one woman he'd ever loved, but he knew he had to be honest and tell her what he felt.

"He let himself down, Roxie. No one can be responsible for the actions of another. We all own our actions. And if he really loved you, would he want you to carry around this guilt? To give up being happy?"

"No. I don't know. I don't know, Cliff."

"Well, I do. You said you love me. Is that true?"

She nodded and he smiled at her. "I'm pretty sure I love you, Roxie. I can't say I know for sure because to be honest, I've never really loved anyone. But what I feel for you is strong and real and I really hope you'll give us a chance to see if it's the kind of feelings that are meant to last. Can you do that? Can you take a gamble on us?"

"I don't know. I want to but..."

"But what?"

"I'm scared."

"Me too," he said with a smile. "But maybe between the two of us we can muster up enough courage to see our way through."

249

Roxie shook her head, a reluctant smile on her face. "You're a real piece of work, Beckett."

"Beckett? We're back to Beckett after I bare my heart and soul? Woman, you wound me."

The slight laugh let him know that the worst of the pain was past. At least for the moment. He longed to kiss her, make love to her and heal the wounds but knew now was not the time.

So instead, he lay back, pulling her to his side. "Sleep, honey. I've got you."

The sigh that preceded her words sounded like relief to his ears. The words, however, sounded like resignation. "Yeah, I guess you do."

Chapter Six

Roxie woke, feeling the steady rise of fall of Cliff's chest beneath her cheek. For a few minutes she lay there, eyes closed, savoring the moment. Then it hit her. She hadn't woken with a feeling of anxiety. The constant weight that had been attached to her for the last five years was gone.

It was almost frightening. She started to rise, but his arm wrapped tighter around her. "Roxie," he murmured, still more asleep than not.

And it hit her. She was free. Somehow, being honest with Cliff had freed her from the prison she'd built around herself. She'd never stop caring about Danny and would always make sure he was taken care of, but the boy she knew was gone and couldn't come back.

The boy she'd loved had left and it was time for her to move on. And the man who'd stolen her heart was there with her, murmuring her name like a caress as he slept.

She was broke, had no home, no possessions and no job, but she was free.

Love welled so strong inside her that she nearly cried. But this wasn't a time for tears. This was the time to celebrate life.

Her hand moved down his chest to the buckle of his belt. Cliff's eyes opened and she sat, undoing his jeans. He helped and soon his clothes were in a heap on the floor. Along with hers.

Cliff started to roll her over on her back but she stopped him. "Huh-uh. My turn."

Without preamble, she climbed on top of him, taking his stiff cock in her hand and rubbing it against her wet sex. Cliff made a sound that had her ready to take all of him inside her.

Trouble was, he was a lot to take.

"Go slow, baby." His voice was raspy from sleep and lust. "You're gonna have to loosen up to take it as hard as I'm gonna give it."

That low croon was like throwing gas on a fire. She felt her pussy grow wet and her belly tighten in need. Their eyes met and in the space of a breath, something happened. Regardless of the fact she was on top of him and initiating the penetration, he was in control. Of that, there was no doubt.

The wonderful thing was that it excited her in a way nothing else ever had. She wanted to impale herself on him in one swift stroke, to ride him hard and fast. But she resisted the urge, working herself slowly onto the length of him.

His eyes locked with hers as his hand moved to her clit, stroking just firmly enough to have her tingling and flushed, wet and hot. She closed her eyes as sensation started to build, anticipating the onset of orgasm.

"Open your eyes, Roxie. Look at me."

She followed his command and his eyes imprisoned hers.

"I want to see you come."

She couldn't even muster a word for the sensation that rioted through her. His finger on her clit, his hard cock inside her pushing deeper as his pelvis rose and fell in a slow, steady rhythm. Her hands moved to her thighs, steadying herself. She was about to go. Her clit was hard as a rock, burning at his touch, and her pussy was already clenching against his cock.

"Not yet," he commanded softly.

"I can't…"

"You can. Let go, honey. Give yourself to me."

Abandon control. Submit. That's how his words translated in her mind. For a split second she was seized with indecision.

Trouble in Chaps

But there was something in his eyes, a promise that was too seductive.

"Yes."

Cliff smiled. Finally. He had her. This time for real. The impact of that knowledge had him wanting to flip her over on her back and ride her like a stallion taking a mare in heat. Fast and hard. But the instant gratification he'd achieve paled in comparison to what she'd just offered.

"I'm going to stop moving. I want you to sink down on me. Take all of it. Don't move anything but the inner muscles of your pussy. I want you to squeeze and release. Nice and steady and slow."

Her eyes never left his as she complied. The first contraction around his dick sent thrill of sensation spiking straight to his balls, making them tighten almost painfully. His fingers continued their assault on her clit, slow and easy.

It wasn't long before he felt a vibration in her body. Her eyes had developed a hooded look, pupils dilated and irises darkened. He could feel her need, feel how close she was.

"Cliff—I... oh damn..."

"Not yet." He eased up on her clit giving her time to recover then started again. Her pussy continued to clench around him, creating delicious waves of sensation that had him as needy as she.

But he wasn't going to give into that need. Not until he was certain that when he let her come it would send her higher than she'd ever imagined.

Over and again, he took her to the edge only to slow and start again. Both of them were slick with sweat, bodies tense with need.

"Please. Oh, damn, Cliff. Please."

Her breathy plea cinched the deal. He increased the pressure on her clit and bucked up inside her. Her body trembled, pussy tightening in quick contractions on his dick. And her scream was the sexiest sound he'd ever heard.

Before her climax could fully crest, he flipped her over on her back and rammed home. Her legs moved to circle his body, heels locking against the small of his back as he rode her.

"Oh god, yes. Yes!"

Her pleas and gasps added sparks of excitement that had him pounding hard. Her legs tightened, heels drumming his back as she met and matched his pace. Breath came hard and fast, words mere gasps and partial syllables.

Her orgasm lasted much longer than he'd counted on. This woman was amazing. He was straining not to come. Not an easy task when she started to gasp, writhe against him and cry out his name as she came.

When her body finally began to relax, he slowed his pace and finally stopped, still inside her. Neither of them moved except their chests and bellies heaving for air.

"Fuck me," she breathed. "That was…incredible."

"That was just the warm up, honey. If you've got more in you."

She grinned up at him, her pussy clenching around him. "Bring it on."

"That's my girl."

"Damn skippy."

Not very romantic, but the sweetest words he'd ever heard. Inspiration hit and he rolled away, pulled her to her feet and headed for the bathroom. "Come on. Shower time."

Roxie protested with a groan. "I like it here."

"You're gonna like this," he promised. "Come on, honey."

By the time they cleared the threshold, he had her in his arms, his lips locked with hers in a passionate kiss. Now that their time had come, there was no holding back for either of them. Kissing, fondling, and he guided her into the bathroom.

Trouble in Chaps

"The bed," she murmured against his lips.

"Huh uh," he argued. "Here I've been thinking about this for a long time. I'm through thinking. Get in the shower."

Something in the soft command of his voice had a thrill running through her. "Or what?" she teased, running her hand down his body to the tip of his erection.

He gave her the most wickedly sexy smile she had ever seen and wrapped both arms around her, cupping her ass to pull her against him. "I guess I'll just have to turn you over my knee and give you a good spanking."

Roxie almost came right then and there. *Damn, who knew she'd be so turned on by the suggestion?* Cliff was bringing out parts of her sexual nature she didn't know existed.

"And you think I'm just going to let you, eh?" she teased, rubbing her pussy against his cock, feeling the erotic thrill of the coarse hair surrounding it as it softly abraded her swollen clit.

He stared deep into her eyes and in that moment, they both found what they had been looking for. "Oh yeah," he breathed, his fingers digging into her ass and pulling her against him even tighter. I think you're not going to just let me. I think that before I'm done, you're going to beg me."

"Promises, promises," she whispered just before his lips claimed hers. With lips locked, he backed her into the shower and turned on the water. She gasped against his mouth as the icy spray rained down on them.

Cliff chuckled, holding her squirming against him as the water warmed then knelt down in front of her. "Spread your legs."

As soon as she did, she felt his tongue, lapping the length of her sex. "Sweet," he said. "Sweet as honey. Turn around, darlin', so I can get to you better."

She turned bent at the waist so that her pussy was at his eye level. He spread her legs wider and then started licking

Ciana Stone

her, sucking the outer lips of her sex until they felt heavy and swollen. His tongue dipped inside her wet channel, probing.

Inside a minute Roxie was hugging the wall, moaning. Every few seconds his tongue would move from her pussy to her clit, making her weak with need. Just as she was about to come, he moved away.

"Hey, no fair leaving a girl stranded." She turned to see him pouring her scented liquid soap into his hands.

"Stand with your back against the wall," he directed.

God, she loved the erotic command in his voice. Her body was already quivering with arousal, her nipples were puckered and hard, and her sex wet. His slick hands started on her shoulders and worked slowly down her arms then back up. As his hands moved to her breasts, palming her nipples in slow circles, she moaned. He stifled her mouth with his mouth. She let him plunder her mouth and then took control, feeding off him.

What had started as a slow burn in her nipples had escalated into a raging fire that was spreading out from the sensitive buds, making her arch against him. His erection pressed against her belly, throbbing.

She reached over and took his cock in one hand, cupping his balls with the other. "Hmmm." She bit at his lip when he moved away from the kiss. He took hold of her wrists to force her hands from him.

"Now did I tell you that you could touch me?" He smiled. "Bad, very bad. I guess I'm going to have to attend to that spanking sooner than I realized."

She thought he was teasing, but soon realized he was not. He turned her around so she faced the wall. "Bend over, baby."

The sexy rasp of his voice was as much of a turn on as his demands. She bent over, bracing her hands on the shower wall. The initial slap on her ass made her jump. The second

Trouble in Chaps

sent a sexual charge through her. He spanked her slowly and precisely, each stoke ending with a caress.

After only a few stokes she was squirming. Her ass cheeks felt as if they were on fire and her sex felt like an inflated balloon between her legs. On one level, she wanted him to stop. But the submissive side of her sexual nature wanted more. "Please," she breathed.

"Please what?" He paused, caressing her ass and running one hand between her legs to stroke the wet folds of her sex. "Please I want more?"

Damn, did she? Could she stand more of it? She didn't know but wanted to find out. "Yes, please."

"That's my girl. Bend your legs for me, honey. Just a little. That's it. Now spread your legs. I want you ass up."

No sooner had she arranged herself into the position he wanted than he delivered the first stroke. It was like a jolt of electricity that ran straight through her body to her pussy. She cried out then inhaled sharply as his soap-slickened finger probed inside her ass.

"Christ, you're tight." His voice was a lusty rasp. "You don't know how many times I've thought about this— imagined it. Baby, you're a fucking wet dream come to life."

She moaned as he stroked in and out, each time going deeper. Her clit was throbbing madly. She reached between her legs to stroke herself and he slapped her ass a strong smack.

"Not yet, baby. You want to use your hands, reach back and spread your ass wider for me. This tight little ass of yours is going to take some time to loosen up enough for me to fuck you."

Roxie did as ordered, her fingers digging into the cheeks of her ass as he inserted two fingers inside her. The sting of the soap added to the pleasure-pain. Her pussy pulsed, her clit throbbed and her breath rasped as Cliff started to work three fingers inside her.

She felt as if she were stretched to the maximum. It was almost too much. Of what, she wasn't sure. The pain and pleasure seemed to be linked.

"Come on, baby, loosen up for me," he crooned in a lover's tone.

"Please," she pleaded. "I can't. It's too much. I can't take it."

"Yes, you can, baby. And you will. Just go with it."

"Oh god," she moaned, "Cliff, it's ..."

"What you want." He finished her sentence. "What I want. You want to give me what I want, don't you?"

"Yes!"

"Then give it to me. Beg me to fuck you up the ass with my fingers while you masturbate and come. I want you to come for me, baby."

"Please."

"Say it, Roxie. Beg for it," he corrected her in a passion-rough voice, with another spank and shoved his fingers deep inside her ass.

"Please, fuck me up the ass with your fingers. Make me come until I pass out. Please, just do it now!"

"My pleasure. Now play with your pussy. I want to see you come."

She reached between her legs and stroked her fingers down her pussy, feeling the swollen folds standing open and ready. Her fingers moved to her swollen clit. It was so aroused that the first touch almost sent her over the edge, but his voice coached her.

"Easy, baby. Not too fast."

His fingers pumped in and out of her sensitive ass as she slowly rolled her fingers back and forth over her clit. She tried to go slow, but she was too far gone.

"Oh god, damn. Cliff ... I can't ..."

Trouble in Chaps

She exploded before she could finish the sentence. Her pussy and ass contracted and pulsed wildly and all the strength went out of her legs. Cliff pulled her up against him when the orgasm finally faded. She sagged back against him, feeling his erection pressing against her. That sparked her energy immediately. She turned and sank to her knees, taking his cock in her hand to guide it to her mouth.

He groaned as she took him in her mouth. Her fingers toyed with his tight balls, slipping behind to play with his ass. He grabbed her hair and pushed deeper into her mouth. "Christ!" he groaned as she slid back on his shaft, letting her tongue circle the swollen head.

She took him to the brink of release twice, each time backing off before he could come. "Jesus, you're killing me," he moaned and pulled her to her feet then up into his arms.

"Honey, slow down," he whispered as she started to guide his cock inside her. "No need to rush. We've got all the time in the world."

Roxie went stone-cold still. His tone was that of a real lover, someone with an emotional investment, someone who was making a promise. Yeah, he'd said he thought he loved her, but his voice now said it without using the words.

It embarrassed her that tears filled her eyes and a small lump lodged in her throat, making her breath hitch. Then it thrilled her when he cupped her face in both hands and his eyes searched hers, looking inside her to places she'd grown accustomed to keeping private.

"It's okay, Roxie," he whispered. "You're safe. I promise."

When his lips met hers, it was a kiss of promise and caring. Passion was there, strong enough to have her eager to feel him strong and hard inside her, but the passion was colored with emotion.

He took his time, exploring and tasting, the kiss tender and slow. It enflamed her, excited and thrilled her. And it frightened her. Not so much what she felt and sensed from him but what it inspired in herself.

God, she was so in love with this man. The fear housed within that realization flared bright and hot then faded like a shooting star. In its place was wonder and excitement. It'd been so long since she'd felt love filling her heart, making her weak in one breath and filled with energy in the next.

She gave herself to the kiss, letting him steer her under the warm spray of water, their bodies pressed together, the heat from their flesh matching the warmth of the liquid that cascaded over them.

Surrendering, she let go of everything else but that moment. It wasn't until the water started to cool that she realized just how long they'd stood there, kissing and touching.

Cliff reached around her to turn off the water. "Want to invite me into your bed?"

"Oh yes."

Cliff grabbed a towel and, with care and tenderness, he dried her, then himself. Tossing the towel on the floor, he scooped her up in his arms and carried her to the bed.

He grabbed a handful of spread and blanket and yanked, sending pillows tumbling to the floor. Then he turned back to her and unfastened the towel she'd wound around her body.

"Before we go any further, I have to say this. We're not having sex or fucking."

Nothing could have shocked her more. "We're not?"

"No. We're making love, honey."

She nearly cried it choked her up so much. He smiled and laid her back on the bed. He sat beside her, letting his fingers trace down her body from face to thigh and then back up. "You are the most incredibly sexy woman I've ever seen in my life, Roxie Ellis. I've dreamed about this moment ever since I first laid eyes on you."

Trouble in Chaps

She smiled up at him. "My friends just call me Roxie. Or Rox."

"What do your lovers call you?"

Her smile faded. "I've only really had one— well one that counted and…and… well, you know how that ended."

"That's the past, baby. This is the right now. And right now I'm asking if you're ready for me. For love."

"I don't know. I think so. But you… you said you thought…I love you Cliff, but I'm scared."

The moment the words were out of her mouth, she knew they were not the right ones. It was clear in the expression on his face.

"Then what do you want, Roxie?"

She couldn't articulate the feelings churning inside her and didn't try. Instead, she sat up, slid her arms around his neck and pulled his head down into a kiss. For her, the kiss was one of offering and surrender. She loosed the restraints on everything inside her, opening herself so that she was emotionally bare for him.

Would he understand what the kiss implied? She didn't know but hoped that on an emotional level he would recognize what she offered. Maybe he did. His arms wrapped around her to pull her close as he deepened the kiss.

And she knew her entire world changed in that moment, in that kiss. The past receded to its proper place and the *now* blossomed. She knew beyond all doubt that she'd beaten the odds. She'd found her man.

With that realization, an urgent need flared. She tore away from the kiss in a rash of impatience born of desperate need. Her lips moved down his neck and chest, tasting and biting until she stopped at his cock. It was like warm silk stretched tight over steel, a curious balance of soft and hard that had her mouth opening, eager to taste.

She ran her tongue over the head then down its length and back up to take him inside her mouth. There was no mistaking the hunger it inspired in him. His hands found their way into her hair, fisting as his body tensed.

Roxie straddled his body, sinking down on him. His hands moved to her hips, aiding as she started a steady rise and fall. She watched, her eyes meeting his and holding. And just as his body started to tense she saw it. This wasn't fucking. This wasn't sex. This really was love.

That sent her spiraling, calling his name. Together they soared. And when it was over, she lay down on him, feeling his arms circle her, hearing him whisper.

"Divorce Danny."

Roxie sat up, not believing what she'd heard. "Divorce? Why?"

"For me. For us. I love you, Roxie."

"But I thought you weren't sure. That you thought—"

"I was scared to admit it. But I know it's true. This is real, Roxie, and we can't let it go. If we do, we'll regret it the rest of our lives. Divorce him, honey. Please. Divorce him and be mine."

She'd never have believed it possible but there was no need for hesitation. She knew what she wanted and what she had to do. "On one condition."

"Name it."

"Go with me to see him. I have to tell him."

"He won't know what you're saying, honey."

"But I will."

"I'll make the arrangements today."

She nodded and sank willingly into his arms. Life was just full of surprises and for the first in a long time, she'd gotten a good one.

Chapter Seven

Roxie rolled over, fumbling for the clock as the shrill, persistent beep shattered the silence. The past few days had been a whirlwind. She and Cliff had returned last night and, despite the lateness of the hour, had spent most of the night making love.

"What time is it?" Cliff asked as she rolled back over next to him.

"Five thirty," she said with a yawn.

"Five thirty? God, who gets up that early?"

"Me." She snuggled over closer to him. "I normally run, but this morning I think I'll skip it. After an hour's sleep I don't think I have the energy for running."

Cliff yawned and ran his arm beneath her. "I don't have the energy for anything."

"Nothing?" She raised her head and looked at him with a suggestive smile as she ran her hand down his body.

"Well, maybe that," he agreed and rolled over with her beneath him.

"Ummm," she purred as his hands moved over her body. "That feels delicious."

"You are delicious," he murmured as he moved his lips down her neck.

Roxie sighed in pleasure, forgetting about the lack of sleep. All time slipped away as they explored each other with their hands. Cliff slid his fingers into the wet folds between her legs. Her body quivered when his fingers slowly slid into her.

He spread her lips and moistened her clit. While his fingers explored between her legs, his tongue slowly circled her nipple, flicking across the hardening flesh.

Cliff gently awakened her body with his touch. Roxie reveled in the sensations, riding the waves of pleasure his hands and mouth created. Her body was his to manipulate, his to explore. For the first time in her life, she had no fear of what surrendering control would bring. Love had changed all that. It changed the quality of a touch from mere physical pleasure to the pleasure that comes from an emotional connection.

His mouth moved from her nipple to the underside of her breast, causing her to arch toward him as she sighed. He ran his tongue up her cleavage to the base of her neck. There he feasted, fueling both their passions.

She grew wetter but he kept the movement of his hands slow and rhythmic. When his body moved up hers, she could feel his hardness against her hip. Her hand traveled down his hard chest and stomach. She stretched her fingers in the tight hair that surrounded the base of his shaft. She stroked his length with her fingertips, circling the pulsing head. Her rhythm of matched his, touch for touch, stroke for stroke. As their mouths met and connected, they pleasured each other with their hands, lovingly fondling one another.

Soon it wasn't enough. Roxie needed that ultimate connection. She needed him inside her. "I need you….in me," she whispered in his ear after her tongue traced his lobe. Her hand guided him into her as he positioned his body between her legs. Her body quivered as he entered her. She moved her hand from his shaft, letting her fingers feel him enter her. He sank in slowly and she sighed in pleasure, savoring the feel of his dick entering her warm, wet core. Her muscles quivered around him, earning her an additional thrill as his dick pulsed in answer to the call of her body.

Roxie kept her fingers between them, rubbing herself to his rhythm. The first orgasm had her whole body tightening around him. Her legs wrapped around his waist, stopping his

Trouble in Chaps

motion until she released. As her legs loosened, he began to move faster and harder in her. She pulled her legs up, giving him deeper access, rocking her hips to meet him. Cliff slipped off the bed and pulled her over to the edge. He went to his knees and buried his face in her. He ran his tongue from her opening to her clit. He lapped at the nub until it hardened. Roxie arched her back, pressing into his tongue. Just as she was tightening to climax, he stood and pushed into her. He rode her climax, letting her push against him as he drove into her. Flesh slapped flesh, an accompaniment to the low gasps and soft groans.

Feeling the pulsing in his groin, Cliff tightened his hands around her hips and drove one final time into her as he stars exploded behind his closed eyes. He pressed into her, wrapping his arms around her. There he held her until the orgasm receded.

Moments later, he withdrew and climbed back into bed with her, spooning around her body. Hours later, the ring of the phone pulled her from a sound sleep. Untangling herself from Cliff's arms she reached for the phone, seeing the lighted display of the clock on the nightstand announcing that it was after ten.

"Hello? Hey, Sam. Yeah, it's Roxie. Yeah, tell her I'll call her in a few minutes." Hanging up the phone, she sat up and brushed her hair back over her shoulders. "Sorry. I didn't even think before I answered. Anyway, that was Sam. Lola was looking for me. I need to call her and Emily and fill them in."

Cliff groaned and pushed himself into a sitting position. "Are you nervous?

"Only that their feelings will be hurt that I didn't tell them before now."

"They're your friends, honey. They'll be happy for you."

"You're right. I just don't want them to be hurt."

"It'll be fine, baby. Oh hell, what time is it?"

"After ten."

Ciana Stone

"God, I'm late," he grumbled. "Got people coming in to do some work on the club today. I need to call and tell them I'm going to be late."

"Okay." She stood and padded naked to the bathroom. "I've got to shower but there's plenty of room if you want to join me."

"As soon as I make this call."

"I'll be waiting."

Cliff watched her firm ass as she crossed the room and blew out a breath. Damn if the woman wasn't too tempting for his own good. And he couldn't be happier.

* * * * *

Roxie waited until they were seated at the table in Cliff's kitchen with plates of sandwiches and chips before she said anything about her mysterious trip with Cliff. He had offered to stay with her but she wanted to do this alone. She, Lola and Emily were best friends. They deserved to hear this from her.

He'd promised he'd be back in a couple of hours. Roxie was pretty sure that in two hours life as they knew it would change dramatically.

It took more than half an hour for her to tell Lola and Emily the whole story. It took two hours of questions before they were ready to move on from the tale of her marriage to Danny.

"Cliff's some guy," Lola commented. "So did you tell Danny you were doing to divorce him?"

"Yeah."

"Do you think he understood?" Emily asked.

Roxie shook her head. "He didn't even know who I was."

"You okay with that?" Emily asked.

"Yes. I am. I never thought I'd hear myself say it, but I'm at peace with it now."

266

Trouble in Chaps

"Damn, honey, I wish you'd told us all this before. You didn't have to bear this by yourself." Lola reached out to cover Roxie's hand with hers.

"Yeah, I did," Roxie said softly. "But I appreciate it. You guys are the greatest. I'm sorry I couldn't tell you before now, but this is something I had to deal with alone."

"Until Cliff," Emily commented.

"Yeah, until Cliff. Which brings me to the second part of my news bulletin."

"Oh god, there's more?" Lola looked around. "Do we need booze for this?"

Roxie suddenly grinned. "Actually, I think we do." She jumped up and hurried to the refrigerator. "Bless you, Beckett," she said as she pulled a bottle of champagne from the refrigerator.

"Champagne?" Emily's eyebrows rose. "In the middle of the day?"

Roxie found glasses, put them on the table and popped the cork. Once the glasses were filled, she took a seat and lifted a glass. "Ladies, say hello to Mrs. Cliff Beckett."

There was total silence. Lola's mouth rounded in an O and Emily's eyes grew wide. Roxie looked at her friends and grinned. "We were married in Vegas two days ago."

The silence was shattered by a high-pitched squeal from Lola. "Ohmygodohmygodohmygod!"

Roxie burst out laughing. "My sentiments exactly when he popped the question."

"You're married?" Emily blurted. "Really married?"

"That I am."

"Well damn!"

Another moment of silence fell only to be broken by all three of them suddenly squealing. Seconds later they were all on their feet, dancing and bouncing in a group hug.

Ciana Stone

"I can't believe it!" Emily exclaimed. "Roxie Ellis, you surprise me."

"Beckett. Roxie Beckett. And sometimes, I surprise even myself."

"Oh, honey!" Lola hugged her again. "I'm so happy for you."

Roxie smiled at her friends. "I'm happy, too. Really happy."

"He really is the one, isn't he?" Emily asked.

"Yes." Even Roxie heard the change in her voice at the answer. "God, Em, I never thought I could love someone like this."

"So, now I guess we're not the only ones who think staying in Mesa Blanco is such a horrible idea, huh?" Lola asked.

Roxie took a seat and sipped her champagne. "That's something else I wanted to talk to you about."

"Should we sit for this?" Emily asked.

"Might as well. We've got this bottle of bubbly that needs drinking. And I have this idea."

"Why did I get a sudden chill up my spine?" Emily teased.

Roxie laughed. "Cliff and I were talking. I don't really want to work at the bar and—oh my god, I didn't tell you. Cliff's loaded."

Both her friends burst out laughing. "What? I'm serious. He...hey, wait, you already knew?"

"Men can't keep secrets near as good as they claim," Lola replied. "Sam told me. Cliff's loaded."

"I nearly fainted when he told me," Roxie admitted.

"Was that before or after you said I do?" Emily asked.

"Oh meow," Roxie, retorted good naturedly. "After. Hell, I'd have married him if he had nothing."

268

Trouble in Chaps

"I believe you," Lola assured her. But you were talking about not wanting to work at the bar?"

"Oh, yeah. He asked what I wanted to do and I told him I'd always wanted to have my own shop—sort of a funky boutique. I know this seems like a strange place for something like that—or not. I mean, since we've been here I've seen Lola being asked for fashion advice a dozen times. So, I thought, how about a boutique that caters to a variety of styles. A little of the glitzy and a little of the homespun?"

Emily pursed her lips. "Not a bad idea. Maybe even add a little day spa for people who want a little pampering?"

"Oh I like that!" Roxie grinned.

"Nails and hair and oh, oh, a masseuse!" Lola added.

"Yes!"

Suddenly they were all chattering a thousand miles an hour, tossing out one idea after another. Before they knew it, the champagne was gone.

"So, I guess this means you like the idea?" Roxie asked.

"Yes!" Lola squealed, followed by a "Definitely," from Emily.

"Then what would you think about being my partners?"

The split second of silence preceded another round of squealing and all three of them jumping up to hug and bounce around.

"Oh my god, no more waiting tables?" Lola heaved a dramatic sigh.

"No more cooking—except when I want to?" Emily added.

Roxie grinned. "Cliff said it would be his wedding present to me, but I said he would invest and we'd pay him back. That okay with you?"

"Absolutely," Emily agreed.

"No problem," Lola added. "We'll make this thing a smash!"

Ciana Stone

"Indeed we will," Roxie replied. "And I was thinking of a name. What do you think about Sequins, Saddles and Spurs?"

Emily and Lola looked at each other then back at Roxie. "I think you better see if there's another bottle of champagne in the fridge," Emily replied. "'Cause, ladies, it's time for a toast."

Roxie dashed for the refrigerator. Minutes later she stood with her best friends, glasses of champagne rose. "A toast," she said.

"To new beginnings," Lola said.

"To friendship," Emily added.

"To love," Roxie offered.

"Amen, sister." Lola clinked her glass to Roxie's then Emily's.

They all drank then Roxie giggled. "What?" Lola asked.

"Who would've thought it would end like this?"

"End?" Roxie jumped when she heard Cliff's voice behind her. "Honey we're just getting started."

Also by Desiree Holt

ഋ

eBooks:

1-800-DOM-help: Delight Me

Cougar Challenge: Hot to Trot

Cupid's Shaft

Dancing With Danger

Diamond Lady

Double Entry

Driven by Hunger

Ellora's Cavemen: Flavors of Ecstasy I *(anthology)*

Emerald Green

Escape the Night

Hot Moon Rising

Hot, Wicked and Wild

I Dare You

Journey to the Pearl

Just Say Yes

Kidnapping the Groom *(with Allie Standifer)*

Letting Go

Line of Sight

Mistletoe Magic 2: Touch of Magic

Mistletoe Magic 4: Elven Magic *(with Regina Carlysle & Cindy Spencer Pape)*

Night Heat

Night Seekers 1: Lust Unleashed

Night Seekers 2: Lust by Moonlight
Once Burned
Once Upon a Wedding
Riding Out the Storm
Rodeo Heat
Seductive Illusion (*with Allie Standifer*)
Sequins, Saddles and Spurs 1: Trouble in Cowboy Boots
Switched
Teaching Molly
Texas Passions 1: Eagle's Run
Turn Up the Heat 1: Scorched (*with Allie Standifer*)
Turn Up the Heat 2: Scalded (*with Allie Standifer*)
Turn Up the Heat 3: Singed (*with Allie Standifer*)
Turn Up the Heat 4: Steamed (*with Allie Standifer*)
Until the Dawn (*with Cerise DeLand*)
Wedding Belles 3: Something Borrowed
Where Danger Hides

Print Books:
Age and Experience (*anthology*)
Candy Caresses (*anthology*)
Demanding Diamonds (*anthology*)
Ellora's Cavemen: Flavors of Ecstasy I (*anthology*)
Erotic Emerald (*anthology*)
Mistletoe Magic (*anthology*)
Naughty Nuptials (*anthology*)
Rodeo Heat
Tease the Cougar (*anthology*)
Where Danger Hides

About the Author

୫ଠ

I always wonder what readers really want to know when I write one of these things. Getting to this point in my career has been an interesting journey. I've managed rock and roll bands and organized concerts. Been the only female on the sports staff of a university newspaper. Immersed myself in Nashville peddling a country singer. Lived in five different states. Married two very interesting but totally different men.

I think I must have lived in Texas in another life, because the minute I set foot on Texas soil I knew I was home. Living in Texas Hill Country gives me inspiration for more stories than I'll probably ever be able to tell, what with all the sexy cowboys who surround me and the gorgeous scenery that provides a great setting.

Each day is a new adventure for me, as my characters come to life on the pages of my current work in progress. I'm absolutely compulsive about it when I'm writing and thank all the gods and goddesses that I have such a terrific husband who encourages my writing and puts up with my obsession. As a multi-published author, I love to hear from my readers. Their input keeps my mind fresh and always hunting for new ideas.

Also by Regina Carlysle

∞

eBooks:

Cougar Challenge: Drilled

Ellora's Cavemen: Flavors of Ecstasy IV *(anthology)*

Mistletoe Magic 1: Breath of Magic

Mistletoe Magic 4: Elven Magic *(with Desiree Holt & Cindy Spencer Pape)*

Feral Moon

High Plains Shifters 1: Highland Beast

High Plains Shifters 2: Lone Star Lycan

High Plains Shifters 3: Ringo's Ride

High Plains Shifters 4: Edge of Nowhere

Jaguar Hunger

Killer Curves

Sequins, Saddles and Spurs 2: Trouble in a Stetson

Spanish Topaz

Tempting Tess

Texas Passions 3: Eagle's Refuge

Print Books:

Aged to Perfection *(anthology)*

Ellora's Cavemen: Flavors of Ecstasy IV *(anthology)*

High Plains Shifters 1 & 2: Lone Star Beasts

High Plains Shifters 3 & 4: Riding the Edge

Mistletoe Magic *(anthology)*
Tempting Turquoise *(anthology)*
Torrid Topaz *(anthology)*

About the Author

ഇ

Regina Carlysle is an award winning, multi-published author. She likes writing that is hot, edgy, and often humorous, and puts this trademark stamp on all of her stories. Regina lives in west Texas with her husband of 25 years and counting and is a doting, fawning, and over-indulgent mother to her two kids. When she's not penning steamy erotic tales or hot contemporary stories, she's indulging in long chats with friends who help her stay sane and keep her laughing.

Also by Ciana Stone

❧

eBooks:

Acid Rayne *(with Nathalie Gray)*

An Unwanted Hunger

Cougar Challenge: Cam's Holiday

Hearts of Fire 1: Memory's Eye

Hearts of Fire 5: Entwined Hearts *(with Nicole Austin, N.J. Walters & TJ Michaels)*

Hot in the Saddle 1: Chase 'n' Ana

Hot in the Saddle 2: Molding Clay

Hot in the Saddle 3: Scout 'n' Cole

Hot in the Saddle 4: Conn 'n' Caleb

Riding Ranger

Sequins, Saddles and Spurs 3: Trouble in Chaps

Sexplorations 2: The Thing About Cowboys

Sexplorations 4: Finding Her Rhythm

Sexplorations 6: Working Up a Sweat

The Hussies: All in Time

The Hussies: A Taste for Jazz

The Hussies: Sin in Jeans

Wyatt's Chance

Print Books:

Acid Rayne (*with Nathalie Gray*)

Cougar Challenge: Tease a Cougar (*anthology*)

Hot in the Saddle 1 & 2: Unbridled

Hot in the Saddle 3 & 4: Unrestrained

Wyatt's Chance

About the Author

๛

Ciana Stone has been reading since the age of three, and wrote her first story at age five. Since then she enjoyed writing as a solitary form of entertainment, before coming out of the closet to share her stories with others. She holds several post graduate degrees and has often been referred to as a professional student. Her latest fields of interest are quantum mechanics and Taoism. When she is not writing (or studying) she enjoys painting (canvas, not walls), sculpting, running, hiking and yoga. She lives with her longtime lover in several locations in the United States.

๛

The authors welcome comments from readers. You can find their websites and email addresses on their author bio pages at www.ellorascave.com.

Tell Us What You Think

We appreciate hearing reader opinions about our books. You can email us at Comments@EllorasCave.com.

Why an electronic book?

We live in the Information Age—an exciting time in the history of human civilization, in which technology rules supreme and continues to progress in leaps and bounds every minute of every day. For a multitude of reasons, more and more avid literary fans are opting to purchase e-books instead of paper books. The question from those not yet initiated into the world of electronic reading is simply: *Why?*

1. *Price.* An electronic title at Ellora's Cave Publishing and Cerridwen Press runs anywhere from 40% to 75% less than the cover price of the exact same title in paperback format. Why? Basic mathematics and cost. It is less expensive to publish an e-book (no paper and printing, no warehousing and shipping) than it is to publish a paperback, so the savings are passed along to the consumer.

2. *Space.* Running out of room in your house for your books? That is one worry you will never have with electronic books. For a low one-time cost, you can purchase a handheld device specifically designed for e-reading. Many e-readers have large, convenient screens for viewing. Better yet, hundreds of titles can be stored within your new library—on a single microchip. There are a variety of e-readers from different manufacturers. You can also read e-books on your PC or laptop computer. (Please note that Ellora's Cave does not endorse any specific brands.

You can check our websites at www.ellorascave.com or www.cerridwenpress.com for information we make available to new consumers.)

3. *Mobility.* Because your new e-library consists of only a microchip within a small, easily transportable e-reader, your entire cache of books can be taken with you wherever you go.

4. ***Personal Viewing Preferences.*** Are the words you are currently reading too small? Too large? Too… ANNOYING? Paperback books cannot be modified according to personal preferences, but e-books can.

5. ***Instant Gratification.*** Is it the middle of the night and all the bookstores near you are closed? Are you tired of waiting days, sometimes weeks, for bookstores to ship the novels you bought? Ellora's Cave Publishing sells instantaneous downloads twenty-four hours a day, seven days a week, every day of the year. Our webstore is never closed. Our e-book delivery system is 100% automated, meaning your order is filled as soon as you pay for it.

Those are a few of the top reasons why electronic books are replacing paperbacks for many avid readers.

As always, Ellora's Cave and Cerridwen Press welcome your questions and comments. We invite you to email us at Comments@ellorascave.com or write to us directly at Ellora's Cave Publishing Inc., 1056 Home Avenue, Akron, OH 44310-3502.

MAKE EACH DAY MORE *EXCITING* WITH OUR

ELLORA'S CAVEMEN

CALENDAR

WWW.ELLORASCAVE.COM

Discover for yourself why readers can't get enough of the multiple award-winning publisher

Ellora's Cave.

Whether you prefer e-books or paperbacks,

be sure to visit EC on the web at
www.ellorascave.com

for an erotic reading experience that will leave you breathless.

Breinigsville, PA USA
06 April 2011
259280BV00001B/249/P